SINFUL KINGDOM

KNIGHT'S RIDGE EMPIRE
BOOK 18

TRACY LORRAINE

1

———

EVIE

Exhaustion like I've never felt before seeps through my bones.

Tears stain my cheeks, but they're nothing compared to the blood running down my skin.

I'm covered in the scratches and deep gouges left behind by the thistles and thorns I've run through.

And my feet...

I can barely stand. The pain is like nothing I've ever experienced.

Give me a ridiculous pair of stripper heels and tell me to dance for twenty-four hours straight. I'd take that over this hell any day.

I'm soaked from head to toe; the rain that started earlier has barely let up in all the time I've been running. It mixes with the blood, turning pink and pooling at the ground.

Stumbling forward, I just about manage to catch myself before I fall flat on my face.

It's dark. Unbelievably so, and cold.

My entire body shakes, my skin is covered in goosebumps, and my teeth chatter.

But there's nothing I can do about it.

There's no shelter, no blankets, no nice warm bath to soothe my aching muscles.

I'm out here, alone, with fuck knows what prowling around me.

We're in England. It can't be that bad. There are no wild bears, lions, or tigers.

But there are the men in masks.

The sun might have set and the hours ticked by, but that doesn't mean they're not still out here searching.

They came here for me. To take me to my rightful owner to embark on a life of Christ knows what. I can't imagine that they'll give up easily.

I search my black surroundings for any sign of light, movement, anything.

But there's nothing.

Nothing but raindrops and the wind that whips around me, ensuring I'm frozen to the bone.

The fear of them returning with search dogs flicker through my mind.

I need to keep moving.

But I can't.

My body is shutting down, no matter how much my brain pushes me forward.

Slumping against a thick tree trunk, I slowly slide down until my arse hits the wet and muddy ground beneath me.

Wrapping my arms around my legs, I curl myself up into the tightest ball I can and let the tears flow.

With my emotions ripped to shreds and my body not far behind it, my sobs soon fade out, overtaken by exhaustion.

Every noise, every howl of the wind and large drop of water startles me.

But there are no voices, and more importantly, there are

no hands lifting me from the ground and dragging me away.

This might be hell, but it could be worse. I could be under the control of the man who paid... I still have no idea how much for me. An eighteen-year-old virgin.

He might be wealthy. He probably lives in a mansion with staff and all those pretentious things. But nothing, nothing is worth losing your free will over.

Alex might have lied, but all he's done is protect me, care for me... love me.

He knows I'm gone. He has to.

He should have returned from his exam hours ago.

He could be running through these woods right now searching for me, or he could be hunting down the men he thinks have me.

There might be a lot I don't know about Alexander Deimos, but I know one thing.

He won't rest until I'm safe.

He did all of this because he cares. It might be naïve or wishful thinking or whatever, but when he told me he loved me yesterday, I believed him.

He won't give up on me. I know he won't.

And nor will the others. They'll all be out searching, doing whatever they can to find me, to bring me back to my family.

Thoughts of Blake and Zay make my sobs return full force.

Do they even know I'm missing?

Will Alex and the guys have kept the intel locked down so they don't scare them? Are they hoping to return with me before Blake realises there's an issue?

Fuck, I hope so.

With my energy depleted, I slump to the side, curling

up in the foetal position as the rain continues to pour and my hope seeps out into the puddle around me.

As soon as the sun rises, you'll find your way out of here...

As long as they don't find you first...

***

Birds are the first thing I hear as the woods surrounding me begin to wake with the rising sun.

Opening my eyes hurts. It gives me very little optimism for what it's going to be like to move the rest of my body.

Right now, I'm so cold I'm numb. And that's probably a very good thing.

I scan my surroundings as the orange hue from the morning sun begins to flood everything around me with light.

The ground is wet and muddy from the storm the day before, but from what I can make out through the gaps in the leaves far above my head, the sky is clear.

At least something is working in my favour this morning.

Sucking in deep breaths, I try to take stock of my body. And after a few seconds, I press my palms into the ground and force myself up.

Something between a roar and a scream rips from my lips as I move. My muscles ache and the cuts and gashes littering my body pull and sting. Some immediately open up with the movement, oozing blood once more.

Checking myself over, I cringe at what I find staring back at me.

But I remind myself that I'm still here, that they never found me, that my life is still my own.

I have the power here.

I need to get out. I need to find a way back to Alex, and then I need to let them do their jobs.

If I'm lucky, they'll have left some kind of evidence behind at the cabin. Something that will help lead the guys straight to them. Anything that will bring this nightmare to an end.

All I wanted was a chance at a new life. Something that Blake and I could make our own. Things were meant to get better for us. Not worse.

Refusing to succumb to my tears once more, I focus on where I need to be.

Alex and Blake.

They're who I need right now.

One will set the world on fire for me. The other will hold me together.

I don't even care which way around they do it, so long as they do.

It takes longer than I want to confess to, but eventually, I manage to get to my feet, although my legs barely have the strength to hold me up.

I move from tree to tree, gripping onto each one as if it's a lifeline.

The sun climbs higher in the sky, and the warmth of it finally creeps through the thick tree cover above me. It feels amazing on my chilled skin and gives me the push I need to keep going.

I feel like I've walked a marathon, but with no markers to tell me how far I've really gone, I fear it may only be a few feet.

I'm so focused on moving that the bark of a dog startles me to the point I let out a high-pitch scream.

Clapping my hand over my mouth, I freeze as fear turns my blood to ice.

They've come for me—and they've brought dogs to ensure they don't leave empty-handed.

Another bark, closer this time, has my breathing increasing to the point I can barely keep control of it.

Silently, I beg. I pray for the dog to turn around, to sniff out something else and lead them in the opposite direction.

But only seconds later there's another yap, followed by the sound of branches cracking underfoot.

No, no. Please.

I made it this far.

Don't let it all be for nothing.

The bush before me rustles and I whimper into my hand, my entire body trembling as the image of a bloodthirsty Rottweiler or something similar plays out in my head.

It rustles again and my knees almost give out before a golden fluffball bursts through the greenery and bounds up to me.

His entire body wags with his happiness as he gazes up at me with what I'm sure is a smile on his cute face.

"Y-you're not here to attack me, are you?" I ask, my voice hoarse.

He stares up at me before sitting down and letting out another bark that startles me again.

"You need to stop doing that," I warn before finally giving in and dropping to the ground.

The second I'm down, the giant soppy thing nuzzles into me.

"Murph," a female voice calls. "MURPHY, where the hell have you gone this time?"

She mutters something I can't make out as naughty Murphy's eyes meet mine.

"Sounds like you're a troublemaker," I tell him, gently stroking his head.

He barks, letting his owner know he's close.

"Murphy, you little shit. What did I tell you last time you did this? Lead walking for a month if you so much as—" The woman's words stop abruptly as she appears in the small clearing before me. "Oh my God, Murphy," she gushes. "Oh, you're such a good boy." She rushes over to me and drops to her knees.

"Are you okay?" she asks in a rush, her eyes darting over every inch of me.

I don't respond. What's the point? She can see very clearly that I am not okay.

As she tracks my injuries, I study her.

If I had to guess, I'd say she was probably in her late thirties. Her brown hair is a little faded, her roots showing some grey she's yet to cover. She's wearing a tank with Murphy's lead hanging around her neck, leggings, and walking boots. But none of those things really capture my attention. It's her eyes that draw me in. They're the most brilliant blue, even in the shade under the trees. And they're so kind. Kind, caring, and the sight has me breaking down in an instant.

"Oh, sweetie. It's okay. Everything is going to be okay," she says, gently pulling me into a hug. "You're freezing. Here," she says, untying a hoodie I didn't see wrapped around her waist.

I wince as the soft fabric brushes over the cuts on my arms, but I happily push that aside for some warmth.

"We need to get you out of here, sweetie. Can you stand?"

I nod, shifting around, ready to push to my feet.

"Here, let me and Murph help."

I nod, putting all my effort into moving instead of talking.

With her arm around my waist and Murphy's support, I manage to stand upright. Together, they lead me out of the woods, which it turns out I was almost at the edge of.

No words are said as I'm led to an old Land Rover and helped into the passenger seat.

Murphy hops in at my feet.

"Murph, get in the back," the woman demands, "give her some space."

But he just sits there and stares back at her, totally unmoving.

"He's okay," I whisper, reaching out to tickle his ear. "My hero."

"He has his good days, don't you, boy," she praises, giving him a treat from her pocket before closing the door and rushing around to her side.

"I'm Trudi, by the way," she says, turning to look at me.

"Evie."

"Okay, Evie. We're about forty-five minutes from the hospital. I'll drive as gently as I can."

"No," I blurt. "I need to go to London. I can... I can give you an address."

"London?"

"Yes. Are we far from—"

"About an hour. But I really think—"

"I know. Trust me, I know how this looks. But there are people I need to get to. People who can keep me safe.

Please, I'll do anything. They'll pay you, for your time and your fuel. I just need—"

"Hey, now," she says softly, reaching over to wipe my tears. "I'll take you wherever you need to go as long as you promise me they'll look after you."

"I promise. Th-they're my f-family. They're going to be worried and—" A sob cuts off my words.

"Okay, can you tell me the address? But I must warn you, if we turn up there and I suspect for a second that—"

"I promise, they'll take care of me. I need them, please," I beg.

With a single nod, she starts the car and opens the maps app on her phone.

"Thank you," I sob, the thought of being wrapped in Alex's arms too much to take, and I break down with Murphy's jaw resting on my thigh supportively.

2

EVIE

The farther we drive, the harder it is to ignore the pain and desperation that seeps through every inch of me.

I close my eyes, wishing that when I open them, I'm pulling up to a house I once prayed I'd never have to see again, but that I now crave for my safety.

Sleep never comes for me, no matter how much I might try.

Instead, I spend my time staring at the map on Trudi's phone, watching the minutes and the miles count down to when I'll be safe, surrounded by those who will do anything to protect me.

I want to be mad at myself for screwing this all up. I thought going outside to do yoga was a risk, but it turns out, it was probably what saved me. If I were inside the cabin when they'd ambushed the place, I'd have had nowhere to hide. They'd have found me, and I'd be in a much worse position than I am right now, I'm sure of it.

Despite my exhaustion, as the clock ticks closer and our surroundings become familiar, my heart starts to race.

I've no idea if Alex will be here, but I know Blake and Zay will. They'll pull me into their arms and look after me. And I've no doubt that Alex won't be far behind. As soon as they call him, give him the news that I'm okay, he'll be there. He'll surround me with his strength and whisper everything I need to hear in my ear.

Trudi remains quiet. She's not happy about this; she wants to be taking me to get medical attention, but thankfully, she's listening to me.

I've no idea who she is or where she came from, but I'll be forever grateful.

It may have turned out that I was right on the edge of those woods, but if I'd turned the wrong way, I could have walked straight back into the thick of it. And then what? I could have been in there for days. Days with no water and no food. A violent shudder rips down my spine as the reality of that settles in.

I could have died in those woods and no one would have known. No one would have found me.

A sob erupts, making Murphy place a giant paw on my knee and Trudi look over.

"We're almost there, sweetie. Just keep it together a little longer."

I nod—not that she can see me as she focuses on the road.

Dropping my attention to Murphy, I stroke the top of his head, silently thanking him for finding me. He stares up at me with huge brown eyes.

"Thanks, pup," I whisper, the familiarity of that name slamming into me.

Please be there. Please be there, I silently beg.

I need you.

"Whoa, can't say this was what I was expecting when

you requested this," Trudi says, her eyes widening as she drives down the street of mostly hidden mansions that Alex grew up on.

I wait a few minutes and then point to the right. "That one."

Sucking in a deep breath, I wait for the house to reveal itself.

The first time I was here, I was terrified of it, of the people I was about to be surrounded by, what I was going to have to do. The second time, there was only one person in my mind, one person I didn't want to see. But hell, I'm so glad I practically ran straight into him.

And now, all I want to do is get inside. The building is no longer petrifying. It's my refuge, my sanctuary from everything I'd just managed to leave behind.

As if someone is expecting us, the second Trudi pulls to a stop, the front door opens.

My heart jumps into my throat and a surge of energy I didn't think I possessed bubbles up from somewhere.

Throwing the door open, my feet hit the gravel and I take off running. And when the figure emerges, my legs only move faster.

He's here and—

My body collides with his in a heartbeat.

"Whoa, steady," he says, stumbling back a little.

Sucking in a deep breath, I savour his scent.

For a minute back there, I didn't think I'd ever get the chance again.

His arms come around me as the sound of a car door slamming hits my ears.

But as grateful as I am for Trudi, she's not my main focus right now.

Pulling my head from his chest, I look up, searching his eyes, letting them ground me.

My body screams as I do it, but I don't care. I need him too much.

After the lies and the fighting, I just need—

I press my lips against his, desperate for a taste of him despite the fact he probably has no desire to do the same seeing as I've spent Christ knows how long running for my life in the woods.

He stills, his body turning to granite beneath me before a shrill female voice echoes around me.

"What the hell do you think you're doing?"

Everything happens too fast for me to process. I'm pulled back, ripped out of Alex's warm arms before a small female steps in front of me.

It takes me a second to recognise her with her face contorted in anger, and it seems that she has the same issue.

Her jaw pops and her nostrils flare before realisation hits and her entire body goes rigid.

"Evie? Oh my God, Evie." Anger forgotten, her eyes quickly sweep over me before I'm pulled into Calli's arms. "BLAKELY," she screams to get my sister's attention, but I barely hear it. I'm already shutting down.

My body knows I'm here. It knows I'm safe and can stop fighting.

Footsteps come running before Blakely screams.

I'm transferred into her arms. She squeezes so tightly a little yelp of pain escapes my lips and she immediately lets go.

"No," I cry, craving the warmth, the security of their arms.

"Evie, what happened? Who did this? Where's Alex?"

Her words float around my head, but none of them register.

"Get out of the way," a deep voice growls. "This isn't helping her."

Suddenly, my feet leave the floor, and when I look up, I find myself in his strong arms once more.

Tucking my face into the crook of his neck, I kiss his warm, comforting skin.

"I missed you," I whisper, loud enough for him to hear. "I'm sorry I said all those things. I love you too."

His body tenses, although his steps don't falter as he carries me wherever we're going. I don't need to question him. I know I'll be safe.

I've no idea if he responds to my confession because the darkness finally takes over, dragging me into his clutches.

You're safe now.

You're in his arms.

The first thing I hear the next time I come to isn't a dog barking, but people talking.

Voices I know. Voices I love.

Opening my eyes takes more effort than I ever thought possible. The room is thankfully dark, but there's enough sunlight streaming through the curtains to allow me to see Blakely and Calli sitting beside me.

Blake looks wrecked. Her eyes are rimmed with red, her cheeks stained with tears as she wrings a ruined tissue with her fingers.

"Still nothing?" Blake asks when Calli wakes her phone up in her lap.

"No. No news is good news. They'll have this under

control." Calli's words are full of confidence that I really want to feel.

Shifting my sore body turns both of their eyes on me.

"Evie," Blakely gasps, jumping to her feet in a heartbeat. "Oh my God, Evie," she sobs, bending over me and resting her brow against mine.

"I'm okay," I force out as tears trickle over my temples, soaking into my hair. "Where's Alex?"

"Evie," Blake warns in a tone I really, really don't like as she lowers herself to the edge of the bed.

"Did he leave? He was here. I remember him."

A warm hand takes mine, and when I rip my eyes from my sister, I find Calli watching me with a similar expression on her face.

"It wasn't Alex, Evie."

"B-but—"

"It was Daemon."

I stare at her in disbelief.

"N-no. It was him."

"Trust me, it was Daemon."

"But—"

"They're twins, babe," Blake says, filling in some of the blanks.

"It was him," I whisper, still refusing to process this information.

Calli shakes her head. "That was my dark knight, not your cheeky one."

My brow furrows as I think back.

His scent. Was it right?

His eyes. Were they the ones I get lost in?

The way he paused when I kissed him.

My eyes find Calli's once more as reality slams into me.

She's right. I was just too relieved and exhausted to see it.

"They're twins. Identical twins," Calli explains.

I think back to the things Alex told me about his brother. I remember him saying they're as much the same as they are different. I didn't think much of it at the time, because that statement could be used to describe me and Blake. But now, it makes so much more sense.

"I'm so sorry," I whisper, feeling the cringe all the way down to my toes.

"It's okay. I told him to stop being an idiot and tell you before you bumped into him."

"Why didn't he?" Blake asks, still looking as fragile as she was when I woke.

"Because he's a frigging idiot?" Calli responds without missing a beat.

Dropping my gaze, my eyes land on a white bandage that's wrapped around my upper arm where one of my worst cuts was.

"Gianna is downstairs," Calli tells me. "She did the best she could to patch you up while you slept."

Embarrassment makes my cheeks burn red as I think back to what happened last time I was in a bed with that woman.

Shaking that memory away, I focus on the issue at hand.

"So, where is he?"

It might be a little presumptuous, but I'm lying here after spending hours running through the woods away from God knows who now wrapped up in bandages. I'd have put any money on him being here and refusing to leave my side. But... he's nowhere to be seen.

He will have been out looking for me. Right?

He'll have come home, alerted everyone, and they'd have been trying to find me.

They—

"He was ambushed when he got back to the house, Evie. They were waiting for him."

All the air rushes out of my lungs as Calli delivers that devastating blow, her eyes swimming with tears.

"No," I cry.

I refused to believe that a guy as well trained as Alex would have been overpowered by whoever that was and—

A scream rips through the air, and it's not until both Blake and Calli squeeze my hands that I realise it came from me.

"They have him?" I ask weakly.

"We believe so."

"You believe so?" I echo. "Why haven't the guys gone storming in to get him back? I need him, Calli. I need him. I —" I break down, falling into my sister's arms as she sobs right alongside me.

"They will get him, Evie. I promise you. Daemon and the guys will do whatever they have to do to bring him back to you. You just have to trust them even if it feels like you want to do the opposite."

"It's not just Alex," Blake whispers brokenly in my ear, making ice flood through my body.

It takes all my strength, but I manage to push her from our embrace so I can look into her eyes.

"What do you mean, it's not just Alex." My heart races so hard it makes my head spin.

There is only one other person who isn't in this room right now that should be. And if—

"They ambushed their car on the way to school," Blake whimpers.

The world falls out from beneath me.

"No," I cry. "No, tell me you're lying."

"Evie," Blake sobs.

"They're both going to be okay," Calli says fiercely. "They have the most dangerous and terrifying men and women in this city fighting for them. We will get them both."

This time when I break, I don't come back from it, and I cry myself to sleep, my heart even more broken than my body.

All I can hope for is that wherever they are, they're together, and they fight with everything they have. Just like I did.

3

———

ALEX

Warmth covers my hand, spreading down my arm and I squeeze, letting her know that I'm here.

My heart swells.

She came back to me. After all that bullshit, she's here. She's holding my hand.

We're going to be okay.

She'll understand why I withheld the truth about the situation we're in, and she'll forgive me.

Then somehow, we'll find the cunts who did this to her, and after we've shown them exactly what we're capable of, we can go skipping off into the sunset.

Maybe we could all return to Vegas and I could really enjoy it this time. I could be the one who comes home with a wife and the promise of forever together.

Mrs. Evie Deimos.

It has a good ring to it.

I'll talk to my dad and Damien, tell them that my time seducing intel out of anyone they deem fit is over, and I'll figure out another way to make myself useful.

Evie and I can start uni. She can move in with me and we can spend our nights studying and fucking and planning our lives together.

Is she a cat or a dog person?

And if it's the latter, like me, can we get one?

We could take him for a walk before classes and watch the sunrise over the city. We could train him together and teach him that Nico is evil and watch him attack—in a friendly way, of course—and laugh as he wrestles with the ball of fur.

We can babysit my niece when she's born, take her to the park and watch her grow.

Double dates with Daemon and Calli.

Holidays as a group. Parties and game nights, football games and movie nights.

I want all of it. I want everything with my girl and my best friends by my side.

But as much as I crave it, something in my subconscious knows it's unreachable as I think about all the possibilities.

It's not, though. It's right there. It's within touching distance.

We just need to take these cunts down. Then, Reid can return home. Luciana can go back to... well, wherever she lives, and our lives can return to normal.

Normal. What a fucking joke.

There's nothing normal about us, about the way we live our lives.

Here I am, planning this future for the two of us, and once Evie is a free woman, she might turn her back on all of this. On me.

It might be too much for her.

No.

No, it's not.

She's strong. Just as strong as the others. Maybe she's not as quick with her fists as Stella and Emmie or has the experience like Calli. But she's got Jodie and Brianna's strength and resistance. And they don't have an issue being on this ride with us.

She fits in. I've already seen that. The others accepted her into our group and have treated her as if she's always been a part of our lives. It's something I'm never going to be able to thank them enough for. The way Emmie and Stella in particular, have been there for her, showing her what our world is about. I fucking love them for it. Even if they allowed her to dance on a tabletop at a Wolves party. But then I guess I should really expect that kind of thing from them. I can only hope she develops a closer bond with Calli. She's less likely to get into trouble with our baby C.

Warmth spreads through me as I think about my family. About their friendship, their loyalty, their... well, everything.

D and I, our real family, are... a weird mix of amazing and awful and everything in between.

Mum is incredible. She's our rock, always has been. Her parents too.

But Dad...

As a little boy, I remember looking up to him like he was the most amazing man in the world. He was my hero. My idol. But then, as the years passed and our grandfather started showing his hand, my opinion began to change.

He knew what was going on, that much was obvious. Although, to this day I'm not sure to what extent.

Our grandfather was training us to be the soldiers he believed we were bred for. He'd done the same to our father. But he never talked about what that looked like for him, and we've never talked about what we were experiencing either.

D and I barely even touched on it. We knew we were being trained differently, but I think both of us were too terrified to dive into the details.

I've seen what he went through. For years, he kept his body hidden, kept his secrets to himself.

Sure, our grandfather raised his hand or belt to me a time or two, but not the extent he did Daemon.

He was training him to be this brutal, terrifying monster, and I had no idea.

I've never felt like a worse brother than when all the truth started unravelling.

And while he was getting tortured, I was treated to the opposite.

Our grandfather didn't want us both to kill and maim. He wanted one lover and one fighter.

The things he had me watching—doing—at such a young and innocent age make me cringe.

I think about Atlas and Zayden, and I can't imagine anything worse than submitting them to the kinds of things we were forced to endure. They're still kids. Although there will always be some kind of training of our young soldiers, it won't be to the extent we received.

With Evie and the possibility of a different future ahead of me, I figure it might just be time that we sat down with our father and finally laid all our cards on the table. Especially with the real possibility of D and Calli's baby being a boy. There is no fucking way any nephew of mine is being treated like that. I might love my father despite everything, but if he ever even mentions putting another kid through that, I'll put a bullet through his skull myself.

My thoughts turn to ones of Daemon with a baby in his arms.

He can be so cold, detached, and quite frankly, terrifying. But that's just one part of him. The other part... well, I'm pretty sure only Calli and I know it exists. Us and their future baby.

He's going to be the most incredible dad, I have no doubt. He might hate hard, but he loves even harder. He's proven that time and time again with Calli. Even when he was pushing her away and trying to do what he thought was right, it was all because he loved her. He always has, and I'm so fucking glad he finally got to discover that she loved him back just as hard.

A contented sigh for both of them slips from my chest and a smile forms on my lips.

"Alex?" a little voice says, bringing me back to reality.

But as much as I might want to open my eyes and turn toward the voice, it's like swimming through tar.

"Alex?" It's more of a whimper this time. The fear within just my name is enough to help drag myself from the clutches of darkness. "I'm scared. Please."

Familiarity tickles my senses, but the only thought I can grasp is that it's not Evie. She's not the one holding my hand and giving me hope that everything is going to be okay between us.

A soft sob hits my ears, and I drag some strength up from the depths and open my eyes.

The sight before me shreds my fucking heart.

"Zayden?" My voice is barely above a whisper, but it doesn't matter.

His familiar blue eyes fill with tears, and his bottom lip trembles.

My body, which previously felt like lead, suddenly jumps into action as he shatters before me.

Wrapping my arms around his trembling body, I clutch him to my chest and hold tight, just like I would if it were his sister breaking down.

"It's okay," I soothe, my own eyes burning red hot as he cries on my chest. "I've got you. I won't let anything happen to you. I promise, Zay. I fucking promise."

His cries continue for long, painful minutes as I rest my cheek on the top of his head, hoping that I can give him even an ounce of comfort that his sisters would if they were here.

I've no idea how to handle kids. The only ones I have experience with are Theo's younger brother and sisters, and they're already a part of this world. Not that I think for a second that they'd know how to handle whatever fucked-up situation we're in the middle of. But they're a little more aware of things.

Zay might have grown up in Lovell, but I also know that his sisters have done everything they can to keep his life as normal and stable as possible, trying to shield him from the worst of what happens in that place.

This kind of thing isn't a part of his life. He hasn't already started training like Atlas has. He has no idea what we're involved in or what our lives are really like. And I really fucking hate that he's about to find it all out like this.

As he clings to me like a lifeline, I look around the room we're in. It's dark and dank. The walls are breeze block, grey, cold and damp. The floor is concrete, and other than the bucket in the corner, the only other piece of furniture is the cot we're both sitting on. And that's not exactly what I'd describe as comfortable.

The air around us is bitter, nothing like the warm

summer days Evie and I had been enjoying on the deck outside the cabin.

A shiver races down my spine, goosebumps erupting over my skin even with Zay's body cuddled into mine.

Glancing down, I find that I'm still wearing my school uniform, only my shirt is covered in dark, dried blood and dirt.

It's the first time since I opened my eyes and saw him that I think about myself.

My face throbs, one of my eyes barely opening enough to see. The rest of me aches just like the morning after a good Circuit fight. Only, I don't remember throwing any punches. Whatever caused the pain was done after they knocked me out.

That thought makes acid burn up my throat.

I've no idea who the cunts are who took me—us—but I know they're not fucking around.

They were waiting for me.

"Evie," I breathe. Did they get Evie?

My blood runs ice cold all over again as I fight the need to run to the bucket to throw up.

Zay needs you to be strong for him.

It's what Evie would have done. It's what you need to do.

"Is she okay?"

But I also can't lie to him. He might be little, but he's not a baby. And if he's going to survive this—which he is because I'll make fucking sure of it—then needs the truth. He deserves the truth.

"Zayden," I say, taking his dirty face in my hands and staring him in the eyes.

He whimpers before I've even said anything, predicting where this is going.

"You're eleven, yeah?" I ask, and he nods slowly.

"Awesome, that means you're man enough to handle all this, right?"

"I-I don't know," he whispers.

"Dude, you're going to be my partner in crime, okay? The Bonnie to my Clyde. The—"

"Who?"

"Uh... the Batman to my Robin?" I ask, suddenly realising that I have no idea what almost-eleven-year-olds watch or read or... any-fucking-thing.

"O-okay."

"And being my partner means that we never lie to each other, okay?"

He nods, his eyes filling with tears again, making my heart crack.

"I don't know what's going on right now," I say honestly. "But we're going to figure it out together, okay?"

4

―――

EVIE

The next time I open my eyes, there's no sunlight sneaking in through the cracks in the curtains and the room is in silence.

It takes a few seconds, but eventually my eyes adjust to the dark room enough to allow me to see that I'm alone.

My heart begins to race, and a surge of heat rushes through my body as panic sets in. I don't want to be alone. I want... I want Alex.

Clapping my hand to my mouth, I smother the sob that wants to break free as memories slam into me.

He's not here. Nor is Zay. Because whoever that was who stormed the house has them.

They're... somewhere. Hopefully together, but probably alone, having fuck knows what done to them.

Those men in that concrete cell may not have touched me, but that's only because one of them was on my side. What would have happened to me if he wasn't there? What would have happened if I was subjected to Mr. Evil and his buddies?

My stomach turns over and I'm out of bed and

clutching the toilet in the bathroom on the other side of the room in seconds.

But it's pointless. I can't remember the last time I ate.

Pain tears up my insides as my body tries to expel all the panic that's taking over.

Tears fall, and I tremble from head to toe as cold sweat covers my skin.

Falling back against the warm floor does nothing as I curl up into a ball. My teeth only pause from chattering so that I can cry.

I don't hear anyone in the bedroom or when they step into the bathroom, but I scream the second a pair of feet appears in front of me.

"Shh, Evie," a soft, kind, and familiar voice says as a warm light illuminates the room around me.

She helps me up, and with an arm around my waist for support, she stands me in front of the basin and helps me brush my teeth and wash my face and hands.

"Thank you," I whisper, my eyes locked on hers in the mirror.

"Oh, honey," she whispers, gently tucking a lock of hair behind my ear. "I'd do anything for my boys, and that now extends to you and Calli."

Another sob erupts.

"I need him," I cry, falling into her arms. "I need him."

"I know, honey." Her arms tighten around me. "You're not the only one."

Her grey eyes hold mine, letting me see her own pain.

My lips part to say something, but she beats me to it.

"Come on, let's get you back to bed."

With me still tucked tightly into her side, she guides me back into the bedroom. One of the bedside lights is on, casting a warm glow around the room. Not that I pay any attention to my surroundings. I'm too numb for that.

Gianna sits on the edge of the bed beside me and waits while I attempt to get comfortable.

Folded on the end of the bed is a black shirt. Immediately, I reach for it, holding it as tight as I would if it were him. Emotion burns up the back of my throat once more.

"Is this..."

"It's Alex's. He still had a few things in his room here. I hope that's okay."

Lifting the fabric, I bring it to my nose and inhale deeply.

It might not be strong, but it's there. His scent washes through me, settling just a tiny part of me.

"They're going to be okay, aren't they?" I plead.

"Evie, my boys are strong. Stronger than anyone I've ever known." She pauses, looking off into the distance as she reminisces.

"When I first met Stefanos, I was blown away," she says absently as if she's not aware the words are even spilling from her lips. "He was every girl's dream. The dangerous bad boy. But unlike everyone saw on the outside, there were cracks. It took a long time for me to dig them out, but I did. He made mistakes and most importantly, he disappointed his father. He was their only son, and the pressure on him was immense. His father wanted him to be perfect. But Stefanos, he's... normal. He has emotions and flaws and all the things his father tried to eradicate from him.'

"Eradicate?"

"It took me a lot of years to learn the truth about the darkness in his life, Evie. Too many years." Sadness darkens her eyes before she hangs her head.

"But my boys... from the day they were born, they were so strong, so fierce. Even Daemon, who had to fight hard in those early months. I don't know if it's because there's two of them, that knowing they always had someone covering their back meant that they didn't have any fear, but Stefanos saw that. He knew how incredible they were going to be, and he tried to harness it to help mould their futures."

I nod, although really, I don't have any understanding of what she's trying to say. I've no idea what Alex's childhood was like really. He's mentioned training and some horrible grandfather, but he's kept most of it brief.

"If I knew the truth of it all, I'd have stopped it. I'd have done anything to have stopped it. But I was kept in the dark about the true ugliness that was happening to my own boys.

"I should have seen it. I did to a point, but I never could have imagined the true horror of the situation."

Lifting her hand, she wipes a tear from her cheek.

"I swear to you, Evie. The day I found out what was really happening, I put an end to it. I just wish I could have done it sooner."

"What?"

She shakes her head.

"Stefanos was trained by his father from a very young age. And while he excelled in a lot of the skills he'd need for the future, he was never good enough for his father."

"Trained?" I ask. "Like taught how to fire a gun and—"

"Yes, but that was only the start of it. Trained is probably the wrong word. Manipulated, corrupted, abused. Any of those would be more adequate. He wanted his boy to be the best, to rise up through the ranks and end up with a senior position in the family. And his upbringing taught him how to raise a fearless soldier, so that's what he did."

I stare at her with my heart pounding in my chest.

"When we first found out I was pregnant, he was so keen to have a daughter. Said he was surrounded by men almost every waking hour and he wanted a mini me to spoil. It was so sweet and he seemed so genuine that I didn't think to question him.

"I knew what he did for a living. I didn't really like it. I wanted to care for people, to make them better, not be a part of something that was doing the opposite, but I was in love. So in love.

"The day I gave birth to two beautiful boys, everything changed.

"He was always overprotective of me, but the way he was with them, it was mind-blowing. Watching him with them melted my heart. He loved them so fiercely. I just had no idea that he was also trying to protect them."

"Protect them from who?" I ask.

"His father."

A violent shiver races down my spine.

"What did he do to them?" I whisper, although I'm not entirely sure I want the answer to that question.

"That's not for me to tell, or to assume. I don't know all of it. Just like I've spent my life trying to protect them, they've done the same for me, so I know that what I've been told barely scratches the surface. I've seen the evidence, though."

"Evidence?"

She shakes her head.

"I've already said too much. You don't need all of this on top of everything else. All I was trying to say is that Alex is strong, honey." She covers my hand with hers and squeezes gently. "He's resilient and smart and knows how to handle himself in situations like this. And the others are just as powerful and capable. Trust them to fix this."

"Zay isn't," I whisper. "He isn't any of those things."

"And how do you know that? Until tested, we have no idea what we're capable of. Just look at you." Reaching out, she smooths down the edge of one of my bandages. "I bet you never thought you'd be able to do what you did."

"It's not the same. They... they could be anywhere."

She holds my eyes, urging me to trust her.

"They will find them. And the first chance they get, they'll take the place to the ground, sending everyone who's done this to hell."

"You promise?"

"I promise." Her words hang heavy around us as the silence stretches on.

I've no idea where everyone else is, but they're not anywhere close, that's for sure.

"It's three AM," Gianna says as if she can read my mind. "Are you hungry? I can go and make you something."

"I..." I pause, trying to focus on anything but the pain, both physically and mentally. "I don't know," I say honestly. "Food is the last thing on my mind right now."

"I understand that, honey. I do. But the last thing either of them will want right now is for you not to be looking after yourself. They're going to need you when they get back."

I nod, knowing she's right even if the idea of food makes my stomach want to revolt again.

"I'll go and grab you a few things."

With another squeeze of my hand, she climbs to her feet and walks to the door. But she pauses before she disappears.

"I know my son, Evie. He'll fight through hell to get back to you."

The second she disappears, pulling the door silently closed behind her, the tears hit.

She saw us together when things were good. She has no idea about the things I said to him, the names I called him after I discovered the truth. Will he still fight as hard to get back to me after I treated him like that?

Fuck. I hope so.

He has to know I didn't mean it, right?

I didn't mean any of it. I was angry and hurt and...

Why didn't I cave the next morning and forgive him before he went off to his exam? Why didn't I tell him how I really felt about him? At least when the worst happened he'd have known that I'd be here waiting for him. Fighting for him.

What if he's... wherever he is, thinking that I hate him?

That thought makes my tears fall faster.

I'm still sobbing into my hands when Gianna returns a few minutes later carrying a tray.

Her soft footsteps pad across the room before she slides the tray onto the bedside table and sits on the edge of the bed, pulling me into her arms and holding me tight.

"You know, I always wanted a daughter. Obviously, I wouldn't trade my boys for anything, but I always wanted someone to share the girly stuff with. I think I might have lucked out with my one day daughter in-laws."

"We had a fight," I confess, my voice broken and rough. "Th-the day before. I f-found out... I found out that he'd been lying to me and..." I sniffle. "I said some really awful things."

"Oh, Evie," she sighs, rubbing my back supportively. "What you've been through over the past week... it would have broken most people. It's been overwhelming and intense, and add a new relationship into that mix and being together twenty-four seven, I'm not surprised things blew up a little. I think that's very normal."

"But what if he thinks I meant all the things I said?"

"He won't. He knows how you feel about him. Just like you know how he feels about you. Fights and things you say in the heat of the moment don't mean anything, not really."

I nod against her shoulder, her t-shirt damp against my skin from my tears.

"Why don't you try to eat something? You might feel a little stronger with some food inside you."

As soon as she releases me, I shake out Alex's shirt that I'm still clinging to and tug it over my head.

"Here." She passes me a glass of orange juice before placing a plate of crackers on my lap. "I can get you something else, but I wasn't sure your tummy would handle it."

"This is perfect, thank you."

Picking up one of the crackers, I nibble the edge. I'm not convinced my stomach will even take this. But I know she's right.

I've no idea what's happening. For all I know, the guys are rescuing the two of them as we speak, working under the cover of darkness to bring them both back to me.

But as I glance at Gianna and catch her with her mask down in a moment of her own worry, I realise it might be wishful thinking.

"You should get some rest," I tell her, remembering that she told me it's the middle of the night.

"I can't sleep. Years of shifts have caused insomnia. Add in worrying about my boys and... yeah," she sighs. "I'd much rather be making use of myself than lying in bed and staring at the ceiling."

I nod, understanding completely. If I weren't so exhausted, I'm not sure sleep would come very easily for me right now.

"Is Blakely sleeping?"

"Yes. She's passed out on the sofa in the den."

"She'll be blaming herself for this. Since our mum died, she's taken on the role for Zay. If anything happens to him, she—"

"Shh." She squeezes my knee. "Nothing is going to happen to him. Especially if my pup has anything to do with it."

"Why do you call him that?" I ask, needing to focus on something else.

"Probably for the exact reason you think. As a young child, he was this over-excited, playful, adorable boy. He reminded me of a boisterous puppy."

I smile, trying to imagine a young Alex racing around with all the energy in the world. It's really not hard to picture.

"Do you have photos?"

"I'm sure I can find some for you. And I did promise to embarrass him with them," she laughs, although the shadows never lift from her eyes.

"Did you used to live here?" I ask.

"Yes. When the boys' grandfather stepped down from his role in the family, they moved out, allowing us to take over."

"It's a beautiful house."

"It is. But I always hated it."

Her honesty takes me back a little.

"I didn't grow up with this kind of wealth, Evie. I was a normal girl from a normal family. Stefanos swept me off my feet. Looking back now, the whole thing was such a whirlwind. I was seventeen when we met, and eighteen when I fell pregnant. Although I would never want to change anything, we were too young. I thought Stefanos was this fiercely independent bad boy, but it was all a front. He was under the control of his father. I had no idea back then, but we were merely puppets, and he was our master. He controlled our every move, every step.

"Moving in here, a place they'd lived their lives, it was just another show of how little control we had over our own. If it weren't for my boys, I'd have left years before I did."

"You didn't love Stefanos?"

"Honey, love is... love is so much more complicated than they show you in the movies. Yes, it's intense and thrilling and exciting. But it's also painful and complicated and confusing.

"I think I fell in love with Stefanos the first day I met him, and I'm not sure I've ever really stopped, if I'm being really honest. But I also don't think we're a good match.

"What we want from life is very different. Our priorities and goals are so far apart. The only thing that kept us together was our boys."

"When you found out what was going on, why didn't you take them and run?" I ask.

She shakes her head, her regrets and pain palpable.

"They were too old by the time I fully learned the truth. They were able to make their own choices. They wanted the life they'd been trained to be a part of, and I don't hold that against them in any way. It's in their blood, and I'd never stop them from doing anything they wanted, no matter how dangerous or stupid I think it is."

"You don't agree with all this?" I ask, gesturing to the house, to their lives.

"Again, it's not that cut and dry. The Family, they do a lot of good in this city. But they're also involved in plenty of bad.

"Do I wish my boys wanted to live normal lives? Of course I do. But I also know they wouldn't be fulfilled by it. They crave the danger, the adrenaline rush of what they do. I see their passion for it shining bright in their eyes whenever they talk about it.

"And more than anything, that's what I want. I want them happy."

Silence falls as I think about her words. I might have only just met Daemon, but I'm aware of what he does. And while I might think he's more than a little crazy, I also understand that he probably wouldn't do something so extreme if he didn't like it. I've also seen that look in Alex's eyes that Gianna is talking about. I see it when he talks about his friends, about uni, and although I know he didn't believe it could be possible, I saw it when I talked about him practising law for the Family.

And Gianna is right. I could also never ask him to walk away from something that quite clearly runs through his veins.

"How are you feeling?" she asks.

"Exhausted. Confused. Scared."

"I gave you some pain relief when I patched you up. Do you need more?"

"Will it make me drowsy?"

"Yes," she says honestly. "But I promise you that if anything happens, I'll wake you."

"Okay, then yes. Everything hurts. And I know you're right. They need me ready to fight when they get back."

5

———

ALEX

Zay cries himself to sleep in my arms. It leaves me feeling weird, knowing that he trusts me enough to do this. I'm so fucking relieved that I'm here for him. But I'm also terrified about what the next few hours, days, weeks, however long might hold for him.

I was put into these kinds of situations when I was about his age. And even though I knew most of them were simulations set up by our cunt of a grandfather, it didn't stop them being any less terrifying.

Daemon and I knew that no matter how hard it got, that we'd walk free at the end. If we were lucky, it would be with praise from that sick fuck. Unlucky, and we'd fail whatever his intended test was and be punished. And that could come in a whole host of different ways.

But right now, I've no idea how it's going to play out. The only thing I do know is what they're trying to achieve.

They want Evie, and they want revenge for intercepting her in the first place.

I knew doing what we did was a risk, but I'd do it a million times over to get that time with her. To keep her out

38

of the clutches of the sick prick who bought her. I'll take the pain, the punishment, the revenge just so she doesn't have to. She and this terrified little boy in my arms.

It hurts like a motherfucker, but somehow, I manage to shuffle backward until I'm resting against the wall.

Every inch of me screams from the beating I must have taken while I was blacked out. Cunts. But I can push all of that aside for him. For her.

Pain is your friend, not your enemy. Embrace it. Use it to make you stronger.

I stare down at Zay, trying to figure out what happened, how he ended up here with me, when something in his hair catches my eye. Reaching into his dark locks, I pull out a bloody bit of shattered glass. From the thickness of it, I'd say it was from a car.

As gently as I can, I check his scalp for injuries, and my blood turns to ice when I find a sizeable cut at the back. My fingers come away red, and despite it not being my own, it makes my stomach turn over and makes my hand tremble.

It's so fucked up that I'm scared of blood. Although, it's only ever been my own until this very moment.

"Shit," I whisper, dropping my head back against the wall and closing my eyes for a few seconds in the hope it'll help calm me.

Dragging my eyelids open, I take stock of the room we're in once more. But there's nothing. Nothing that can help a bleeding fucking head wound.

I look down at my shirt, but I've no chance of ripping a bit free to use as a bandage while he's in my arms.

"Zay," I say quietly, knowing that I need to wake him. I might not be an expert, but I've picked up enough over the years to know that if he has a concussion then he shouldn't be sleeping. "Zay, buddy. I need you to wake up for me."

He doesn't stir, but I can feel the warmth of his breath on my neck, making relief rush through me.

It's not enough, though. He needs checking over.

As best I can, I look over the rest of him.

He's still wearing his uniform, and although his shirt is ripped in places, I think it might have protected him enough that I don't see any more blood. His trousers are the same, and he seems to be missing a shoe. And other than scratches on his hands and the cuts and bruises I saw on his terrified little face when I came to, I'm hopeful that he's okay.

Still debating the idea of waking him up versus letting him block all this out with sleep, I sit there watching him.

The clunk of a lock being pulled back puts my heart in my throat, but thankfully, Zay doesn't even flinch.

My grip on him tightens as the door opens and my pulse takes off like a fucking jet plane.

If he were awake, I'd have him behind me already, but as it is, I do what I can.

A man dressed in all black with a balaclava on his face steps into the room with two bottles of water in his giant hand.

He doesn't say anything, but his cold, hard eyes hold mine.

"He's got a head wound," I say, my voice steady and determined. "Do you have a nurse or a doctor?"

He continues to stare. Fucking buffoon.

"He's a kid, man. He's innocent in all of this," I plead.

I'll do anything if it means he gets help and gets out of here, but I'm not about to show that hand quite yet.

The guy grunts before dumping the water on the end of the bed and disappearing as quickly as he arrived.

Okay, so that could have been worse.

Using my foot, I manage to hook the bottle closer.

After inspecting the lid to make sure it's new, I open it, as confident as I can be that it hasn't been spiked with anything that's going to fuck me up, and I take a sip.

The first mouthful is fucking heaven, making me realise just how gross the state of my mouth was.

My eyes catch on my bare wrists and anger curls even more fiercely inside me. Fucking cunts have stolen my watch.

I'll be having that back before I watch this fucking place —wherever the hell it is—burn to the ground with every motherfucker who did this to Zay, to Evie, to anyone whose lives they've fucked up inside it.

Dropping the empty bottle to the floor, I focus back on Zay, who's still sleeping soundly on my chest.

Lifting my hand, I gently press my fingers to the back of his head to check the bleeding.

I grit my teeth when I hold them in front of me and find them coated in red once more.

"We need to get that fixed up somehow, bud." Where the fuck is my mother when I need her?

Resting my head back against the wall, I close my eyes and only one person's face fills my mind.

Where are you, Evie?

Did they get you?

And if they did, I hope you're putting up one hell of a fight.

I don't know if I was wrong about the water, or if the beating took it out of me more than I anticipated, but I somehow manage to fall asleep, shivering cold.

I wake when the door unlocks sometime later, and this time, it makes Zay stir.

Another man head to toe in black steps into the room. I've no idea if it's the same one as before, and quite honestly,

I don't care. As far as I'm concerned, they're all on borrowed time.

My boys will already know I'm missing, I'm sure of it. They'll know where I am. Where we are.

They could be outside right now ready to storm the place to get us back...

The guy has a pile of things in his hand, but again, he doesn't say a word. He just lowers everything to the end of the bed and then leaves once again.

"What's that?" Zay asks in a weak voice.

"I... um... I'm not sure, bud. How are you feeling?" I ask, checking over his face. His cheek is red and swollen, his right eye darkening, and his bottom lip has a nasty-looking split in it.

"Bad."

"What happened?" I ask, slipping from beneath him to see what we've had delivered.

"A big black truck drove into the car on the way to school. It drove us off the road. The... the car flipped a few times." He shakes his head as his eyes fill with tears. "I hit my head really hard against the window. I think I passed out. Then I woke up here with you." His bottom lip trembles as he wrings his hands in his lap. "I'm so glad you're here."

"Me too. If we're together, everything will be okay. Okay?"

He nods, although he doesn't look entirely convinced.

"My friends, my family, they'll be working out how to get us out of this and get revenge on the men who did it," I say confidently.

"I hope so. I miss Blake and Evie."

"Me too, bud. Evie more than Blake," I confess, making him smile.

Sifting through the medical supplies the man brought, I glance between surgical wipes and Zay.

My hands begin to tremble again as I consider what I'm going to have to do.

He really needs to hope that some of Mum's skills have rubbed off on me over the years.

"What's all that?" he asks as I start laying gauze and wipes and things out.

"Um... You know you said you hit your head? Well, you've got a cut that I really need to clean up."

He frowns before lifting his hand to the back of his head. He winces as he finds it before sobbing when he sees his fingers covered in blood.

I try not to look, and instead I focus on what he needs me to do.

Right now, he only has me to rely on, and I need to do everything I can to make this bearable.

"Can you lie down on your front? I need to see it."

"D-do you know what you're doing?" he asks, following my instruction.

"Of course," I lie. "My mum's a nurse. She's taught me everything."

Ripping open a wipe, I lower myself to my knees beside him and suck in a deep breath through my nose and out through my mouth.

You can do this, Alex. It's just a little bit of blood. No big deal.

With another steadying breath, I lean over Zay and gently part his hair, searching for the wound.

"Is it bad?" Zay asks, his voice trembling.

He can sense your fear, you pussy.

You've patched up D and the guys plenty of times. Why is this any different?

"No. It's barely anything," I lie, hanging my head as the pressure gets to me. "I'm really sorry, Zay. But this is probably going to hurt."

"I can handle it."

"I know you can, bud."

The second I press my fingers against his hair to get a better look and clean him up, he winces. But that's the only reaction he has as I work.

"I'm going to need to glue this together, bud. You okay there?"

"Glue?" he asks, sounding horrified.

"Would you rather I try my hand with a needle and thread?"

"Umm..."

"Exactly. It's just going to seal the wound and stop it from bleeding. You ready?" I ask, pulling the lid from the tube of glue with my teeth. Probably not the most hygienic way of doing it, but what other choice do I have? Leave it to get infected and turn gross?

"Just do it."

Getting as much of his hair out of the way as possible, I warn him before pushing the skin together to close the wound and running a generous amount of glue across the seam.

He groans in pain, but he barely flinches as he tries to stay strong for me.

"Okay. We just need to let this set and you're done."

"Okay," he whimpers.

"I'm sorry, bud. I know this sucks."

"We're locked in a concrete cell by God knows who and I've got glue holding my head together. I'm not sure saying it sucks is the best description."

"No, you're probably right."

"They're coming for us, aren't they?"

"Of course they are. We just need to bide our time and conserve our energy."

Silence falls between us, the weight of my possible lies pressing down on my shoulders.

Have faith, Alex.

No one is going to forget about us and leave us here.

"I think you're good to move now," I say, helping him out and grabbing the blanket the man also left. "Here." I wrap it around his shoulders before passing him the other bottle of water. "They didn't bring painkillers."

"It's okay." He sips at the water as I stand in the middle of the freezing cold room, feeling completely out of my depth.

I know there's nothing I can do, but that's not good enough.

Rushing to the door, I pull at the handle, slamming my fists against it in the hope of getting some arsehole down here.

If someone's here and the door's open, then there's a chance we can—

"Alex, stop, please," Zay begs behind me. "We need to wait and conserve our energy, remember?"

His words steal every ounce of my determination, and my arms fall still at my sides as my brow presses against the cold, steel door before me.

Closing my eyes, I whisper, "I remember."

"Freaking out isn't going to help. If you really believe they're coming then you need to have faith."

"Aren't I meant to be the older, wiser one?" I ask without turning around.

"We can be a team. Just like me, Blake and Evie are. Teamwork makes the dream work."

A smile curls at my lips.

"Yeah, bud. It does." Stepping back from the door, I turn around as he opens the blanket for me to join him. "I'm sorry you're having to deal with this," I say after getting settled with him on the cot.

"You make Evie happy, Alex. It'll be worth it to see her smile like she does when she's with you."

6

———

EVIE

When I wake again, the pain and exhaustion isn't quite as all-consuming as the times before.

With my eyes still closed, I think over everything that happened that led me here, allowing myself to experience the fear of being chased through those woods from the safety of this bed.

I was scared. There is no doubting that. But looking back now, only hours after the event, and I already can't believe I did it. I outran... whoever they were, and I made it back here to my family.

That fear grips me in a tight hold once again, its icy claws digging into my skin until it physically hurts.

Not all my family.

Please let Alex be with Zay. Please, I silently beg. If they're together, then maybe things will be okay.

"Evie, I know you're awake," a quiet voice says, making my eyes pop open.

Lying on the pillow next to me is Blakely. Her big blue eyes show her own torment as she watches me.

Gianna might have said she was sleeping on the sofa, but it doesn't look like she's had any rest. Dark circles surround her bloodshot eyes, and there are tear tracks down her cheeks.

"Hi," I whisper, instantly calmed by her presence.

"How are you feeling?"

"Better, I think."

She nods, continuing to study my face for lies.

"I can't believe you beat them. Do you have any idea how dangerous those men were?"

"No, not really. Do you?"

"Well, no. But Stef and the guys, they seem to think—"

"Stef?"

She rolls her eyes. "Stefanos. Alex's dad."

"Yeah, I know who he is. I just wasn't expecting you to have given him a nickname already." I raise a brow at her.

"It's not. It..." She sighs. "All the guys call him it. It's just... easier, I guess."

"So you're one of the guys now?" I ask, more happy to dive into this distraction.

"No, I'm not, I'm just... We've been living here, Evie. While you've been loving life with your sexy boy in that insane cabin. I'm just making the best of it." Her eyes fill with tears, making my heart knot up. I'm the worst sister in the world.

"I'm sorry. I know. I'm sure you've been doing a fantastic job as his housekeeper."

She holds my stare for a beat before she barks out a laugh.

"A good job? Have you met me? I'm pretty sure I'm the worst housekeeper he's ever had."

"Why did Derek get you the job? If he knew he was se... selling off then..."

"I've thought about this a lot and asked Stefanos," she says, making a point of using his whole name. "He said that Derek has found him housekeepers before, and he gets a decent cut out of it. I think it might just be a coincidence that I'm out of action as a dancer and Stefanos needed someone."

"So all of Stefanos' past housekeepers were retired dancers?" I ask, remembering just how serious Alex's warning had been about keeping her distance from his dad.

Have they all been hot like my sister? Is that why he clearly can't keep his hands to himself?

"Seems that way."

"Well, isn't Stefanos a lucky boy," I tease. "Your cleaning might not be up to scratch, but it seems there are some perks to having you around." My eyes drop to her cleavage spilling from her tank with the way she's lying and then to her booty shorts.

"What? You might not know it from in here, but it's baking outside."

"Sure, that's the reason you're walking around looking like sex on legs. Because it's sunny." I roll my eyes at her. "You can't fool me, Blakely Moore."

"I'm not trying to fool anyone. Jeez, you're as bad as Alex."

"So you're not fucking Stef?" I ask outright.

"No."

"And he hasn't tried it on?"

"No," she huffs, giving me a little insight into how this whole situation is playing out.

"But you have?"

"Doesn't matter what I have or haven't done. He's not interested."

"No one told me he was blind," I mutter.

"He's not. He's... He's a good man, Evie."

I think back to some of the things Gianna told me about her ex-husband, about the things he's been through, the guilt he suffers because of what he allowed his boys to experience as well. I also vividly remember her telling me she'd probably always love him.

"I'm sure he is, Blake. Just be careful, yeah?"

She narrows her eyes at me.

"I can handle myself with the likes of Stefanos," she counters.

"I'm not suggesting you can't. It's just..." She raises a brow. "Everything here is complicated. The world they're a part of, it's dangerous and—"

"Evie, look at us right now. I know all of this. Just... trust me, yeah?"

"Of course. You know I do."

She falls quiet, content with my words.

"I really need to pee," I whisper, mostly to myself in the hope the words spur my body into action.

"You need help?" Blake offers.

"To pee? No, I think I'm good."

I wait two more seconds before forcing my body into action, flipping the covers off and swinging my legs over the edge of the bed.

Before finding my way to the bathroom, I find myself at the curtain-covered window. Suddenly, my need to see the sun is bigger than my need to use the toilet.

Throwing the heavy blackout material aside, warmth washes over my body. It doesn't fix anything, but it does help, just a little bit.

I take a few moments to appreciate their well-tended garden before I turn around for my first proper look at the room I'm in.

"Oh my God," I gasp, realisation dawning on me as I scan the photos on the shelves, the framed football shirt hanging on the wall, the couple of barely dressed girls pinned to a board behind a desk.

"We thought you'd want to be in this room if you were given the choice," Blakely explains.

Being surrounded by all his things, his childhood memories, makes his absence right now that much more painful.

Walking over to one of the photos, I study the two identical boys.

They're probably seven or eight. They're wearing different coloured t-shirts, but that's about where the differences end. It's almost impossible to tell them apart.

"They're really quite something, huh?" Blakely asks, her voice closer than I was expecting.

Her warmth covers my back as she wraps her arm around my waist and rests her chin on my shoulder.

"You knew?" I whisper.

"I've been living in this house since they discovered what happened to you, Eve. Of course I knew."

"And you didn't want to tell me?"

She chuckles. "Not my story. And plus, I was a little distracted by the fact someone had purchased my sweet and innocent little sister to really care all that much."

"Not so sweet and innocent anymore," I mutter sadly.

She doesn't say the words that I know are on the tip of her tongue.

He'll be okay.

It's all fake promises and false hope.

None of us know the outcome of this. All we can do is pray. But the harsh reality is that nothing could be okay ever again after this.

Tears burn the backs of my eyes as a huge lump crawls up my throat. But I fight it.

Crying is going to get us nowhere.

If the guys do figure a way to get them out of this, if Alex and I have some kind of future ahead of us, then I need to be stronger.

I'd be naïve to think this is a one-off incident. They all live dangerous lives, and I can only assume that this kind of situation is fairly normal for them. Which means, if he can forgive me for the things I said, for the way I treated him, then it's going to be my life too.

"I still need to pee," I say, trying not to lose myself in all the what-ifs here.

Releasing me, Blakely takes a step back as I move across the room.

I don't look back. I don't need to to know that she's watching me closely.

"I'm okay," I say quietly before slipping into the room and closing the door behind me.

More of Alex's things that I didn't see when I was in here in the middle of the night make themselves known. And no sooner have I done what I came in here for than I find myself with his shower gel bottle under my nose, losing myself in his scent.

Come back to me.

I'm sorry for everything I said. I didn't mean it.

I've no idea how long I stand there for, lost in memories of our time together, but a knock on the door startles me.

Not needing to be invited in, Blakely slowly pushes the door open and pokes her head inside.

Her expression turns sombre when she sees what I'm doing.

"Oh, Evie," she says, rushing inside, taking the bottle from my hand and gathering me up in her arms.

But still, I refuse to let the tears fall.

I need to do something more productive than cry.

"Gianna and Calli want to know if you're hungry," she whispers.

"Umm..."

"They're baking up a storm in the kitchen."

"Where's Stefanos and Daemon and—"

"Some big meeting somewhere. It's just us girls."

I nod, liking the sound of being surrounded by fierce females who understand all of this.

"The others?"

"Stella and Emmie are at school, but they're coming as soon as they're done. Jodie is on her way with more icing sugar."

"Have you met them already?"

"They were here while you were sleeping."

"They're good people."

"Totally terrifying, but yeah, good people. They're exactly who you need in your corner right now."

Those words are the reminder I don't need that while Alex and Zay might be the ones at the mercy of whoever wants me, I'm still at risk. I'm the one they really want, and one wrong move and I'll find myself plucked from life as I know it to start over. And something tells me that if they get me, no one will ever find me.

A pained sigh slips past my lips.

"What is it?"

"I really need to shower. I'm all kinds of gross."

"You can't get your bandages wet. If those cuts get infected then—"

"Will you help me? Then I'll come eat."

"Evie," she whispers. "You know I'd do anything for you. Gianna left some plastic wrap stuff. We can cover what we can then be careful with the rest."

Nodding, I step up to the basin to brush my teeth while she goes to find it.

Blakely faffs around, turning the shower on and getting the temperature right before she helps me undress, wraps the bandages that are covering more of my body than I realised, and helps me into the shower.

The warmth of the water on my skin is incredible, but nothing is better than the moment she rinses through my hair. Little twigs and leaves land by my feet, the water dark and murky with a mixture of blood and dirt.

It's a harsh reminder of what I went through.

"You did so good, babe," Blakely tells me as if she can read my mind.

"Alex is going to be so proud of you for getting away like you did."

I suck in a sharp breath.

"What?"

"He might not know," I whisper. "Wherever he is, he might think they have me too. He might not be trying to get away because he's trying to rescue me." My breaths come faster, my chest moving more rapidly as my heart races.

"Whoa, calm down, Evie. Just breathe, yeah?" Placing her hands on my shoulders, she stares into my eyes. "With me. Breathe in, and out. In, and out."

It takes a few seconds, but I finally get myself under control.

"Trust him, Evie. Trust them."

I nod, because, what else is there to do?

Everything feels utterly hopeless. And right now, I'm totally useless while the man I love and my little brother are... fuck knows where.

Please be together, I silently beg once more. Please let Alex be with Zay, keeping him safe and making him smile.

7

———

ALEX

The slam of the door jolts us both awake, and when I open my eyes, I find five hooded men staring down at us.

"What do you want?" I bark, sitting up and keeping Zay behind me.

They don't respond—not that I really expected them to. Instead, three of them reach for me.

"Get the fuck off me," I grunt, fighting back the best I can with three sets of hands on my body and my head still hazy with sleep.

"Ugh, you little cunt," one barks when I manage to kick him in the shin.

"No," Zayden wails behind me.

"Get off him. He has nothing to do with this. Let him go."

"No can do. Our little Greek friend is exactly where we need him," one sneers.

"Fuck you, prick." I spit at him before his eyes drop down my body.

"I've heard about your skills, pretty boy. But if it's all the same, I think I'll wait for my turn with your little lady."

The roar that rips from my throat doesn't sound human.

"You keep your motherfucking hands off my girl."

I kick and fight, but their grip only tightens before one of them throws a punch that makes the world spin around me.

"Alex," a little voice cries, bringing me back.

"Let him go. Please, just—"

Darkness cuts off my vision as Zay continues to cry out.

"It's okay, bud. I won't let them hurt you. Ooof." All the air rushes from my lungs and someone punches me so hard in the stomach I fold over, falling to my knees.

"Alex," he cries.

"I'm okay. I'm okay," I assure him as I'm hauled from the ground and dragged from the cell we'd been locked in. "Don't you dare split us up," I warn as he continues to whimper behind me.

"You'll do as you're fucking told," someone grunts.

Despite trying to find some purpose, my legs continue to flail around as I'm dragged fuck knows where. That is, until a van door opens and I'm thrown inside, quickly followed by Zay.

"Where are you taking us?" I demand, but the only answer I'm met with is the slamming of the door followed by a loud fist on the side of the van that makes Zay scream in fright.

"It's okay, bud," I say, ripping the sack off my head before removing his.

"Where are they taking us?" he asks, his eyes wide with fear.

"I've no idea." I wrap my arm around his shoulder and pull him close.

"They're not taking us home, are they?"

"I highly doubt it," I mutter as the engine comes to life and the van takes off.

The drive is bumpy as hell. My head bounces off the side of the van more than once, making me see stars while Zay trembles against me.

"They're never going to find us if they keep moving us."

"It might be a trick. We might end back up in the exact same place," I say, thinking about some of the games we use to disorientate people.

"Really? Seems like a lot of effort."

"Anything could be happening. Keep an open mind."

"I'm trying."

I've no idea how much time passes before the van finally pulls to a stop and the back door is ripped open, allowing some sunlight in before our heads are covered once more and we're dragged back out.

It soon becomes obvious that I was wrong about them throwing us back into the same cold, dark cell, because the one we find ourselves in once we're left alone again is even more depressing.

There's a leak above us somewhere, which results in a river of water running down the wall that also has mould growing out of it. The floor is disgusting, and this time, there's no uncomfortable cot to sit on or sleep in. There is nothing.

"I guess we shouldn't have hated on the first place so much, huh?" Zay asks, looking around with his arms wrapped around himself and his top lip curled up in disgust. "I didn't think there was anywhere worse than Lovell. Guess I was wrong. What is that for?" he asks, looking up at a heavy chain I hadn't seen hanging from the ceiling. "Oh, and those?"

My eyes find the two large hooks screwed into the old concrete wall, and I swallow nervously.

"Umm..." I rub the back of my neck, not wanting to explain to an innocent child that they could well both be used to torture us.

"This place isn't going to be enjoyable, is it?"

"No, it's not."

"Do we really just have to sit and wait for them to find us?"

"Did you have a better idea?" I ask, genuinely interested in what he's thinking about all of this.

"You any good at digging through concrete with your hands?"

"Sadly not. You?"

He shakes his head and takes another step into the gloomy room.

"They're going to come for us soon. We can do this." His voice might be full of confidence, but when he looks back, I see the truth in his eyes, and it damn near kills me.

Evie is relying on me to protect him the best way I can, and right now, I can't help but feel like I'm failing.

We huddle in the corner, and with nothing else to do, we just wait.

The second the sliding of a bolt echoes through the silence, I jump to my feet, keeping Zay behind me when he follows suit.

My body trembles with the need for food. The one bottle of water we've had hasn't really cut it.

The door swings open and I grit my teeth, ready to go head-to-head with these pricks.

"Alexander Deimos, I must say, it's such a privilege to have you staying with us," the tallest of the men who step into the small room says, moving ahead of the others. "It really is a pleasure to welcome you to our sanctuary."

"I can't say I'm overly enjoying it, to be honest," I mutter.

He studies me from behind his mask. Fucking pussies. If they were brave, they'd show their faces, but instead, they're standing before me like fucking mice, ready to run away and hide.

It's how I know they won't win.

Damien, Dad, the guys... they'll already be on to them. They'll know exactly where we are, and they'll be busy running intel and getting everything in place. And we're just the tip of the iceberg. They also have Reid and Luciana after their blood. No motherfucker is going to get away. We'll be dancing in their blood by the time this is all over.

"That's a shame. We're going to have so much fun together."

He jerks his chin in instruction to the goons at his side, and before I know what's happening, they have my arms in their grip. The sound of heavy chains fills the air before something cold is wrapped around my wrists.

"No," Zay cries, rushing forward to protect me as I'm dragged into the centre of the room.

I could fight them. I'm not that weak, not yet. But now isn't the time. I might beat them, but there's no way they're not the only ones. If this guy is the boss, he'll have more than two henchmen protecting him.

"Please no, let him go," Zay begs.

"It's okay, bud. I can take whatever they want to dish out."

One of the men chuckles darkly at my confidence. But I stand by it—as long as they're delivering punishments to me and not Zay.

"No, it's not fair. You haven't done anything."

He rushes over, prepared to fight for me, but the goon to my left isn't having anything. His arm whips out and he backhands Zay, sending him flying back into the wall.

"You motherfucker," I bellow, using the other guy's shock to my advantage and twisting around to headbutt the cunt who just hurt Zay.

Pain shoots through my skull and down my spine, but the crack of bone and rush of blood from the prick's nose before he roars in anger is more than worth it.

"You stupid fucking cunt," the boss says calmly. "You're going to pay for that."

"Where is she?" I demand. "Where's Evie?"

Ninety percent of his face might be covered, but I don't need to see it all to know he's smirking at me. I see it in the twinkle of his eyes.

"Don't worry, we're taking real good care of your girl. Isn't that right, boys?"

Acid rushes up my throat at the thought of them being anywhere near her.

"I will fucking kill you if you so much as lay a finger on her."

He stalks closer as my arms are wrenched above my head and secured from the chain Zay found when we first entered.

"Is that right?" he taunts. "You see, it doesn't seem like you're able to do much right about now."

"You're all going to die for this."

Cool air wraps around my torso as one of the guys rips my shirt away.

"Look at that," the other taunts. "Barely a mark on him. Nothing like his brother."

My entire body jolts at the mention of Daemon's scars.

"Aw, you think we're clueless idiots. No, no, Alexander. We're far from that."

"What do you want from us?" I demand. "You wanted Evie back. Sounds to me like you've got her. What more do you want?"

The boss chuckles.

"You stole her from me, Alexander. I paid good money for that curvy little body and tight virginal cunt, and you went and stole her."

My chest heaves, my nostrils flaring at his words.

"You and your little friends need to learn who's really in charge here."

I snarl at him as something heavy is clamped around my ankles.

"We know what Ricardo and his men did to your brother for sticking his nose in their business. And guess what? We're going to do the same to you. After all, identical twins do like to look the same, right?"

The second he finishes speaking, something cracks across my shoulder blades, making the skin burn red hot.

"No, please, no," Zay cries, watching us with wide, terrified eyes.

"It's okay," I force through gritted teeth.

They're coming. They already know where we are. They're going to get us.

They're going to get Evie. They might have even done so already.

While they're in here, they could be sneaking her out.

"ARGH," I cry this time when the whip hits lower, slicing into my skin.

Zay screams, his own pain at being forced to watch this outweighing his ability to stay quiet.

"Bud," I say, through clenched teeth. "Squeeze your eyes tight and put your hands over your ears for me, yeah?" I ask. In reality, it'll do very little, I'm sure. But I need to do something. Watching this is going to fuck him up. I should know. I've seen first-hand what this kind of treatment did to Daemon, and I wouldn't wish that on anyone. Especially a young, innocent child. "Please, Zay. For Evie, yeah?"

He nods and does as I say a beat before the next lash cuts through my skin and I roar in pain.

They're coming. They're coming. They're coming.

Closing my eyes, I repeat that mantra over and over as images of being with Evie play out in my mind, taking me off to a different place where these cunts can't hurt me.

8

———

EVIE

The second I step foot in the kitchen, I'm engulfed in a set of arms.

Calli doesn't say anything. She doesn't make me any false promises, and I love her that little bit more for it.

"Whatever you need, I'm here. We all are."

"Thank you."

"Okay, so we have pancakes, waffles, cupcakes, cookies. You name it, we've baked it."

Jodie reaches for my hand as I pass, and she squeezes it in support as I take the stool next to her.

"Umm... coffee?" I ask.

"Yes," Calli hisses. "We totally have that too." She hops around the kitchen like a little pregnant Duracell bunny.

"Is she okay?" I ask.

"Too much sugar," Blakely says. "She was already eating icing when I came down earlier."

"I couldn't sleep. Daemon was out all night with the guys and I just... I needed to help."

"Calli, you're pregnant, you need to rest," I say, concern

64

twisting up my insides that she's doing too much. That I'm putting too much stress on her and the baby.

"I promise, I'm okay," she says, sliding a steaming mug of coffee my way. "I just need… I don't know what I need. But no one will allow me to go running out there wielding a gun, so I'm baking. Everyone is going to be hungry, right?"

"You didn't do this when Daemon was…" Jodie trails off, making me more than curious.

"No, that was different."

"Where did he go?" I ask, needing to dive into something, anything but the current situation.

"Are you two okay if Evie and I—"

"Go," my sister says. "We've got all this covered." She wipes her finger along the counter before licking it. "And not just in icing sugar." She raises a brow.

"I'm a messy cook," Calli admits with a shrug.

Grabbing a bottle of water, she nods toward the back of the house and takes off. With my hands wrapped around my coffee, I follow her down to a massive sunroom and then out through open double doors to the patio.

"Wow," I breathe. The garden looked impressive from the window, but it's nothing compared to down here with the comfortable furniture laid out in the shade. There are brightly coloured flowers everywhere.

"It's my favourite spot in the whole house. Not that I really spend much time here."

"Is Stefanos a keen gardener?" I ask, making her burst out laughing.

"Hell no. That man wouldn't know a daisy from a rose if they smacked him in the face."

"But this is—"

"He has a gardener. And I think his last housekeeper enjoyed being out here."

"I can assure you that his new one won't be deadheaded anything," I say, my fingers delicately stroking a vibrant orange rose petal. Thinking about my sister spending her day cleaning is a push, but gardening...

I shake my head.

We've lived in that flat in Lovell all our lives. Any plant that ever found its way inside ended up dead within a week

"Give your sister some credit," Calli says with a smile. "Stefanos seems to love having her around."

"Anything to do with the booty shorts and overflowing cleavage, by any chance?"

"Huh," Calli says, tilting her head to the side. "And here I thought it was her skills with a feather duster."

"My sister might have skills, but I can assure you, they don't involve a feather duster. Or," I say in a rush, "at least not doing what she should be with it."

Calli laughs as I take a seat on the other end of the outdoor sofa to her. I attempt to curl my legs beneath me and tuck into the corner, but one of the cuts across my thigh pulls and I'm forced to sit a little more sensibly.

"Still hurting?"

I shrug. "It could be worse," I say absently, staring out at the perfect lawn and endless flowers before us.

"A few months ago, Daemon was taken by the Italians," Calli says, dragging my attention back to her. "We had a Family event for my mother's birthday and they attacked.

"We had no idea if he was alive. My dad died that night, I lost my boyfriend—a boyfriend no one but Alex knew I had—and I discovered I was pregnant. It was—"

"Horrendous?" I finished for her.

She smiles despite the nightmare she's explaining. "Yeah, that about sums it up."

"The guys rescued him?" I ask, assuming there's a

happy ending here, seeing as I ran into his arms when I got back.

"No, actually. He was locked up with Ant after they discovered he was a traitor. They escaped."

"Wow."

"Yeah, it was pretty impressive. They were... they were a mess. But he came back to me." Her hand gently rubs over her small bump as she talks. "I know everyone keeps saying that it'll be okay, and I know how it feels to hear that when everything feels so hopeless and out of your control. But you need to have faith."

"Daemon won't rest until they have them back. None of the guys will, I can promise you that."

"Daemon and Alex... do they... can they feel if something is wrong? You know, like twins on the TV?"

"Sometimes. Alex never once gave up on D when he was gone. He knew he was okay and that he would be back. D feels the same right now."

"That's reassuring."

Sipping my coffee, I soak up Calli's strength and support. She doesn't need to say anything. I feel it.

"Did they hurt him?"

She rubs her belly again.

"Yeah. Daemon was already forced to bear the horrors of his past on his body, and they just added to that."

I stare at her, a few of the things Gianna said to me while I was barely with it coming back to me.

"Their grandad?"

Calli's eyes widen in surprise. "Alex told you?"

"He mentioned him not being a good person. But it was Gianna who said something about how he treated Stefanos and her boys."

Fire burns through her eyes, a wave of protectiveness so strong it's almost intimidating.

"If that man weren't already worm food, I'd have been the one to make it happen."

"I think Gianna might have beaten you to it."

She blinks at me.

"N-no. He had a heart attack."

"Oh, okay. Fair enough." I sip my coffee again while Calli gets lost in her own thoughts.

"Do you think... do you think she had something to do with it?"

"I don't know. I wasn't exactly in a great place when she was telling me all this. I might be reading too much into things."

"What else did she say?" Calli asks.

I relay what I can remember.

"She hasn't told you these things?" I ask.

"Not quite like that, no. But I've grown up with Alex and Daemon. I guess she doesn't feel the need to explain how things went down quite in the same way. I already know they're two of the strongest, most capable guys in the city. It's interesting to hear it, though. Stefanos, Alex and D have a strange relationship."

"Strange?"

"They've all suffered at the hands of Stefanos's father. I guess that mutual pain could have brought them together, but I think Stefanos's guilt keeps him from making the most of the relationship he could have with his boys."

"That's sad," I say. "My mum died in a car crash when I was younger."

Calli nods. "Blakely told me. Sounds like things were tough."

"Yeah, they were. But she's incredible. I owe her so much."

Footsteps bring our conversation to a close, and when I look up, Gianna is smiling as she moves toward us with a tray in her hand.

She looks incredible with her dark hair curled over her shoulders and a flowy summer dress that highlights her figure. She might still have dark circles under her eyes, but she looks fresher than she did in the middle of the night. I hope that means she managed to get some rest.

"How are my girls doing?" she asks, lowering the tray to the table before us, then sitting in a chair opposite.

Calli beams at her with love filling her blue eyes. It's obvious they have a special kind of connection. One I can only hope to find with the mother of the man I love.

"We're okay, G," Calli says, rubbing her belly once more.

"Evie?" she asks.

"Yeah, you know. Coffee helps."

"Always. Make sure you eat too." She pushes the tray closer, and I reach out to grab a plate full of waffles, fresh fruit, and whipped cream.

Unable to deny how good it looks or the way my stomach growls, I fill my fork with sweet goodness and moan when I get my first taste.

"You can make a good waffle, Calli."

She blushes at my praise. "Jocelyn taught me everything I know," she says with a smile.

"How's she doing without having to dote on your mother twenty-four seven?" Gianna asks, giving me a clue as to who Jocelyn might be.

"Good. She's too good a person to put up with that woman's crap."

"I'm sensing you didn't get on with your mother," I muse.

"That's a story for another day. Let's just say she's where she deserves to be."

"And if you ever wondered, Calli is a bad-arse just like my boys," Gianna adds.

"I'm not sure about that," Calli smiles. "But I appreciate it."

"Don't underestimate yourself. It takes one very strong girl to put up with Daemon."

"He's a teddy bear really."

"There are a lot of people in this city who would argue with that."

"Is there any news?" I ask. As much as I love finding out more about Alex and his life, right now, the present is more important.

"I haven't heard anything. But if I do, you'll be the first person I tell," she says softly as more voices fill the air.

"Look out, trouble's here."

Not five seconds later do Emmie and Stella spill into the garden and immediately rush toward me.

"Evie, how are you feeling?" Emmie asks.

"Been better," I say honestly. "Have you heard anything?"

"No, sorry. The guys were gone all night. Still haven't seen or heard anything from them."

"They've got to know something though, right?"

"Yeah, they should. We're all tracked. Unless those who have Alex have blockers in place, they should know exactly where he is."

It takes a few seconds for Emmie's words to register.

"If they know, then they might already have them, right?"

Emmie sits down beside me and takes my hand while Stella lowers her arse to the table in front of me.

"We don't know, Evie," Emmie says. "But what we do know is that they all know what they're doing and we have to trust them. I know it's hard. We're worried too. But they wouldn't do anything to put Alex and Zay at more risk than they already are."

"They're going to get them back, and they're going to destroy this human trafficking ring in the process," Stella says confidently.

Jodie and Blakely join us with fresh coffees for everyone, and we spend the rest of the afternoon and evening sitting outside in the sun, all of us anxiously waiting for news.

Brianna joins us, completing our group. It's a weird yet comforting feeling being surrounded by so many fierce women when growing up it was just me and Blake.

I'm in awe of each and every one of them. And I couldn't wish for anyone better to have my back right now.

As the sun begins to sink behind the trees at the end of the garden, my eyes are so heavy that I can barely keep them open.

"You should go and get some rest," Blakely says.

"I don't want to miss anything if they come back."

"We won't let that happen," Stella assures me. "But Blakely is right, you need to rest."

I look around at all the glum, concerned faces around me.

"Promise you'll come and wake me if anything happens."

"We promise," Gianna assures me.

"Come on," Calli says. "I could do with a lie down too. That's if you want company."

'Thank you,' I mouth.

Together, we make our way through the quiet house and up the stairs. Calli follows me into Alex's room.

"I can go to D's room if you want to be alone," she offers as I head for the bathroom.

"I'd rather not be, if that's okay with you."

"Of course."

I duck into the bathroom, and when I emerge, I find her standing at Alex's desk, looking at the photos I was studying earlier.

"They're really something, huh?" I ask.

"You've no idea," she laughs. "All six of them, they're… everything."

"You all are too. They're lucky to have you."

"We're a bizarre little family, but I wouldn't have it any other way."

A yawn cuts off any response I might have to that comment. With a concerned look, Calli takes my hand and leads me to Alex's bed.

"Rest. If anything happens, we'll wake you."

Curling up under the sheets, I bury my nose in the pillow, breathing in the faint scent of Alex that lingers.

"Have faith," Calli whispers. "He'll come back to you."

The room is in darkness when I wake. Calli is still out cold next to me, her nap seemingly turned into a full night's sleep.

My skin prickles with the awareness that I'm being watched, and slowly, I turn around and look at the chairs that were still pulled up beside the bed.

My breath catches when I find a dark figure sitting in one.

"It's okay, Evie. It's just me," he whispers.

"No wonder everyone is terrified of you. Jesus," I mutter, covering my racing heart with my palm.

"Sorry, I didn't mean to scare you. Just... yeah," he says, his eyes lifting to the sleeping girl behind me.

"She's okay," I assure him. "She came to lie down with me. I think we both might have underestimated how tired we were."

The sliver of moonlight that cuts across the room allows me to see the smile that curls at his lips as I talk about Calli. It doesn't diminish the dark look in his eyes, though.

"Have you found them? Got them? Anything?"

He sits back with a sigh. "Trust us, Evie. Let us do our jobs."

"Easier said than done."

"I know. Believe me, I do."

"He's okay though. You'd know if he wasn't, right?"

"He's fine. It'll take more than this to bring any of us down."

His words should reassure me, but I can't help but feel like he's saying them to make me feel better.

"I'm sorry," I blurt. "About what happened when I first saw you."

He chuckles darkly. "I told him it was a bad idea. Warned him that you'd take one look at me and realise you'd chosen wrong."

I smile, wishing I could have experienced that brotherly banter before all of this.

"I love him, Daemon." The words are out of my mouth before I've even thought them. "We fought before all this, and I never got the chance to tell him."

"He knows. When it's real, you don't need words, Evie."

I fall silent, the weight of that statement stealing any response I might have had.

"We've met before, you know that?"

"No. When?"

"That first night you were here working. We had a conversation in the kitchen. You thought I was him."

My lips open to respond, but I quickly close them again as I vaguely remember the conversation in question. Although, I can barely recall what we said to each other.

"He was enthralled with you from the moment he saw you that night. He couldn't take his eyes off you."

My cheeks burn up, and I send up a silent thank you for the darkness.

"I had no idea he was looking for you after, though. We haven't always been as close as we probably should be."

"Things have been tough, from what I've heard. It's understandable."

"Know all my secrets, huh?"

"No, no. That's not what—"

"I'm joking, Evie. I've nothing to hide from my family. Calli has taught me a lot in a few short months. I'm trying to be a better brother and boyfriend. Friend."

"For what it's worth, I think you're doing a pretty good job."

"I'll bring them back to you."

"I know. I have faith."

He scratches at his jaw, pausing as if he can't quite believe those words.

"Nikolas," Calli moans behind me, and I still.

Did she just say another guy's name in her sleep?

"I'm here, Angel."

Frowning, I watch as he pushes to his feet and walks around the bed.

"She hasn't told you all my secrets, I see," he comments, able to read my confusion. "I'm taking my girl. Are you going to be okay?" he asks before sliding his arms under her body and lifting her to his chest without any effort.

I don't speak until he gets to the door.

"Daemon?" I whisper, making him pause. "He's lucky to have you. They all are. Never forget that."

He nods once and then disappears from the room, leaving me alone for the first time in a while.

Sitting up in the middle of the bed, I clutch the covers tight as I send up another prayer to anyone who might be willing to listen that we're all going to come out of this unscathed.

9

———

ALEX

Something warm hits my shoulder before running over my arm. It makes a shiver rip down my spine, but as my body shudders, pain erupts. Memories of what happened slam into me. They're so visceral, so real, it's as if it's happening right now.

Something hits me again and my eyes ping open in confusion.

My heart splinters right down the centre at the sight of Zay sitting over me protectively, crying.

"I'm okay," I whisper. My voice is hoarse, and I can only imagine why.

I remember shutting down. In my head, I was back on the deck of the cabin with Evie, rolling around on that outside sunbed, while my body was screaming in pain. Zay was doing the same thing, making it hard to stay in my fantasy, but I did what I could.

What else could I do?

Blinking back the sleep, my eyes catch on his hands. Both of them are bright red with blood.

My stomach turns over, and my heart rate increases.

"Is that... is that mine?"

He glances down at them.

"Yeah. It won't stop, and I've no idea what to do."

Sucking in a deep breath, willing my panic and fear to stay down, I reach out and take his bloody hand.

"You don't need to do anything," I assure him. "Just being here..." I shake my head.

"I can't believe they did that," he whispers, another tear dripping from his jaw.

As if they're watching us—which they probably are— footsteps pound outside the door before the locks are pulled back and two men step inside.

I want to say I'm on my feet in a heartbeat, shoving Zay behind me and standing tall, but something tells me it might be a lie. The burning pain from my back sure clues me into the fact that I'm not being as slick as I'd normally be.

"What do you want?" I growl as the warmth of my own blood trickles down my back.

My hands tremble at my sides as my head spins. But succumbing to my own fears right now isn't going to help anyone. And if they were to learn my weakness... No, just fucking no.

"You want to see your girl?" one of them growls, fully distracting me from the blood.

"Yes," I state simply.

"Okay, then come with us."

I stare at them for a beat before looking back.

Zay holds my eyes then nods, telling me to go.

"No, I can't—"

"We might not offer again," one of the men warns darkly. "The kid will be okay."

I've no idea if these are two of the men who tied me up and whipped me—it's impossible to tell with only their eyes showing in darkness. Not that it matters. I don't trust any of them. Especially not with Zay.

"It's okay," Zay whispers. "Go make sure she's okay."

"I'd do as he says if I were you," the other guy states. Something tells me that if his face weren't covered, he'd be smirking.

I hesitate, fear that this might all be a ruse to get me away from Zay growing.

"Go, Alex. I can handle it," he says firmly.

My leg moves of its own accord, taking me closer to the men, and hopefully my girl.

"Let's go then. And I swear to God, if you've hurt her, I will gut both of you alive."

One of them chuckles darkly and the other steps around me, slamming his palms against my ruined back and shoving me face-first into the wall so he can cuff me.

"Cunt," I hiss with my cheek pressed against the cold concrete wall.

"Be nice, or we might change our minds."

I keep my mouth shut, because I can't risk that happening.

I need to know if Evie is here or if they're just baiting me. I need to know if she's okay, and if she's not, then I need to figure out a way to bring this place to the ground, with or without the help of my body.

I'm marched from the room, shouting back for Zay to be strong. The hallways I'm taken down are about as depressing as the room we're locked in.

It's so cold that we have to be underground. It's summer on the outside. Even the solid walls caging me in shouldn't keep the warmth out quite so effectively, unless we're that far away from the sun.

But before I get to figure it all out, I'm shoved into a

room that looks a lot like the one I've just left, only this one has a single chair in the middle and screens attached to every wall.

"What the hell is this?" I demand.

"We told you, we brought you to see your girl."

This wasn't what I had in fucking mind, arsehole, I seethe silently.

"Take a seat," the other says, shoving me into the chair, making my eyes water with pain when I'm dragged back into it. "You wouldn't want to miss the show."

The screens flicker to life one by one, capturing my attention so fully, I don't notice them cuff me to the chair.

"Ready?" I grunt in response, too desperate to find out what the fuck they're playing at. "Time for action."

The second Evie appears on screen, lying on a bed in a sexy nightie, I roar in anger, desperation, and fucking fear.

"Where is she?" I demand, my eyes scanning every inch of the screen, but my panic is too strong to really register any of it.

"She's right there," one mocks in my ear. "And I don't know about you, but we're going to enjoy the show."

They both step back. I've no idea if they leave or just slip into the shadows. I don't really give a fuck.

The girl on the screen, though. Fuck.

She's so fucking beautiful, mesmerising, and sexy.

Her lips move as she speaks, but there's no volume. I crave the sound of her voice, and as if they can read my thoughts, the speakers crackle and I get exactly what I need.

"How are you doing? Have you had a good day?" she purrs. I recognise that sexy voice from when I locked myself in the bathroom in The Empire and had some one-on-one time with her like a creep.

My lips part to answer despite knowing that she's not actually talking to me. And then the inevitable happens and the world crashes down around me.

"It's better for seeing you, sweetheart. What about you?" a deep voice asks through the screen.

She stares right at the camera, right into my eyes. It's as if I'm the only one in the world, and it makes my heart race and my palms sweat despite how fucked up this whole situation is.

"Yeah, it's been good. Busy," she replies.

I study her, really fucking study her, trying to pinpoint when this might have been done.

Was it after we started spending time together? Or was it before?

Or... my blood runs cold... is it more recent?

I search for any indication that it could have happened while I've been here, but I don't even know what I'm looking for.

"I hope you haven't been keeping others entertained in my absence," he teases.

My teeth clench and my fists curl, knowing that whoever this motherfucker is was filming my girl.

She trusted him enough to do this, and he totally fucking betrayed her.

They talk back and forth about bullshit as she drives him—and me—wild with innocent touches of her body.

The white satin she has wrapped around her body is sinful. If I really study the screen, I can see the blush of her nipples behind it. And it's sitting so high on her thighs that one move and I'd get to see everything I've been missing.

"Why are you doing this?" I demand.

Someone behind me chuckles.

"We thought you should know how much we're

enjoying spending time with your girl in your absence. She sure knows how to put on a show."

My teeth grind so hard I'm surprised I don't crack one.

"She's really quite something. So sweet. So innocent. Can totally understand why you're so enthralled with her."

"Hell knows I'd have a go on that if I had the chance," the other adds helpfully. "Unlike you though, I value my own life enough not to get involved."

Pussy, I want to spit at him, but everything vanishes as Evie shifts a little on the bed she's lying on. Arching her back, she shows off her body, making her even more tempting than before.

My cock swells just watching her, and I've no doubt the cunt on the other end of this call is having the same reaction.

"You want me to take this off... Daddy?" she purrs.

Bile washes through my stomach.

Fuck yes, I want her to take it off.

But this isn't for me.

Squeezing my eyes closed for a beat, I realise for the first time why they brought me in here, and quite frankly, for as much as I love watching her, I think I'd prefer another round with the whip.

"You know I do, beautiful. Let me see what's hiding behind that teasing nightie." As he speaks, I try to focus on his voice. There's a faint recognition niggling at the back of my mind, but I can't place it.

Vincent?

Derek?

Any of the cunts who've visited Zay and me over the past few hours... days?

My fingers curl so tightly, my nails dig into my palms.

But the pain barely scratches the surface of what listening and watching this does to me.

"So beautiful," he murmurs as she pulls the fabric aside, exposing herself to him.

Acid burns up my throat, and my mouth waters, ready to puke all over myself.

Sucking in a deep breath through my nose, I force myself not to react.

It's what they want. They want to torture me, hurt me for taking something that belonged to... whom? Their boss? Fuck knows. But there's no fucking way I will allow them to see that it's working.

"Fuck, yeah," he grunts like a sick fuck when she finally stops teasing him and reveals her tits to him.

Fuck you, arsehole. You might get to see her, but I've touched, tasted and devoured every inch of that body.

I bark out a laugh when their time runs out and he begs like a pussy to have longer with her.

"Fucking loser, paying for a woman who would never look twice at you in real life," I spit.

"Where do you think your girl is right now, Deimos?" one of the men snarls. "She's locked away somewhere you're never going to find her while she goes to town on Daddy's dick instead of yours."

Anger rushes through me, and I jolt in the chair with my need to get to them.

"Good luck with that, prick."

Laughter follows, but the second voices come back through the speakers again, my eyes focus on one of the many, many screens all showing the same video of my girl.

"Now, where were we, beautiful?" he murmurs.

"She really is beautiful, huh?" one of them says behind me.

"Sure wouldn't say no. Wouldn't fucking pay for it, though. I can think of more entertaining ways of making her bend to my will. Boss sure has more patience and willpower than I do."

"You also wouldn't care about waiting until she was eighteen, you sick fuck."

"She's legal. Why wait? Nothing but a waste of a good pussy, if you ask me."

The second her voice fills the room, I manage to tune the two goons out, although I begin to regret it when I hear what she has to say. "Tell me what you want from me, Daddy,"

"YOU MOTHERFUCKER," I roar, no longer able to keep a lid on the anger that's bubbling up inside me, much to my audience's amusement.

"Fucking knew you'd enjoy this."

"Lie on your back and pull your nightie up. I want to see that pretty pussy you're hiding between your thighs," he demands.

"Someone means business tonight," she whispers seductively, following orders and angling herself so he—and I— have a perfect view of her flawless body.

I can't help but groan at the sight, my cock painful in the confines of my trousers. And I can't even fucking reach for it.

A deep growl rumbles in my throat.

"You're a tease, beautiful."

"And you're a fucking sick cunt," I spit.

"I think you like that about me, Daddy. You know you shouldn't be looking, and it makes it so much hotter."

"You've no idea," he drawls, and she begins to tease herself over the lace of her knickers.

Oh, baby, please. Please don't give him the satisfaction of watching you fall.

It's so fucking beautiful, and he doesn't deserve any of it.

As if she can't look at him on the screen, she slowly lowers her eyelids, cutting herself off from the situation she's in the middle of.

That's it, Vixen. Get all up in your own head. We all know who lives in there, and it's not this twisted motherfucker on your cam call.

Just like that afternoon at The Empire, I'm fucking enthralled watching her on screen.

Her fingers work smoothly and confidently as she pleasures herself.

Are you thinking about me, Vixen? Hell knows I'm hard as fuck for you right now.

With nothing but heavy breathing coming through the speakers, it's easy to imagine myself in an entirely different situation.

That is, until someone fucking speaks.

"Fucking tease. Let's see that pussy, whore."

"Will you shut the fuck up?" I bellow, my heart racing, my entire body trembling with barely restrained fury.

"Oh, someone's getting a little frustrated. You close to coming in your pants yet, kid?"

"Fuck you."

"That's what I'm talking about," the prick on the screen growls as Evie tucks her thumbs into the sides of her knickers and pushes them down her thighs.

"Fuck yeah, look at this virgin pussy. I bet she's so fucking tight."

The roar that erupts from my throat doesn't sound human as I fight with everything I have to break free.

The chair that was bolted to the floor starts to rock as I throw all my weight into it.

I crash to the floor with a roar, pain exploding through my shoulder.

The second I roll to the side, I realise just how badly the rookies fucked up, because both my wrists and ankles come free.

Without considering the kind of disadvantage I'm at, I climb to my feet and fly at both of them.

I manage to get a few solid hits in with their confusion and lack of appreciation for just how fiercely I'm willing to fight for my girl.

But I only have the upper hand for so long. Before I know it, something hard collides with my temple, and I'm lost to the darkness.

10

EVIE

Still shrouded in darkness, I pull the bedroom door open and slip out into the equally dark and silent hallway.

My eyes linger on the bedroom door next to the one I just walked through. It's Daemon's. The thought of him in there with Calli sends a wave of security through me.

I might not know him like... at all, but I don't need to to know that he'd protect me just as fiercely as Alex would if he were here.

Pain slices through me as I wonder where he could be right this second, how he could be being treated.

As I descend the stairs, a soft light comes from a room I didn't venture into earlier. Silently, I walk up to the door and peer around.

My breath catches at the sight of Stefanos sitting in the middle of a dark sofa with a glass of amber liquid resting on his thigh, his head resting back and his eyes focused on the ceiling.

I should move, I know I should. But after talking to

Gianna, Calli and Blake about him, I can't help but be intrigued by this enigma of a man.

I give myself a few minutes to study him before I take a step back, intending on finding a drink and then locking myself away in Alex's room once more.

Only before I get a chance to escape, his deep, rumbling voice makes me stop dead in my tracks.

"You don't need to run."

All my breath rushes past my lips as if someone's punched it straight out of my lungs.

"Um..."

"I promise I won't bite, Evie."

Looking back over my shoulder, I find that he's sat forward, resting his elbows on his knees, his drink now hanging between them. His shoulders are wide, his features sharp, terrifying, deadly. But it's the look in his eyes that makes me spin around and step into the room. He looks as defeated and stressed as everyone else.

"When did you last sleep?" I ask, mentally kicking myself. Telling your boyfriend's father that he looks terrible in not so many words is not the best way to build any kind of relationship.

He shakes his head as if he can't remember. "Not since we knew they were gone."

The fact he doesn't just mention Alex, but Zay too, makes my heart swell.

Blake and Zay may have only been staying here a few days really, but maybe our little brother has softened a part of this cold, hard man.

We can only hope, because we need all the luck we can get to find them both.

"How are you feeling? I heard you weren't in a great state when you arrived."

A smile kicks up one corner of my mouth as I come to an awkward stop at the side of the sofa opposite him. "You could say that. I've certainly been better."

He studies me closely. I've no idea what he's looking for, but my skin prickles, making me want to curl in on myself.

"I'm not going to hurt you, Evie. I'm on your side here."

"I-I know, I'm sorry. I—"

"Please, take a seat," he says, unfolding his body and standing at full height. "Can I get you a drink?"

After downing what's left of his, he walks toward his bar and grabs an extra glass before I've even said anything.

"I... um... what is it?" I ask when he walks back toward me with a small amount of amber liquid in both glasses.

"Scotch. It was my father's favourite. Very expensive. When he died, I took every bottle he'd collected, and when something bad happens, I open one. Curse him out."

My lips open and close like a goldfish, but no words come out.

"It's either that or pour it all away out of spite, but it's too good for that. He'd hate that I was drinking it after he saved it all for so long."

"Don't most people save special bottles for happy events?" I ask, taking the glass and giving it a hesitant sniff.

"You may have noticed," he starts, lowering himself back to the sofa and swirling his drink around the glass, "we're not normal people."

Tipping his glass up, he drinks the lot in one big swallow.

Curious, I take a sip.

Oh, holy crap on a cracker. What even is that?

"Not a fan?" he asks with a smirk, my face clearly giving away my immediate thoughts of that engine fuel he just made me drink.

"I'm not sure it's for me," I confess, leaning forward to place it on the coffee table between us.

"Shame Blakely isn't awake. She makes incredible cocktails."

My brows lift slightly at his mention of my sister.

He doesn't say anything for a few seconds, losing himself in his thoughts.

"Your sister, she's... also not normal."

I can't help but bark out a very unladylike laugh.

"Can't argue with that."

"What about you, Evie? From what I've seen and heard, my son is quite enamoured with you."

My cheeks burn at his question as his intense stare continues.

"Umm... I'm not sure what there is to say."

"You're a dancer. I remember the night you both met."

Why did you even consider looking into this room, Evie?

"I... um... I'm not really a dancer."

"No, a cam girl."

"Blakely and Zayden have always been the most important people in my life. I will do anything to support them, to ensure they can live the life they deserve. And if dancing and camming earns me—"

"Whoa," Stefanos says, placing his empty glass down and holding up his hands in surrender. Something I can't imagine he does to many people. "I wasn't judging you, Evie."

"Really?" I ask, my brows almost in my hairline. "Most would."

"We all do things that may not be our first choice, that others may judge us for. That doesn't make it wrong."

I study him just like he has been me since I walked in here.

"I guess. Doesn't mean you want your son to be with a dancer and cammer, though."

"I want my son to be with someone who loves him. Who accepts him for what he is and the things he does. I want him to be with someone who won't judge him for the past, and what the future will inevitably hold. "

His words feel like a test, and the way his eyes drill into mine, and the unspoken words in his statement only confirm that suspicion.

Sitting up straighter, I hold my head high and square my shoulders.

"I have no issues with anything Alex has done, or will do," I say honestly. "How he chooses to live his life is his decision, just like mine is my own. I will support him in whatever he wants to do." And as for the first comment, I promise there and then that the next person I confess my feelings about Alex to will be, well... Alex.

Stefanos nods.

"Understood." Pushing to the sofa's edge, he collects his glass and gets to his feet. "Now, if you'll excuse me, I need to shower." He walks to the door but pauses when he gets there.

"I don't know what Alex has told you about me, Evie. But I want you to know that my boys are the two most important people in my life. I'm aware that my actions don't always lead people to believe that, but it's true nonetheless, and I will not rest until he's back here with us. With you. And I also promise that anyone who has been involved in this, anyone who has hurt you, him, or anyone you love will be dealt with."

Before I figure out what the hell I'm meant to say to any of that, he's gone, almost like he was never here in the first place and I imagined it all.

With a sigh, I fall back into the sofa, exhaustion hitting me all over again.

———

Voices wake me, and when I open my eyes, I realise that I'm exactly where I crashed last night. The only difference is that I've got a blanket over me.

Pushing up onto my elbow, I glance out the window at the early morning sun.

I've no idea what time I came down here and ended up having a one-to-one with Alex's dad, but something tells me that not many hours have passed.

Rubbing the sleep from my eyes, I sit up, focusing on the deep rumble of voices.

There are multiple, and they don't exactly sound happy.

Pushing the blanket aside, I get to my feet and walk to the door.

I know I probably shouldn't, but if they're discussing where Alex and Zay are, then I'm all ears.

"That's bullshit," an angry, familiar voice barks. "You can't sit there and tell me that you actually agree with this plan."

"It doesn't matter what I think. The boss has spoken. It's what we're doing."

"He's wrong," the first voice states.

"Matter of opinion," Stefanos mutters, sounding utterly exhausted.

"For the record," someone else says in a thick American accent, "I'm with Daemon. We have their location and know the most important players will be there. I'm done fucking waiting."

My breath catches. They know where Alex and Zay are and they're just sitting here having a fucking meeting?

"You agreed," Stefanos growls angrily.

"I've also been searching for these motherfuckers for months. I'm done waiting. Done letting them hurt people. Our families. Come on. They want a trade, so let's fucking give it to them."

A loud bang makes me jump, but as skittish as I might be, nothing could scare me away from this right now.

"No," Stefanos barks fiercely. "I am not letting you send Evie into that shitshow. It. Is. Not. Happening."

I stand there stunned, utterly dumbfounded that he would protect me quite so fiercely when I could be the key to getting his son back.

"We wouldn't have to actually let her go, just make it look like we were and then storm the place."

"No," Stefanos growls again. "The boss has a plan. We follow his command. I don't know how you handle your shit over the pond, but here, we follow orders."

"I'm usually the one giving out the fucking orders."

Silence follows. I picture a room full of terrifying men all glaring at each other. I might be willing to eavesdrop on them, but fuck being in there.

"I'm calling my boys in. When we get permission to end this, we need all the men we can get."

"I'll let the boss know."

"And Luciana?" the yank reminds him.

"Of course. I know how to do my job, kid."

"I might have lived a few less decades than you, old man, but don't fucking patronise me. I could get this job done with or without your help."

"Is that why you're here needing our support?" Stefanos quips.

Footsteps descend the stairs, dragging my attention from the bickering men in favour of who's about to catch me snooping.

"Evie," my sister says suspiciously. "What are you doing?"

"For the record, I think waiting is the wrong thing to do. We don't know what they're planning. We—"

"Evie," Blakely hisses. "Are you eavesdropping?"

"They're missing, Blake. Our brother and my... my... Alex. I think I have every right to understand even a little bit of what's going on."

"It's none of our business, Eve."

"I don't care. I need him. Them. The longer this goes on, the more they could be hurt and—"

"Fuck. Come on," she says, wrapping her hand around my arm and tugging me toward the kitchen when a heavy chair scrapes against the wooden floor in the room I'm spying on.

"Ow, Blake," I complain as her fingers dig into one of my cuts.

"I don't want to sound unsympathetic here, but I think you'd prefer that to an entire room of deadly men catching you listening in on them."

My mouth opens to argue, to tell her about Stefanos protecting me, but for some reason, the words never appear.

She stares at me expectantly, but then a door opens and deep male voices float down to us.

"Shit," she hisses, jumping into action, grabbing a mug and kickstarting the coffee machine as the rumble of voices get louder.

Stepping up beside her, I watch the hallway as shadows get closer and then a group of tired, suited men step into the room. And I swear, as they do so, they suck the air right out of it.

Stefanos's eyes lock on mine for a beat before shifting to my sister.

"Coffee?" she asks.

"Please."

Daemon, Theo, and Nico follow, all heading in my direction before another man enters.

"Who the holy hell is that?" Blake whisper-hisses as the only man not dressed in a sharp black suit stalks through the large space.

"That is Reid Harris," Theo says.

"And don't get any ideas, he's very much taken," Nico warns.

"Pfft, he might be hot, but he's too young for Blakely, ain't that right, Sis?" I tease.

"Careful, don't let my brother hear you confess to things like that," Daemon warns darkly.

"He doesn't need to worry. He might be pretty, but he's not Alex."

"You hear that, Reid?" Nico calls. "Alex's girl reckons the twins are hotter than you."

The hot, dangerous guy in question glances over at us, raises a brow and smirks.

"I think I just came," my sister quips, making Nico and Theo laugh.

"Someone's lacking action."

"As she should be, living here with my father," Daemon states.

"Oh, don't start that again." She waves Daemon off before focusing on Reid. "Can I interest you in a coffee?" she asks as Nico snorts 'slag' like an immature child.

"Coffee sounds great, thanks."

"Oh, and he's American."

Ignoring her, I focus on Daemon.

"What's going on? Do you have any news?"

He stares at me, his mask firmly in place, but there's something in his eyes letting me know that he wants to tell me something but can't. If it weren't for knowing Alex as intimately as I do, then I'd probably miss the look, but I recognise it now.

"Nothing we can act on right away, but things are moving in the right direction."

"You found them? Are they safe?" Blakely asks in a rush.

With Daemon and my sister distracted, I watch as Reid disappears out the door, heading in the opposite direction to Stefanos.

The second the coffee in the machine is done, I grab the mug and slip away.

At first, I don't find him, but then a familiar scent hits my nose followed by a faint puff of smoke. Following it, I round the corner and find him tucked into the shadows, smoking a joint.

"You didn't say how you liked it, so I guessed black and strong."

"What gave me away?" he says coldly.

"Your exuberant personality," I say with a smile.

He snorts, dropping what's left of his joint and crushing it into the ground with his heavy boot.

"So you're Evie," he says, his eyes tracking down my body that's only covered by another of Alex's shirts.

"Yep. All of this," I say, holding my arms out at my sides, "my fault."

"Nah," he says, scratching his scruff-heavy jaw. "You've

no idea how much you've helped me out. Because of you, we might just end all this bullshit."

"Then I guess... you're welcome."

I shift awkwardly on my feet as he continues studying me. There's no interest there, confirming what Nico said inside about him being taken. It's more... curiosity.

He just saw me standing like this beside my bombshell of a sister. It's a look I'm fairly used to.

"How are you feeling? I heard you've been through it."

"Just a few scratches," I say with a shrug. "Could have been worse."

"You were lucky. The men chasing you, they're dangerous."

Dropping my eyes, I look at my bare feet as fear rocks me to my core.

"They've got my boyfriend and brother," I whisper.

He doesn't say anything. What is there to say? And honestly, I wasn't expecting anything. It's not like he gives off 'I'm friendly, please talk to me' vibes.

Sucking in some strength, I keep my thoughts to myself. The silence between us grows—so does the awkwardness—but I don't back down.

I've got two guys out there who need me to be strong, to fight for them. And I want to prove to Alex that what I said, or more so, what I didn't say, doesn't mean I don't care. I do. More than anything. And I'm in this with him one hundred percent.

I meant what I said to Stefanos last night, and I want to do what I can to help.

"I... um... I was listening. Earlier, I mean. When you were all talking in Stefanos's office. I know that you know where they are and that they want you to trade me for them." If he's shocked by my confession, then he doesn't show it. His face is as blank as when I first walked up to him. "And I know you want to do it. That you want to end this."

"Evie," he growls in warning. I probably should be scared. Terrified actually. But I know who the enemy is here, and it's not this inked-up, cold-eyed, dangerous American in front of me.

"Take me there. Make the trade," I say, holding his eyes firmly so he can see how serious I am.

"You've no idea what you're asking."

"He's just a kid, Reid," I plead. "And while Alex might be trained for this kind of thing, he doesn't deserve to suffer it because of me. He saved me. Protected me. And look where it got him."

Ripping his eyes from mine, he stares out over the garden. "If I were running this show, I'd already have you in the trunk of my car. I'm over this bullshit and ready to watch the entire organisation burn to the ground," he confesses. "But I'm not. I'm on Cirillo and Rivera territory, and I need to pull rank. Sorry, kid."

He pushes from the wall and takes two huge steps to rejoin the others. In a panic, I reach out, wrapping my fingers around his forearm.

His stills, his jaw ticking with irritation.

"Please. I don't care what they do to me. I need both of them out of there. This is my mess; I should be the one dealing with it."

He shakes his head then turns to me, his dark eyes boring down into mine.

"I can't take you there."

"Maybe not. But I'm sure there is something you can do," I challenge.

11

ALEX

I don't remember being brought back to the cell I'm sharing with Zay. But it's where I wake up, with him once again watching over me with cheeks damp with tears and concern and fear in his eyes.

I hate this. I fucking hate that my world, my life is fucking up another young boy.

They might have barely laid a hand on him, but there's no way that this whole experience isn't going to fuck with his head. How can it not?

He has no idea if his sister is safe and no idea what the hell is going to happen with us.

They've given us no clue about the game plan here. We're just stuck in limbo.

At least if they told me something, anything, then I might have something to work with.

Are they keeping us here to lure the Family here? If they already have Evie, then it's not like they can offer a trade.

My heart pounds as images from that cam video play out in my mind. Although I don't focus on the best bits, on the moments I want to lose myself in like she's my ultimate happy place. I'm trying to look deeper, find clues. But I'm struggling.

The lack of food, sleep, and one too many beatings is fucking with my head.

It's what they want, to make me weak. But why?

Is it just a power trip, or are there bigger things at play here?

This time when the bolts keeping the door closed clank, I barely react. I don't have the energy to fight right now, so if that's what they're here for, then they can have at it.

To my surprise though, that isn't what follows.

A masked man steps inside, but he's alone and holding a tray.

"Food," Zay practically sings as he lowers it to the floor and pushes it closer to where we're huddled in the corner.

He dives for it like a starved bear cub and immediately stuffs a piece of bread into his mouth.

There's a warning on the tip of my tongue that it could be poisoned, but it's too late. It's gone. And for the first time since I woke and found him here with me, there's a twinkle of his normal self in his eyes.

Holding my hand out, he places some bread on my fingers and I join him.

Silently, we sit side by side, eating our meal of bread and water. It's not exactly luxury, but compared to the lack of anything else we've received other than bottles of water since we've been here, it's practically five-star.

He eats half and then stops, pushing the plate closer to me.

Every inch of me hurts. Even holding my hand up to my lips to take a bite is excruciating.

I need the sustenance, I know I do. But fuck. I just want

to curl up and go back to sleep again. I want to drift off into a place full of dreams of my girl, not be forced to endure this bullshit.

"It's okay," I say, my head dropping back against the wall. "You have it."

"Alex, no. You need—"

"You need it more. The second we get the chance to leave this place, you need all your energy to run as fast as you fucking can. You got that?"

He nods, but there isn't much confidence in it.

"You think they're going to let us go?" he asks quietly.

Dropping my head, I stare down at my busted knuckles and let out a pained sigh.

"Honestly, Zay, I've no idea what they're going to do. Nothing makes any sense, and I can't help thinking that they're just playing with us for their own amusement."

"Well, that's... great. What happened when they took you? Aside from the obvious," he says, his eyes tracking my injuries.

I haven't looked at myself—we haven't been granted the privilege of a bathroom with an actual mirror—but I don't need to to know what kind of mess I'm in. I've been in enough fights over the years to know how bad this kind of pain looks.

Dropping my gaze from his innocent eyes, I try to come up with something that isn't an outright lie, but that also isn't the whole truth either.

"They forced me into a chair and made me watch a video of Evie at work to rile me up."

"At work?" he asks, his voice laced with confusion. "You mean camming?"

My chin drops as my eyes dart to his.

"You know?" I study him, looking deeper than I have before.

"I might only be eleven, Alex, but I'm not blind or stupid."

My lips open and close like a fish, the splits in them cracking every time I do.

"I hate it. But I also understand what Evie and Blake do to keep our house, to protect me."

"Jesus, Zay. You shouldn't have the weight of all this on your shoulders," I mutter.

"But it's okay for them?" he asks innocently.

"They're older, they—"

"Are doing all of it for me. I hate it."

"Shit, bud. I don't know what to say."

He holds my eyes, words right on the tip of his tongue, but he holds them back for some reason.

"Go on," I encourage.

"Can you tell me what's happened? What's really happened? I know it's to do with Dad. That's why Blake and I had to leave the flat. I didn't believe the gas leak story for a second, but I was willing to go along with it for them. Then Atlas said all this stuff, and honestly, I had no idea if he was lying or what. But this... it all fits his words and—"

My need to protect him wars with my need to treat him like the mature young man that he is.

Clearly, he's far from naïve with the life they all live. But will telling him everything do more harm than good?

Can there be any more harm than this?

"Yeah, bud. It was your father. He put Evie up for sale on the dark web."

His brows pinch together as he tries to process those words.

"He... what a fucking arsehole."

My eyes widen at his outburst, but I also can't stop my smile from spreading.

"Zayden," I half warn, half laugh.

"What? He's a prick. I have no good memory of the man. He's a drunk, and a crook, and clearly the worst father in the entire world. How could he do that to Evie?" His eyes fill with tears as he thinks about her.

"I'm sorry, Zay."

"It's okay. It's always been okay because I have Blake and Evie. They make up for all his flaws."

"They're pretty incredible," I agree.

"So what happened? How did we end up here?"

Shifting on the hard concrete floor, I turn to look at him properly before I give him the CliffsNotes of the events that lead to us sitting here together.

"So they have us here because they don't have her?" he asks hopefully.

"Her bracelet," I blurt, startling him.

In that video, she wasn't wearing the bracelet I bought her, or the necklace from her mother that Blake gave her on her birthday.

That video was old.

They don't have her. If they did, they'd be torturing me with live feeds and proof. Right?

"Alex?" Zay asks while my head spins with a million thoughts.

"You're right. I don't think they have her," I whisper. "That video, it was old. She's not here. They don't have her."

He nods, lost in his own thoughts.

"Okay, so what does that mean?"

"It means exactly what you said. We're here because she's not. They probably want to trade us for her."

"Your Family, they'll probably do that, right? To get their soldier back?"

I narrow my eyes on him. "Just how much did Atlas tell you?"

He smirks, a soft laugh spilling from his lips.

"My Family, they might be a lot of things, but that word is at their heart. We are a family, and whatever they're planning right now, Evie, Blake, and you, will be a part of that.

"They're not going to storm in here, take me, and leave you all to your fate. It's just not going to happen."

"You promise?"

"They're also not going to trade us for her," I add. "They'll figure out a way to protect us all. I promise."

He nods, accepting my words as gospel.

Now all I have to do is wait and see if I'm right.

I fucking pray I am, because the last thing I want is to hurt him more than he already has been.

We finish eating our delightful meal before coldness and silence is the only thing surrounding us once more.

"What day do you think it is?" Zay asks.

"I've no idea," I mutter, my exhaustion getting the better of me again, those few mouthfuls of bread having very little impact on my energy levels.

"You need to rest," Zay says, watching me closely as I crash.

"Yeah," I say, slumping down the wall until I'm curled up on my side. Pain shoots around every inch of my body, but it's not enough to stop the darkness from creeping in. And when it does, she's there, waiting for me like an angel in white silk.

Fucking heaven.

I'm so lost in images of Evie dancing for me up in her cage that it takes longer than it should to register that I'm moving.

"No, leave him alone. Put him down," Zay screams, breaking through the fog of sleep.

I rip my eyes open just in time to see two guys grab him.

"NO," I roar, but my voice is quickly cut off when someone wraps a rag around my head, tying it tightly and stopping me from saying anything.

Zay continues to scream and shout until they've no choice but to do the same to him. It doesn't stop him from trying to fight them off, though. I've no idea if it's because he's small, but he manages to free his arms and legs more often than the men holding him would like and he kicks and punches, achieving more than a few grunts of pain.

Give them hell, little buddy.

I, however, don't waste my energy on fighting. There's no point. Even if I were to break free, there's enough of them to overpower me.

Instead, I hang like a dead weight as they carry me wherever it is they're taking me.

There will be a better opportunity than this, I have to believe that, and I have to just wait for it.

It will come. It has to.

I refuse to just sit here like waiting ducks to be rescued. There has to be something I can do to save us.

Daemon did it...

No, he had inside help in the form of Enzo.

That's what I need. To make a friend. To find an ally.

We move through the old, cold building, through narrow corridor after narrow corridor.

The old stone walls out here are damaged and crooked, and when we get to a small spiral staircase, it gets even more decrepit.

With a grunt of annoyance, the man holding my legs unceremoniously drops them to the floor while the guy holding my shoulders pushes me upright.

His grip on my upper arms gets tighter, his fingers digging into my skin before he grunts for me to move and shoves me closer to the stairs.

They're not the easiest thing to navigate on a good day, but with a body that's barely willing to do anything I tell it, they're almost impossible.

As if he cares, the guy holding me stops me from face planting more than a handful of times as we make our way up.

More of the same dark and dank hallways greet us, but we don't move toward them. Instead, I'm shoved toward an old heavy wooden door.

Another man darts around us and pulls it open, using the huge wrought iron handle. The hinges squeak so loudly announcing our arrival that I actually cringe at the sound. It's like nails on a chalkboard.

"Go," the man holding me grunts, and I stumble forward. My shoulder crashes into the half-open door, sending another bolt of pain shooting down my arm before I fall to my knees in the middle of... of a church.

I blink in confusion, taking in the old stained glass windows that cast colourful light around the vast space.

But that elaborate architecture—unlike everything I've seen downstairs—isn't what really captures my attention. That would be the men standing before me.

All but one are covered head to toe in black, their identities concealed.

The unmasked man steps forward. But despite having never seen his face before, I know who he is before he opens his mouth.

"Alexander Deimos, you really have been a thorn in my side, young man."

12

———

EVIE

Reid left me standing there without any kind of suggestion to help.

I got it. I did. They'd been told to follow orders, and I guess even the baddest of gangsters have to follow the rules sometimes.

With my tail between my legs and any hope of helping with Alex and Zay's freedom dashed, I headed back inside.

Stefanos and Reid were nowhere to be seen, but the guys were sitting around the table chatting to Blake as if they were all lifelong friends.

They might not have been their normal boisterous selves, but seeing them smile and joking about hurt. It really fucking hurt.

The second Blake spotted me, she watched me with concerned eyes, but that's nothing new. It's been the same since I woke here.

After refusing her offer of help, I made myself a coffee and disappeared upstairs.

My head was spinning, and with everything I'd heard, I

didn't want to sit around laughing and joking while the two most important men in my life were likely suffering.

What I needed was a plan.

They wanted me in exchange for their freedom.

I'd damn well let them have me in a heartbeat to protect both of them.

The only problem is, I've no idea how to find out where they are to even think about getting there and handing myself over.

I laid in Alex's bed, staring up at the ceiling for the longest time.

Blake came to check on me. It was the only time I closed my eyes as I pretended to be asleep. I felt awful for doing it, but I wasn't in the right place to talk to her—or anyone, for that matter.

Voices rumbled downstairs, doors closed, and cars came and went, but I never once stepped out of the room.

Well, that is until the house falls silent and my need to find out more about what's going on gets the better of me.

With ninja-like skills I didn't know I possessed, I make my way downstairs. One look out of the hallway window tells me what I already suspect. All the cars in the driveway are gone. The sun is high in the sky, and I can only assume that means Blakely is out sunbathing instead of doing her job while Stefanos is out ruling the city.

The second I hit the ground floor, I dart across the hallway to Stefanos's office. I don't knock or even double-check there's no one inside before I slip through the gap.

I stand there just inside the doorway as memories from the last time I was in here fill my mind. Staring at the desk, the image of the two of us together plays out like a movie.

I knew Alex was dangerous. I didn't need to hear his angry words to know that. One look at his sinful face alone after what had happened between us the first time we met was enough to know that. I just never could have imagined what an impact he was going to have on my life, and on my heart.

Shaking those thoughts from my head, I focus on the task at hand.

I'm not stupid enough to think that Stefanos will have left a map of their location sitting on his desk, but there could be something. Anything.

Lowering my arse to this chair, I begin searching through the papers.

"Shit," I hiss when nothing shows me anything useful. I don't even know what most of this is. Spreadsheets and data and ugh.

I continue riffling through everything before lifting a ridiculously ugly paperweight. Only, I totally underestimate just how heavy it is, and as soon as I've lifted it from the desk it slips from my fingers, bouncing on the edge of the tabletop and plummeting to the floor.

It lands on the thin rug beneath my feet with an almighty thud.

My heart jumps into my throat and my hands tremble. If I get caught in here, even if it's by Blake, then I'm fucked. She'll make me talk, and my chances of doing this will be less than they are now.

"Hello?" a soft voice calls out. Only, it's not Blake, it's Calli.

"Oh, shit, shit, shit," I hiss, looking for the best place to hide on the off chance she comes in here to check something weird isn't happening, which of course, it totally is.

"You go, I'll check it out," someone says before heavy footsteps, I was clearly too distracted to notice earlier, move closer.

A quick glance at the window shows the arrival of a fancy black car.

"Fuck, fuck, fuck." I can't imagine Daemon will be too impressed if he catches me in here.

With my heart in my throat, I drop to my hands and knees and crawl under the desk just as the door creaks open and a pair of black boots and jeans appear merely a few feet away.

'Oh my God,' I mouth to myself as my heart pounds so hard in my chest I'm sure he can hear it.

He moves closer before rounding the desk and stopping right beside the paperweight.

Why did you move that, you stupid cow? I chastise.

Trying to curl in on myself as if it'll make me invisible, I hold my breath as he bends down, but as predicted, long before his fingers connect with the heavy rock thing, his eyes collide with me.

All the air comes rushing out of my lungs, but the fear isn't quite as potent as I was expecting, because the eyes staring back at me aren't a pair of dark grey angry ones that belong to the devil. They're softer.

"Ant?" I breathe, my panic ebbing away slightly.

"Hey, Buttercup. How's it going?" he asks, holding his hand out to help me out from my hiding spot.

"Umm..."

The second I'm standing before him, his eyes drop to Alex's shirt, and they darken a shade as sadness and fear flicker through them.

"So I'm assuming that Stefanos doesn't know you're snooping in his office?"

I bite down on my bottom lip and shake my head, shame rolling over me.

"Did you find what you were looking for?"

"No, I—"

A car engine rumbles close and both our heads snap to the window.

I've no idea who it is, but anyone else who drives a blacked-out car catching me in here isn't a good thing.

"Come on, before someone else finds us."

He takes my hand and tugs me from the room, stopping in the doorway to make sure the coast is clear.

Then, without any hesitation, he pulls me toward the stairs. We hit the top floor as the front door opens and heavy footsteps thud down the hallway.

"There you are. I thought you were going home," Daemon says, relief clear in his tone.

"I bumped into Ant. We came to check in on Evie."

"They upstairs?" Daemon asks, making my eyes dart to Ant's.

He smirks at me before pulling his phone from his pocket and shooting off a message.

Calli's phone dings beneath us.

"Seems that way," she says. "You want a coffee?" she offers, not in the least suspicious.

"I can do it. You rest."

"Aw, Devil Boy, you're such a softie," she breathes.

"And I've heard enough," Ant says, dragging me forward. "Which room?"

I point to Alex's door. "You haven't been here before?"

"Not up here, no. Whenever we've hung out it's been at his flat."

Memories of the short time I spent there make me miss him and the little slice of heaven we found together all that much more.

"Hey, it's going to be okay, Evie," Ant assures me, reading my mind.

Pushing the door open, we walk inside Alex's room. Ant's eyes are everywhere, but they home in on those photos.

"So he's always been ugly then," he teases.

I laugh, but it's strained.

I miss him so much. More than I ever thought it was possible to miss another person.

Before I realise it's happening, a sob bubbles up my throat.

"Oh shit," Ant breathes, rushing to my side and pulling me into his chest.

I've only met him once, and very briefly, but his unquestioning support tells me everything I need to know about the kind of person and friend he is.

Turning into his body, I press my face into the softness of his t-shirt and cry.

"I miss him. Them," I wail, too distraught to care that I'm currently covering a stranger's t-shirt in snot and tears.

"I know, Buttercup. We all do."

He presses a soft kiss on the top of my head as he continues to hold me.

Once I've calmed down, I relax in his arms and look up at him.

"I know," I whisper, searching his dark eyes.

If I weren't pressed up against him and wrapped in his arms, then I wouldn't know he'd reacted to those words. But as it is, I feel his muscles lock up the second they roll off my tongue.

"Evie," he says hesitantly, his arm dropping as if he's about to bolt.

"It's okay," I say in a rush. "I don't... I understand."

"Shit," he breathes, releasing me and dropping his head

into his hands. "This is not how meeting one of your closest friends' girlfriends should go," he mumbles.

"What? You haven't had this happen before?" I deadpan, trying to lighten the mood.

"Can't say that I have, no," he confesses, lowering his hand but keeping his eyes locked on the window. "How much do you know?" he asks hesitantly.

"Everything, I think."

"Brilliant," he mutters under his breath. "Evie, I—"

He turns to me, his eyes full of fear and his expression wrought with unease.

"I don't... Alex and I... it's not—"

Resting my hand over his, I cut off his words.

"I know. I'm not worried that you're about to go running off into the sunset together. And not just because he's not here right now," I add when his lips part. "You had fun. Experimented a little. There's nothing wrong with that."

He stares at me while a million and one thoughts spin behind his eyes.

"Have you spoken to anyone about this?" I ask in concern.

"A few people know, yeah."

"Not what I meant." I raise my brow and give him a pointed look. "Talking about what you did and how it makes you feel are two very different things. Trust me, with everything I've done in the past few months, I know."

He nods, letting me know that he's aware of what I've been up to as well.

"No," he whispers. "I wouldn't even know where to start."

Taking his hand in mine, I squeeze it in support.

It should be scary how relaxed I feel in his company, but it's not. Just like with any of Alex's friends, I feel like I belong, like I'm exactly where I need to be. And right now is no different.

With my heart racing, I look into his eyes, hoping that he can see the same kind of connection and friendship I feel with him.

He's hot, sure, there's no arguing that. But he's not Alex. I don't feel *that* kind of connection with him.

"I need some help with something," I confess. "Maybe I can help you figure out what's going on up in your head, and you can assist me with my little issue." Shamelessly, I bat my lashes at him, taking a trick out of Alex's book of using seduction to get what you want.

He sighs, resigning himself to my request. I just about manage to keep in my burst of excitement. He has no idea what he's just agreed to. And something tells me that he's going to really, really regret it.

"What do you need, Evie?" he asks, searching my eyes.

"They're offering a trade. Me for them. I—"

"No," he barks, jumping to his feet and crossing his arms over his chest. "Absolutely, one hundred percent no, Evie. Alex would kill me. No, not just kill me, he'd skin me alive and carve out each of my organs while demanding I watch."

My lip curls in disgust at his vivid description.

"I'm not even joking, Evie. If he found out that I put you in danger..."

"They know where they are, Ant. And they're just leaving them there, waiting for fuck knows what."

He stares at me, his expression hard and unwavering.

"Do you remember what they did to you?" I ask, my eyes dropping to his body where I know he still bears the scars of his ordeal.

His jaw pops and his throat ripples with a rough swallow.

"You've got a little sister, right?" I ask, vaguely remembering when Alex tried to explain the Mariano Family tree.

His jaw tics again, giving me his answer.

"If they had her, what would you do?"

"Evie," he growls.

"What would you do?" I push.

"Rip the place a-fucking-part to get her."

"Exactly," I state, pushing to my feet, going toe-to-toe with him. "But they don't just have my little brother. They have Alex too. If I can get there, they'll trade me for them, give you all an extra soldier with knowledge of the inside, and then you can bust me straight out again. Kill them all, burn it to the ground. Whatever you want."

Lifting his hands, he combs his fingers through his hair and looks up at the ceiling.

"It's not going to be that easy, though."

"Why not? Don't you know where they are?"

His eyes meet mine and I get my answer.

He knows. He knows everything.

13

EVIE

"Get dressed."

"What?" I blurt as he stalks toward the bags of my clothes sitting ignored in front of Alex's wardrobe.

One Blakely grabbed from our flat when I got back here, the other Theo and Emmie brought after they swept the cabin for evidence.

He rummages through and pulls out a pair of leggings and some flip-flops.

"Get dressed. We're leaving."

"You're agreeing? You're going to take me—"

He turns to look at me, the fierce expression on his face immediately making my words falter.

"Just get dressed. And... don't make me regret this."

I take the leggings before rummaging in the same bag for a clean pair of knickers and a bra. If I'm going to do this, then it isn't going to be without underwear.

I'm not changing Alex's shirt, though. I'll wear that as armour in the hope of channelling some of his strength and confidence.

Pulling his phone from his pocket, he taps at the screen and lifts it to his ear before I slip into the bathroom to clean up.

I'm still a mess. Cuts and scabs still litter my body, and the bags under my eyes are beyond insane. But it won't stop me from doing what needs to be done.

By the time I emerge, Ant is off the phone and waiting by the door.

"Come on, we're going for a little road trip."

Excitement flutters in my belly. I should be scared— terrified—of what I'm about to do. But I'm not.

Alex has done so much for me in such a short space of time. Now, I need to step up and do the same. For him and Zay.

Knowing that they're both safe will make all of what might happen next worth it.

My heart jumps into my throat when we get to the bottom of the stairs to find Calli and Daemon about to head up.

They both look at Ant before their eyes turn to me.

I swallow nervously, any words I should be saying right now seeming to shrivel and die on my tongue.

Wrapping his arm around my shoulders, Ant pulls me into his side protectively.

"We're going for a drive," he states. To anyone else, I'm sure his tone would leave no room for argument. But not with these two.

"Is that a good idea?" Calli asks as Daemon studies Ant with a deadly glint in his eye.

"I'm not going to do anything to put her at risk," he assures both of them.

Calli and Ant share a look before she nods.

"It'll probably do you good to get a change of scenery," she concedes.

"Yeah, I need to clear my head," I lie, aware that I need to say something.

Ant tugs me forward, but Daemon's deep voice stops us before we get to the front door.

"Do anything stupid and Alex will kill you with his bare hands," he warns.

"I'm aware."

"And she's tracked. So we'll know if you do something untoward."

"I'm what?" I gasp.

"They did it when you were out of it," Calli says softly, as if that'll make this any easier to swallow.

My lips open to say something, but there are no words.

I'm not shocked. Not really. I guess this is normal in their world.

"We're all tracked," Calli adds. "It stops these possessive arseholes from freaking out when we leave the house. And it ensures we can all be found at all times. Just in case."

"Right," I mutter.

"Come on, let's hit the road," Ant says, pulling the door open and leaving the two of them behind.

"Am I really tracked?" I whisper once we're far enough away that they can't hear me.

"Yes."

"This is a really bad idea, isn't it?"

"Wanting to help is never a bad thing, Buttercup."

He holds his passenger door open for me like a gentleman before stalking around the bonnet to join me.

"You look like you're about to cover my dash in vomit," he points out helpfully.

A pained laugh spills from my lips.

He glances over with a grimace, but it doesn't stop him from starting the engine and rolling out of Stefanos's driveway.

The farther we get away from the house, the harder my heart pounds and the more violently my hands tremble.

I'm unfamiliar with this part of the city, so I've no idea where we're going. I don't really know what I was expecting, but staying in the city wasn't it. When people get abducted, don't they usually get taken to the middle of nowhere where they're unlikely to be discovered?

Ant chuckles. "How many crime documentaries have you watched, exactly?"

"Uh..." I start, turning to look at him.

"Yeah, you asked that question out loud."

"Right."

"You're right, though. People don't usually hide in plain sight. Most are too scared to even try it."

"But these guys aren't scared?"

"Yes and no," he mutters.

"Cryptic much," I scoff, folding my arms over my chest in the hope of hiding my trembling hands.

"They're not in the city," he confesses. "You're right, they're in the middle of nowhere."

"So why are we—" My words cut off when a sign up ahead comes into view. "What are you doing, Ant?" I ask, my voice quieter and weaker than just a few moments ago.

"I'm doing this the right way, Evie. If you're willing to get in the middle of this, then you need someone with a lot more authority than me to agree to it. I don't have a fucking death wish, and that's exactly what I'd be signing if I took you to make the trade."

"Traitor," I mutter.

"No, Evie. That's exactly what I'm not."

"I asked Reid to help me," I confess. "He refused."

"Smart man."

Slowing the car, he turns into The Empire's underground car park and drives straight into one of the reserved spaces.

"Alex's," he explains when I narrow my eyes at him suspiciously.

I know that things between the Cirillos and the Marianos are okay now, but I'm not naïve enough to think they're suddenly best friends who give each other personal parking spaces.

"Of course," I whisper, desperately trying to dig up some of my inner Stella and Emmie so that I can step out of this car and face whoever Ant has brought me to see.

I don't realise he's killed the engine and got out until he opens my door and appears before me.

"Are you sure you want to do this?" he asks. "I could just take you home and allow Calli and D to believe we really did just go for a drive."

"They're stalking me. They already know we're here," I say confidently.

There's no way they didn't deliver that warning about the tracker to then ignore it.

"I'd put money on it. We'd better move before they catch up and try and stop you. That's if you're really serious about this." His eyes bounce between mine, searching for any sign that I might be about to back down.

While it might have been easier to convince myself that this was a good idea in the safety of Alex's bedroom, standing here now on the cusp of making it a reality is a very different thing.

Holding my head high and squaring my shoulders, I stare him dead in the eyes. "I'm serious."

I take off toward the lift I can see over his shoulder before he's expecting me to.

"I can see why Alex likes you," he confesses as he catches up with me. "You've got the same butter-wouldn't-melt face as he does, but under the surface, you're a force to be reckoned with."

"Let's hope it's enough to get me what I want then, huh?"

We step into the lift together after the doors open. I expect him to punch a button to the floor we need. What I'm not expecting is for him to reveal some secret panel and tap in a code to give us access to where most mere mortals aren't allowed.

"I hope you're ready for this," Ant warns darkly.

"I can honestly say that I am not."

He laughs as the lift ascends through the building, and sensing that I need something to help give me the confidence I need, he slips his hand into mine and squeezes gently.

"He'd be so proud of you right now. You need to know that."

"I'll do anything," I confess. "Anything to get them both out."

He nods, but neither of us says anything again as we head toward our destination.

My resolve to appear strong and sure of myself falters the second I walk into some kind of security room with Ant.

It's full of computer screens and suited men. All of whom turn around to stare at me.

I can only assume they don't have a lot of females up here. Intrigue and amusement fill their eyes as we walk past them, heading to a set of double doors at the back of the room.

Just before we get there, Ant dips his head. "I'm assuming you haven't met Damien Cirillo before?"

"N-no," I stutter as he lifts his hand and knocks.

Each thud of his fists against the door rocks through me, making my heart miss a beat.

I have no idea what lies beyond that door, other than the fact it's almost as terrifying as if Ant had dropped me off wherever Alex and Zay are to do the trade.

"Come in," a deep voice rumbles.

"Ready?"

"Is that a rhetorical question?"

He chuckles before pushing the door open, pressing his palm against my lower back and giving me little choice but to move forward.

I don't breathe as I cross the threshold, and it only gets worse when I find multiple sets of curious eyes staring back at me.

"Evie, this is Damien, the Cirillo boss. Matteo, the Mariano boss. Luciana from the Riveras, and Reid. But I believe you've already met."

What the fuck have I got myself into?

"You also know Stefanos," he says, pointing to where more men stand to the side of Damien's desk. "That's

Galen, Stella and Toby's father. And Charon, the Cirillo consigliere."

"The what?" I ask, a deep frown lining my brows.

A rumble of deep laughter fills the room.

"Their advisor."

"Right," I mutter. I have never felt more out of my depth in my entire life.

I thought getting up on a table to dance or climbing into a cage at a club was terrifying, but it really has nothing on this right now.

Any of these men, and woman, could kill me with one swift move and not lose one wink of sleep over it.

"Ant said you have something you'd like to discuss with us, Evie," Damien says, sitting behind his massive mahogany desk looking as formidable as I'd expect being head of the Family.

"Umm..."

I stand there in the middle of this massive office filled with deadly gangsters, wondering what the hell happened to my quiet—albeit boring—life.

Unable to hold Damien's eyes any longer, I look down at my feet, my gaze snagging on the gaudy carpet in surprise.

Ant's shoulder brushes mine, dragging my thoughts back to this current moment.

"You want this, you need to prove you can handle it."

Sucking in a deep breath, I lift my eyes once more, only this time, I catch Luciana's large blue ones. Her beauty is breathtaking, but it's her strength and confidence that really shine through. I've no doubt that if she wanted to, she could have all the men bending to her every whim.

"It's okay, sweetie. We're all on the same team here," she says in a soft American accent.

Rolling my shoulders back, I look every single one of them in the eyes before I state, "I want you to make the trade."

"No way," Stefanos growls behind me. "Boss, we agreed that—"

Damien lifts his hand, silencing his capo in an instant.

"Let the girl speak."

"Err... I didn't really have any more than that to say."

Reid smirks, while Luciana's eyes lighten almost in pride.

"They want me in order to release them. So take me. I'll do anything."

"Do you know what you're asking? What they're likely to do with you in there?"

"I don't care. Zay... he's only eleven. What would you be doing right now if it were Atlas?"

His jaw tics as I mention his youngest son who's become good friends with Zay in the short time Alex and I were at the cabin.

"I can't hide out here, knowing they're suffering in there because of me."

"It's not your fault," Reid growls.

"Y-yeah, I know that. But it's not their fault either."

"Okay, say we do this," Matteo says, breaking the stalemate. "There's no guarantee that they'll release Alex and Zayden like they've promised. They could end up with all of you."

"So, don't you have the manpower to overthrow them? Correct me if I'm wrong, but there are four of you, and only one of them."

"We want to ensure we get all of them. This ends here. I will not leave one sick cunt still breathing when I get on a plane," Reid growls.

"We'll get them," Luciana promises fiercely before turning to me. "Are you sure you can handle whatever might be on the other side of that door?"

Lifting my chin, I hold her eyes steady.

"For those two, I can handle anything," I promise.

"Evie," Damien growls, earning my attention once more. "Take a seat. It seems we might have some planning to do."

14

ALEX

Multiple sets of hands grab me on the cunt's instruction, and the gag is ripped from my mouth.

"Get the fuck off me," I bellow the second the fabric clears my lips, my voice echoing around the vast space.

It's beautifully harrowing.

I've never really thought about how and where I might die. But I guess having it happen while being looked down on by God—assuming he exists—can't be a bad way to go. Maybe if I apologise enough, I might not even be sent to hell for everything I've done.

"Fight all you like, young man. We're in control now."

I'm pulled down the aisle, my knees and feet dragging over the stonework beneath me, adding to the cuts and bruises that already litter my body.

Zay cries behind me, but his words are muffled by the gag.

I try to look back, to see what they're doing to him, but I'm unable to see with the number of masked men that are following me.

It's something akin to a procession. And I won't lie, a shiver of fear races down my spine as I think about what could be waiting for me at the end of this.

It certainly isn't going to be my girl in a white dress, that's for sure.

"I hope we made the right size," he drawls as we come to a stop at the foot of my fate.

Looking up, my mouth runs dry at the sheer size of the wooden cross that stands before me.

Straps hang loosely from the arms, longer ones down the length.

I guess I should be grateful at the sight. At least it means they're not going to nail me to the fucking thing.

"What are we waiting for, gentlemen? It's more than time our entertainment started."

Zay continues to scream and sob behind me as I'm lifted from the floor once more.

I don't fight. There are more important things to worry about right now.

"Let him go," I demand as I'm hoisted up in the air. "He doesn't deserve this. Please, let him go."

Now that they've spun me around, I can see Zay clearly, standing at the very end of the aisle with two masked men holding him still.

His eyes are wide as he stares at me, tears streaking down his cheeks.

"Please," I beg. "He doesn't need to witness this. Please."

But it's pointless. No one listens to me.

Evie, I'm sorry. I'm so fucking sorry.

With half the men holding my weight, the others strap me to the cross before stepping away and leaving me more helpless than I've ever been in my life.

My chest heaves as the pain saturates my body. The cuts across my back rub against the wooden frame and the straps dig into my skin. It's not going to take long for them to cut through, leaving me hanging here, bleeding out for their sick pleasure.

Ignoring every set of eyes locked on me, I keep my gaze on Zay's, silently promising him that everything is going to be okay.

They're going to come.

They're going to come.

They have to fucking come, because I refuse to bow out like this. I refuse to allow him to watch as they do whatever the fuck it is they've planned to do with me.

Footsteps echo through the space as all the masked men back away.

Foreboding washes over me as the echoing steps get louder and the tension amongst the men before me seems to crackle with the intensity of an incoming storm.

After what feels like an eternity, two dark figures emerge from the shadows.

The second I clock one of their identities, a bitter laugh tumbles from my lips.

"Ah, good. You remember my business partner," the man from the video sneers.

"Yeah. Only the last time I saw him, he was bleeding out at my feet," I spit, remembering all too well how it felt to get the opportunity to throw my fist into his face for a second time in only a few months. "I'm disappointed to see you've healed so well."

Grant steps forward, joining the first man with nothing but pure hatred etched into every inch of his still slightly bruised face as he stares up at me.

"Alexander Deimos, how wonderful it is to see you

again. I would shake your hand, put all that bullshit behind us, but it seems you're incapable to do so right now."

The need to ask him what the fuck he wants is right on the tip of my tongue. But I already know the answer.

Revenge.

Suddenly, everything is starting to make so much sense.

Not only did I steal their newest, most precious purchase, but I humiliated Grant. Twice.

And I'm not even fucking sorry for it.

He deserved it. The only thing I regret is that I didn't put him in the ground.

If I had, then this could have all been avoided.

"Let him go," I demand again, jerking my chin in Zay's direction once more.

"Who, the kid?" Grant snarls. "I don't think so. I believe Zayden needs to be here to learn a very important lesson."

"He's already learned enough. Now let him go before you fuck up the rest of his life just like you have thousands of other innocent people."

He tsks before beginning to pace before me.

"We don't deal with people who have lives that can be fucked up any more than they already are," he confesses like he's actually doing people a fucking favour by putting them up for sale and letting them go for the highest price.

"Bullshit," I bark. "Evie's life was never fucked up. She has a loving family. People who care about her. A future, you sick fuck."

"Ah, alas. Evie Moore was special," he muses. "I knew from the moment I saw her photo that she was going to be worth so much more than all the rest."

Anger burns through me as his eyes glaze over as if he's imagining doing all kinds of wicked things to her.

"She's mine," I roar.

He chuckles as if all of this is nothing but a joke to him.

"You can believe that all you want, but I have a contract that says differently."

"That means nothing. That contract isn't legally binding. You cannot buy a person."

"Ah yes, Alexander Deimos, the future lawyer. Isn't that right?"

My teeth grind as he lays out evidence that he knows me.

"It's cute that you still think you have a chance."

"They're going to come for you," I warn, "and when they do—"

Clapping cuts off my words.

"You think they're coming?" the prick from the video interrupts. "It's Peter, by the way," he explains when I narrow my eyes at him. "Don't you think they'd be here by now if they cared? Maybe you're not that useful to your beloved Family after all. I mean, you're just a rent boy, are you not?"

The growl that rips from my throat echoes around the old church, making me almost sound as furious as I feel.

"You're a dime a dozen, you know that, right?"

"Fuck you. You're not going to win this. You fucked with the wrong girl, and we're going to take you down. Both of us will be dancing over your fucking grave when this is all done."

The cunt just grins back at me, his confidence shining through.

"Why her?" I ask. "What about all the others? There must be loads. This isn't a first for you lot. You've been trafficking people for years with the help of Victor Harris. Why Evie?"

"Grant was right," Vincent pipes up for the first time

after being happy hiding behind these two pricks. "Evie was special. And to think, Derek tried to refuse to hand her over to us."

"What?"

"Yeah," Vincent laughs, "I was shocked to discover that he has a decent bone in his body too. Or maybe it's just a soft spot for our little Evie. She is rather tempting, after all."

"Why didn't he want to hand her over?"

He shakes his head. "Told us we were stupid to trade someone who would be missed. Knew she'd cause trouble."

"So why did you?"

"Alexander," he mutters darkly, "something tells me that you know exactly why. An innocent, pure young woman like that comes with a hefty price tag, and lucky for me, these two gentlemen here were more than willing to pay the price I put on her head. If only you took me up on the offer the night we met. She could have been yours."

"You're sick. All of you are fucking sick."

"Rich, really, coming from a Cirillo soldier, don't you think? Just think of all the things you've done over the years... I'd say we're in good company, all of us right now," Vincent states.

I can't help but laugh at his assumption. "I've never once harmed an innocent woman," I argue.

"What about a guilty one?"

My teeth grind once again. They know as well as I do that we don't discriminate by sex when we've been wronged. Fuck us over and we'll fuck you right back, gender be damned.

Movement behind my three-man firing squad catches my eye, and my gaze lands on Zay wiping tears from his cheeks.

"Let him go. I don't care what you do to me. Just let him go. Please," I beg.

His tired eyes find mine, and I swear my heart splits in two.

Every time I've looked into his eyes, I've seen a little more of his innocence vanish. It reminds me of being a kid and looking at my other half.

Daemon got darker and more detached with every visit to our grandparents. I hated every moment, but I knew there was nothing I could do about it.

Right now, though, I can do something. And I will. I'll do anything to get him away from all this.

No one responds to my demands. And from the blank expressions on their faces, I'm not even sure they hear my pleas.

The guys and I might be cold, Daemon especially, but we'd never, ever force a child to suffer like this.

They stare up at me with excitement twinkling in their eyes, and I can't lie, it brings me so fucking close to giving up.

There is literally nothing I can do, hanging up here. If they decide to hurt Zay, there is fuck all I can do about it other than be forced to watch.

"Right then," Grant says, clapping his hands together. "Shall we?"

My blood runs cold as a million and one possibilities run through my head.

"NO," I roar when the two guards protecting Zay drag him to his feet.

"Scream all you like," Grant taunts. "No one can hear you, and no one is coming."

I thrash against my bindings, desperate to get free, to help him.

But the only thing I achieve is slicing my skin up with the straps, causing blood to run faster over my body, dripping onto the stone floor beneath.

"We'll be back." Peter's dark voice echoes through the space before they all disappear, leaving nothing but the crash of a slamming door behind them.

"NOOOO," I cry. "ZAYDEN. DON'T YOU DARE FUCKING TOUCH HIM."

My chest heaves, pain flooding through every inch of my body.

But there's nothing I can do. Literally fucking nothing but hang here and hope that I'll still be coherent when they get back.

Each second feels like an hour, each minute a day, each hour...

I've no idea how long I hang there with any kind of hope draining out of me that my boys are going to come, that I'm going to be rescued before I bleed out here. All I can hope is that they're treating Evie well. That they're giving her everything she needs, everything she deserves.

Squeezing my eyes closed, I think back over every moment we've had together, forcing my brain to take me from this hopeless situation to happier times.

She's not here. She's not here, I repeat over and over.

I've no idea how long passes, and I'm not entirely sure if I'm asleep or losing the will to live when the slamming of a heavy door somewhere in the distance grabs my attention.

Footsteps and loud voices filter down to me, although they're not loud enough for me to actually hear anything, to make out what's going on.

All I can do is pray that it has nothing to do with Zay.

I suck in a deep breath and roll my neck. It's the only

thing I have control of right now, but it does little to make me feel any better or give my body any relief.

My heart continues to race, beating completely out of rhythm. Fear knots up at my inside—not for me, though. For Zay. And emotion burns up the back of my throat, making my nose itch and my eyes red hot.

It's hopeless. Utterly hopeless.

I wince as I glance at my right arm. The straps were wrapped tight anyway, but add my weight and they're cutting through my skin like it's nothing more than tissue paper.

My stomach turns over at the sight of the blood dripping from my arms. My vision begins to fade out a little.

I want to fight it, the inevitable darkness. Allow it to consume me and take me away.

It'll be easier that way.

But I can't. Not while they have Zay. Not until I know he's safe.

Not until...

I come back to with a start. It takes me a few seconds to realise it was pain that woke me.

Opening my eyes, I find two masked men before me with an array of weapons in their hands.

I've no idea what they just used to bring me to, but I'm confident it wasn't the metal bar in one of their hands, because I don't think anything hurts badly enough for it to be broken.

My teeth grind as I snarl at them. Not that I'm in any way scary, trapped up here, but that doesn't mean I'm not going to try.

"Oh good. You're awake," Grant booms, his footsteps getting closer before he emerges out of the shadows. "Did you know," he taunts, "today is your lucky day?"

I scoff, hardly able to believe that's the case.

"I think our definitions of lucky are vastly different," I spit, my voice hoarse.

"Oh, I don't know. I think we're very similar, you and me. We certainly want the same things."

"Never," I hiss.

"You sure about that?"

Movement rips my attention from him, and I find more men filling the room.

"Where's Zay? What have you done with him?"

"Oh, don't worry, Alexander. Your little buddy is quite safe right now. But if you want him here, that's your decision to make."

My nostrils flare as he taunts me.

I don't trust a single word that spills from his lips, but there's a huge part of me that I can't ignore screaming at me to leave him where he is. He doesn't need to witness whatever these twisted fucks have planned. I'll just have to pray that wherever they have him, he's not experiencing worse than I'm about to.

"What do you want?" I snarl.

He chuckles darkly.

"I had all these plans for you, kid. Beautiful, wonderful, plans. But then something turned up and threw a spanner in the works. Only that spanner wasn't a bad thing. It was a very, very good thing, because it's going to make this so much more exciting."

"Stop talking in fucking riddles," I snap.

"You know, it's a good job you're pretty. You're not much good for anything else, are you, Deimos?"

"I dunno, I overpowered you in a fight pretty quickly."

He smirks, rubbing the back of his neck. "Because I let you."

"Bullshit. You're a pussy. Just like him," I sneer, jerking my head toward Peter. "He couldn't even show his face. Instead, he hid behind a camera screen. Probably for the best, to be fair. No girl, no matter how inexperienced, would want his small cock anywhere near her."

I roar in pain as something thrashes against my bound legs, but I don't look down to see what their goons are doing. Instead, I keep my eyes focused on them.

"Do your worst," I tell them. "I can take everything you throw at me."

"Is that right?" Grant mutters with a smirk.

With his eyes still locked on mine, he bellows three words that make my heart drop into my feet.

"Bring her in."

A heavy door crashes open before my worst fucking nightmare plays out right in front of me.

Two masked men march my girl, who's bound and gagged, down the aisle toward me.

Her eyes are impossibly wide, tears flooding her cheeks as she stares at me.

It rips me in fucking two.

Sucking in a deep breath, I try to force down all my feelings and over-the-top reactions that want to spill from me.

If I show them weakness, this will only end worse.

They'll enjoy watching me break, and it's not going to fucking happen.

"Oh, what?" Grant taunts. "Did you think we didn't have her?"

15

EVIE

The discussion that followed my announcement that I wanted to put myself right in the middle of all this in the hope of ending it didn't last half as long as I was expecting it to. It also wasn't as terrifying as it probably should have been. But the things being discussed didn't seem real. It was more like they were discussing a movie plot than they were my life. It was bizarre. But I'm grateful that listening to them was a distraction, because the last thing I needed to do was think too hard about the motions I'd just kick-started.

With a plan in place, Ant directed me out the way we came and back to the car park.

A man in a van was waiting for me, much like the one I was delivered to the cabin in. Only this man didn't have his face covered.

Ant pulled me in for a hug, made me promise that I wouldn't do anything even more stupid than I already was and assured me that they'd all meet me on the other side.

All I had to do as I walked away from him was pray he was right, that there would be another side.

He helped me inside, and with a final good luck, the door was pulled closed and I was shrouded in darkness.

I tucked myself back into the corner and wrapped my arms around my legs as the van rumbled to life, taking me toward my fate.

Whether I'd live to tell the tale was yet to be seen.

The journey toward wherever they're keeping Alex and Zay feels like it goes on forever, until the van finally rolls to a stop, and the engine cuts out.

And the second that happens, I realise it has actually been the fastest trip of my life.

My heart's in my throat as I sit and wait to be dragged out, my entire body trembling.

You're doing this for Alex and Zay. Be strong.

They have a plan. It'll all be fine.

Have faith.

I wince the second the van door is ripped open, allowing the low summer sun to flood the space around me, making my eyes water with the sudden brightness.

The man whose face I could clearly see before we left the hotel is now covered with a balaclava, leaving only his dark eyes visible.

"Ready?" he asks, his voice softer than his appearance would lead anyone to believe.

Sucking in a deep breath, I steel myself for the performance of my life.

"Let's go."

None too gently, he drags me from inside the van, his fingertips digging into my upper arms before I'm thrown across the gravel.

My palms and knees burn with the impact, and my leggings immediately rip.

Tears fill my eyes as pain shoots through my body, but I use it to my advantage.

Play the game, Evie. Play the—

I'm snatched from the ground by the back of Alex's shirt before he restrains my hands behind my back, making my shoulders smart.

"I'm sorry," he whispers in my ear before his fingers twist so tightly in my hair that the tears filling my eyes spill over.

He marches me toward an old church. I'm sure back in the day it was probably beautiful, but right now, it's nothing but harrowing with the low sunlight glinting in the stained glass windows, making the dark stonework even more terrifying.

I can't say I'm surprised, though. These men are more than happy playing God. It's actually quite fitting for them to be here.

Long before we get to the colossal double doors, they creak open slowly, proving our assumptions of being watched from the moment we drove through the gate correct.

"Delivery," the guy grunts before throwing me forward into the waiting arms of two other masked men.

Thankfully, they catch me before I hit the stone entryway.

"Who are you?" they bark at the man.

"No one. And I can assure you, after doing this, you won't see me again."

I'm jostled around enough to catch sight of him running back to the van.

"Boss," one of the guys says, pressing his finger against an earpiece. "We have company. We need the grounds swept."

I glance up when silence falls. I can't read anything in his cold, dark eyes as he listens to whoever is on the other end of his comms.

But a violent shudder rips through me the second they run over my body like I'm nothing more than a toy that has just been delivered purely for his pleasure.

"We have the girl."

My entire body jolts, hearing those words.

Play the game, Evie.

But while I might tell myself that, there is nothing fake about the whimper that spills from my lips as I'm shoved forward.

"You got it, boss. We'll be right there."

One of the men holds me tightly while the other pulls rope from his pocket.

He binds my wrists together behind my back while I whimper in pain.

"That's enough," he snaps before wrapping the second length around my head, gagging me.

I cry out and try to fight against them, but I'm no match for their strength.

And it's in that moment that I really understand just how much of a stupid idea this might have been.

Happy with their work, they each wrap a hand around my upper arms and march me through the church entrance toward another set of doors.

"It seems you've timed your arrival perfectly," the one who wasn't speaking into his earpiece growls. "The show is just about to start."

My stomach bottoms out at what those words could mean as another terrified whimper rumbles in my throat.

Please, please, please let them be okay.

As they wrap their free hands around the massive door

knobs that I assume lead to the church's heart, I'm grateful they're holding me up.

I've no idea what it is, but I have a very deep sense of something horrific being right on the other side of those doors. Despite everything I've told myself, since overhearing Stefanos and the guys' conversation earlier today, I'm not sure I can do it.

And if I can't do this, then I've failed them.

You won't fail them, Evie. You're here for them.

Have faith.

You will all get out of this.

I keep my eyes locked on the floor as the doors open, too terrified to look up and discover my fate, or the fate of those I love.

But I'm unable to remain naïve to what they're dragging me into after we've stepped over the threshold and I look up

The second I do, it's like the world is ripped clean from beneath me.

Alex.

A scream rips from my throat as I take in his battered and bruised body strapped to a huge cross behind the altar.

Tears cascade down my cheeks as I'm dragged forward.

As the distance between us reduces, I'm able to get a better look at what they've done to him—what they're doing to him.

Blood drips from his arms and runs down his body, pooling on the floor beneath his feet.

"Oh, what? Did you think we didn't have her?" a familiar voice taunts.

I try to look around to see who it belongs to, but the guards holding me don't allow it.

Alex doesn't react to his words. His eyes just hold mine.

He might not be saying anything, but I hear everything he's thinking loud and clear.

I'll kill every single one of these cunts for this.

Be strong, baby. You can do this.

As subtly as I can, I nod. I need him to know that I'm here, that I understand him and that we're in this together.

Footsteps move closer before two men walk around my guards and make themselves known.

The second I see their faces, my knees buckle. They must feel me sag and decide to let gravity do its thing, because the next thing I know, I'm crashing to the unforgiving floor. I cry out, but with the gag between my lips, it's nowhere near as loud as I need it to be.

"Good evening, Evie. Long time, no see," Pete says. "Oh, how I've missed you."

He steps closer as if he's about to reach out and touch me, and I panic.

Falling on my arse, I kick out my legs as fast as I can, shuffling away from him.

Seeing as I've only ever seen him through a screen, it was easy enough to pretend he didn't really exist. That all the lies he clearly spewed were the truth. That he was some sex-starved middle-aged man who lost his wife to cancer.

Stupid, stupid girl.

"What's wrong, sweetheart?" he asks, softening his voice in a way I remember all too well. Only now, it makes my stomach revolt.

"Stay away from me," I try to say as he continues to prowl closer like a lion stalking its prey.

Alex watches our exchange with fury burning in his eyes. I don't need to look up to see it. I feel it.

It gives me the strength I need to get my legs beneath me once more and clumsily climb to my feet.

For all of about three seconds, I might have a little control over the situation, but then I back up and gasp when I collide with a body.

"There, there, Evie," Grant purrs, reaching up to pull my hair away from my neck. Dipping low, he drags his nose up the column of my throat, breathing me in. "As sweet as ever," he murmurs.

My mouth waters as bile burns up my throat.

"I told you she was beautiful," Pete says, his eyes eating up every inch of me. "And more than worth the money that stupid prick put on her head."

I whimper as Pete pulls a knife from somewhere and holds it up in front of me.

"You've made us work for it, haven't you, sweetheart? And while we understand that we might not quite be getting what we paid for, I think it might actually work out for the best.

"You see... that... that boy up there," Pete says, pointing back at Alex. "He seems to think that you're his. But that's not true, is it, sweetheart?"

I have to fight not to vomit all over myself when he reaches out and brushes his knuckles down my cheek, his knife still in his hand.

Grant's fingers dig deeper into my arms before he presses the length of his body harder against me, allowing me to feel just how much he's enjoying this.

I glance up at Alex over Pete's shoulder. He might still be silent, but he's on the verge of losing his shit. It's bubbling up behind his eyes.

I want to tell him that it's okay. That I'm not alone. That soon, everyone who loves him as much as I do is going to storm this place and get us all out of here.

My breath catches as realisation slams into me.

Zay.

Where the fuck is Zay?

I frantically look around for any sign of him. But there's nothing.

"You want him in here?" Pete offers. "He's been so brave. You'll be so proud of him."

At the mention of Zay, Alex breaks.

"No," he roars. "Leave him out of this."

Despite knowing he can't get down, Alex thrashes against his bindings.

As much as the sight rips me apart, it also makes my heart swell for how fiercely he's willing to fight for my little brother.

With drool now running from the corners of my gagged mouth, I silently beg him to stop. The more he fights, the more he bleeds, and the more of that he loses, the weaker he's going to be.

We're going to win this fight. We are. I have to believe that. And when it happens, he's going to want to be standing beside his brothers, watching this place go up in smoke.

A door opens somewhere to the side of me, and I look over.

A scream of horror rips from my lips at the sight of my sweet, innocent little brother also bound and gagged. Tears stream from his petrified eyes.

It's okay, Zay. I'm here. I'm going to fix it all.

With his eyes locked on me, he breaks down in the arms of the man who's pushing him forward.

I thought I'd felt pain in my life. But nothing I have been through comes anywhere near close to watching the two men I love more than anything in my life hurt.

It proves to me that doing this, that putting myself here

in the middle of this, no matter what happens next, was the right thing to do.

While we're in here, they're all out there, waiting to strike.

Zay's moved into a row of pews and he sits there as if he's waiting for a service to begin, too afraid to do anything but what he's told.

I can understand why. I don't need to look at Alex to know I've no idea what they've been through.

"Now everyone is here... where were we?" Pete lifts the knife again, and it glints off the low light and candles that are flickering ominously throughout the vast space around us. "Oh yes. We're about to remind everyone exactly who you belong to."

Before he's finished speaking, he pulls Alex's shirt from my body and slices straight up the middle, exposing my bra to them.

Alex roars like a wild animal, but I don't make a sound. Not even a whimper leaves my throat as I resign myself to what will probably happen.

All I can do is hope that everyone on the outside moves in quickly enough to stop the inevitable. Because if it happens, I've no idea how any of us will come back from it.

16

—

ALEX

The second Zay's name was mentioned, any hope that I was going to be able to keep my shit together throughout this withered and died.

I knew it wouldn't help. That it would only make this victory sweeter for them. But I couldn't stop myself.

He doesn't deserve this.

She doesn't deserve this.

But while I'm stuck up here, there's very little I can do about any of it.

Why is she even here?

She shouldn't fucking be here.

If they had her, they never would have shown me an old video of her camming. They'd have found a more up to date way of torturing me. Just like they are now.

Evie stands strong between the two sick fucks as they strip my shirt from her body.

It's another piece of evidence to point toward her not always being here. The last time I saw that t-shirt, I was putting it in the laundry at Dad's.

There's no reason for her to have it unless she's been there.

Unless they've been taking care of her.

And if that's the case, then why the fuck have they allowed her to walk in here and put herself in the firing line?

She's not stupid. She had to have been aware of what might happen should she come anywhere near these pricks.

But she's done it.

She's done it for you, a little voice shouts in the back of my head.

She's here for you. For you and Zay.

As much as I hope that thought is right, I really fucking hate it, because watching as they strip my shirt from her body and drag her leggings from her feet, all I want to do is rip the two of them limb from limb for touching what's mine. I don't care how much they've paid for her. She's mine.

Mine.

"Leave her alone. You don't need to do this," I bellow, my voice hoarse from lack of water and too much shouting.

Grant chuckles.

"That's where you're wrong, kid. We paid for this sweet, sweet piece of arse, so we get to do exactly what we want to do. And right now, we're going to take her for a test drive. And guess what? You get to watch. You all get to watch just in case anyone thinks for even one fucking second that she might belong to anyone else but us."

"No, she'll never be yours. Even if you do this. Her heart is mine."

Evie's eyes find mine as they move her closer to me, letting me know that my words are true.

My heart aches, my need to get to her, to protect her all-consuming.

Please be outside. Be fucking be outside, I silently beg.

Burn this place to the ground with us all inside it if you have to. Just fucking stop them from doing this.

"Such a shame to ruin this flawless skin with so many cuts and bruises." At Peter's words, my eyes drop from Evie's to discover what he's talking about.

My breath catches when I find her beautiful body littered with cuts and bruises. Nowhere near as bad as mine, but still worse than should ever be inflicted on her.

"No, please," I beg like a pussy as they lift her from the ground and carry her even closer, laying her on the altar at my feet. "No. Let her go, don't do this."

Along with my pleas for them to stop, the sound of sobbing ripples through the church.

Without moving my eyes from Evie, I speak to Zay. "Bud, you need to close your eyes, okay?" His sniffle is the only kind of answer I get before he continues sobbing. But without being able to speak to me, I've no idea if he's listened.

Risking a glance up, I find he's curled himself up into a ball on the pew and has his eyes squeezed tight. I just wish he could cover his ears, too.

"Fuck, yeah. You were worth the money, sweetheart," Peter groans before me, dragging my eyes back to my girl.

She's on her back, her bound arms beneath her as they touch her. They're gentler than ever thought I'd give them credit for, but it doesn't matter. I feel their unwanted touches right down to my soul.

I've experienced it enough in the past, as my grandfather was training me, to understand exactly how sick she feels right now.

"Evie, give me your eyes," I command when I find hers closed, as if she's submitting to her fate with these two disgusting men.

It takes her a few seconds, but finally, her eyelashes flutter open. Her eyes are flooded with tears as hands continue to paw at her. Her teeth grind, making her jaw pop with anger and despair, but there's nothing either of us can do about it.

If I thought I was useless pacing back and forth in Harry Reid while trying to get back for her, then it was nothing compared to this agonising situation where she's right there, right fucking there, and I can't get to her. I can't do anything.

The two men continue talking, but I zone them out, just like I hope Evie does as she stares deep into my eyes.

'I love you,' I mouth. 'I love you so much. I'm sorry. I'm so fucking sorry.'

It's almost unbearable to stare into the pain that's filling her eyes, but I don't look anywhere else. I can't. I need her to know that I'm here, and that I will continue to be here when this is over.

None of this changes anything for me.

Nothing.

The sound of fabric ripping makes my teeth grind so hard I'm amazed one doesn't crack. But I still don't look to see what they're doing.

Evie's body jerks in disgust, her eyelids lowering.

I do the same in warning.

Don't you dare take those beautiful eyes from me, baby. I'm right there. Right by your side.

Tears continue to spill over her temples and into her hair, but still, she doesn't say a word, doesn't whimper or cry out.

She's strong, so fucking strong, not allowing them to see that they're affecting her as they—

A wave of nausea rushes through me at the thought of them doing this, of stealing something so precious from her.

All this time I've been worried about what this situation might do to Zay and how it might change his future. What about Evie?

If she was ever going to change her mind about me, then surely something like this would help do it.

Not that I'd be able to blame her if she walked away.

I might have not been the one to start all of this. But I sure didn't help when I got myself in the middle of it.

They still would have hurt her. She still would have ended up here, only, she'd have never known how deep your love truly runs.

Finally, it all gets too much for her, and her eyelids lower, cutting her off from me.

I want to scream, roar, rip the fucking world apart, but I can't. I'm stuck here watching them with my girl, and I can't do anything.

Dragging my eyes from her face, I find the two monsters who are willing to use her for their own pleasure.

Peter has his hands on her breasts, the cups of her bra ripped away while Grant is between her legs, her pussy now bare for them.

He fists his cock as he stares down at her like a lion would its kill.

Desperation like I've never felt before rocks through me and I roar out in anger, needing to do something to dispel the energy racing around inside me.

I want to maim, kill, destroy, but I can't. I can't fucking do the one thing I promised I'd do for her.

Protect her.

The echoes of my voice barely fade away when I hear something.

Please, please, please be here.

I don't look around. I can't. If I'm right, then I can't cause suspicion.

But then, I notice something else, something that makes all the air rush out of my lungs and hope flood through my veins.

There's a small red laser light on the back of Grant's head.

Daemon.

He's here.

There's another noise. It's louder this time, and one of the masked men also hears it.

"Boss, what was—"

"Quiet," Grant roars, too impatient to ruin my girl to take his warning seriously.

Stupid, stupid prick.

"Boss, I really think—"

Two shots land their intended targets, and Evie finally makes a noise. A blood-curdling scream rips from her throat as she's covered with blood and brain matter from both Pete and Grant.

Zay follows. Despite the gag in his mouth, he screams bloody murder for his sister.

"ZAYDEN," I bellow. "Get down between the pews and don't poke your head up until someone gets you."

Just as I've finished, doors slam open around the church and footsteps pile in before bullets start flying.

Each time someone notices me, they still for a beat in disbelief.

I get it. Trust me, I fucking get it. But I don't need their shock or sympathy right now. I just need my fucking girl and her brother taken care of.

"Evie," I shout. "Someone get Evie."

Heels click on the stone floor and when I look up, I find the queen of death herself walking toward me.

She glances at me, but her face shows nothing as she moves closer, a gun in each hand.

Someone ducks down behind the pews to her right, but she doesn't miss it. Her arm lifts and she fires off two rounds before a body hits the ground.

She moves so calmly, so confidently, it's awe-inspiring.

If she has any concern for the bullets flying around or the men who are fighting, then she doesn't show it.

"Evie, sweetie," she says, rolling Grant away with her foot, looking disgusted that she allowed her shoe to touch such a repulsive piece of shit. "It's okay. We're going to get you out of here."

Placing her guns on the altar, she shrugs her jacket off. She drapes it around Evie's shoulders once she's sitting before pulling a knife from somewhere and releasing her wrists and gag.

The second she can speak, it's my name passing her lips.

"Alex. You need to get Alex," she begs, staring up at me. "Please. I need him. Look at him."

"Evie," Luciana says, holding her face in her hands. "They'll get Alex, I promise you. But right now, I need to get you and Zay out, okay?"

Despite Luciana wanting her attention, Evie's eyes are still locked on mine.

"Go, baby. She'll look after you," I force out, my throat raw as fuck from all the shouting.

But Evie still doesn't look convinced. Well, until

Luciana spots someone behind her and quickly lifts her gun and shoots the motherfucker behind Evie's back

Evie screams, throwing her arms around Luciana for dear life.

"I'm coming for you, Vixen. I fucking promise."

Thankfully, she agrees, and a few seconds later, I'm watching Luciana guide Evie down the aisle. The second they get to where Zayden is hiding, Evie drags him into her arms, holding him tighter than I'm sure she ever has before.

The sound of gunfire, grunts, groans, and bodies hitting the ground continue to sound out around me. I get a view of some of it from my vantage point, but from the noises echoing around me, I think this is a bigger fight than it looks.

Just before Luciana ushers both Evie and Zay out of the main doors, hopefully to safety, Evie looks back.

'I love you,' she mouths, making my heart shatter in my chest before she vanishes from my sight.

One more loud gunshot rings out in the main church before pounding footsteps close in on me.

My heart jumps into my throat that they might not belong to the men I want, but the second I glance to my left, my eyes land on a pair so familiar to mine that everything knotted up inside me begins to relax.

"D," I breathe, my relief palpable.

"We got you, Bro," he assures me before more people surround me.

Seb, Theo, Nico, Toby, Ant, and Dad are all there, ready to get me down.

"Steps," I croak, jerking my head in the direction the men stacked them after they got me up here.

In only a minute, they're on top of them. Seb, Alex and

Nico hold me while the others work their way through all the straps holding me.

The pain is fucking unbearable as they undo each one, and I don't need to look to know how much blood I'm losing. I can feel it running down my body, and my head is getting light as fuck.

"These scars are going to look sick, man," Seb says, trying to keep the mood as light as possible.

"They'll get me all the girls, yeah?" I croak quietly.

"Dunno about that, Bro," Daemon says, unstrapping the belt around my waist. "I'm pretty sure there's only one you need to pay attention to."

I groan, closing my eyes as I think about how beautiful she is. How fucking strong she was only minutes ago down there.

"She's incredible," I whisper.

"Mate, you have no fucking idea," Ant says, making my eyes pop open. "I'll explain later."

I nod, silently taking him up on that offer as Seb, Theo, and Nico take more of my weight as I'm released with a pained groan.

"We got you, man. It's over," Theo assures me.

The second I'm on my feet, Dad stands before me.

His eyes search mine, allowing me to see the paternal concern that's always there, hidden right under the surface.

"I'm okay," I assure him.

I'm not sure if he thinks my knees buckle—to be fair, that could be the reason—but I throw myself into his body and wrap my fucked-up arms around him.

He stiffens against me. We've never really been all that affectionate with hugs. That's Mum's department. But right now, I fucking need it.

"Come on, Son. Let's get you out of here. Your mum is waiting."

With Dad and Daemon on either side of me, we make our way back down the aisle, leaving that fucking cross and this whole shitshow behind us.

"Did you get them all?" I ask roughly.

"You fucking know it," Daemon agrees proudly. "All present, accounted for, and deader than a fucking dodo."

"But just in case one is still breathing, we have one final gift for them," Nico says, sounding utterly deranged.

It takes all my effort, but when I look back, I find him smiling like a maniac.

As we burst through the main entrance to the church, more figures dressed head to toe in black with guns and knives in hand come running forward.

"They let you party with the big boys again, huh?"

"Like they could fucking stop us," Stella says, her wide-arse grin matching Emmie's before someone else comes running.

"Mum," I breathe, taking in her wide, terrified eyes. "I'm okay. I'm o—"

17

EVIE

Zay trembles in my arms violently as I hold him tightly against my chest.

"It's okay. It's okay. It's over," I whisper into the top of his head.

We're in the back of one of the cars that was parked outside the church entrance when we stumbled out with Luciana.

I thought she was a bad-arse when I met her in Damien's office earlier, but I was not prepared to see her in action.

She was fierce and strong and confident—everything I've always wanted to be from having a role model like Blakely as an older sister, only, she was fucking dangerous. Deadly. She shot those men without question or doubt. She knew they'd hurt us, were a part of all of this, and she took them down without a second thought.

Maybe it makes me as twisted as her, but I loved it.

"Evie," Zay whimpers, clutching me tighter as if he can't believe I'm here.

"I've got you, bud. I'm here."

"Alex," he whimpers.

I slam my eyes closed as the image of him strapped up against that cross with blood covering every inch of his body fills my mind.

A sob threatens to erupt from me, and as if she can sense it, Luciana reaches over and squeezes my shoulder in support.

Opening my eyes, I find hers. Even in the darkness of the car, the blue seems to shine. And despite knowing exactly what she's capable of, I find something very, very comforting about her.

"Thank you," I whisper.

"Anything. And they'll get Alex, Zayden. Don't you worry."

He whimpers in relief but doesn't lessen his hold.

"You want to wait to see him come out?" she asks me.

I nod. I might be selfish not to take Zay back to Blakely immediately, but I need to see Alex leave that church with my own eyes. I want to be with him. Every inch of me begs to be beside him. But he's got his boys, his dad, and Luciana has assured me that Gianna is here waiting to help him.

The person who needs me most right now is curled up on my lap, and I need to focus on him. Not me.

Alex will be fine. He's surrounded by people who love him.

But all that blood...

There are so many things I want to say, so many questions I want to ask. But none of them find their way past my lips. The three of us sit there with only Zay's quiet sobs filling our ears as men run in and out of the church.

But eventually, a small crowd emerge from inside the building, earning everyone's attention.

My breath catches and I lean forward as if it'll help me get a better look.

Come on, Alex. I need to see you.

My heart pounds in my chest, and the second it happens, the moment he emerges, I swear it stops.

With Stefanos and Daemon at his sides and the others behind him, they make their way out.

He's a mess. But he's awake. And for the first time, I allow myself to believe he might be okay.

Two slim figures approach him, and he just about manages to smile at the sight of Stella and Emmie looking as bad-arse as the woman beside me. I was floored when I saw them dressed head to toe in black with guns in hand. I couldn't believe that Theo and Seb would allow it. But then I remembered who they were and that they'd hardly take no for an answer.

And then someone else goes running, and the second I see Gianna, the tears filling my eyes spill over.

In full-on nurse mode, she starts bossing everyone around, and in only seconds, Stefanos and Daemon are loading Alex into the back of a blacked-out van which I can only assume is an undercover ambulance of sorts.

"They'll bring him back as soon as they can. Are you ready to head out?" Luciana asks me softly.

There's a huge part of me that wants to say no. But then Zay lifts his head from the crook of my neck, his big blue, exhausted and terrified eyes staring up at me, and I know I can't.

"You ready for a hug from Blakely, bud?"

He nods, his bottom lip trembling.

"Let's go then. She's waiting for you."

Luciana instructs our driver to go, and with one last look at the van hiding Alex from me, we head for home.

The second our car pulls into Stefanos's driveway, Blakely runs frantically from the house.

Ripping open my door, her eyes land on Zay, and she immediately bursts into tears.

"Zayden," she cries, pulling him from my lap and into her arms.

The pair of them sob loudly, clinging to each other for dear life.

"You okay?" Luciana asks softly as I study them.

"Ask me again in a few hours when Alex is home."

"Evie," Blake sobs, reaching her hand out for me.

Wrapping Luciana's jacket around me tighter so I don't flash anyone, I climb out and find myself immediately pulled into a group hug.

"I could kill you for that stunt you pulled, Evie Moore," she warns.

"Got results, didn't it?" I ask cockily, pushing aside how I really feel about what I just did.

She studies me, her eyes searching deep in mine.

"Are you okay?"

"Good as new," I lie.

She glances down at the jacket I'm wearing in question, but she doesn't say anything.

"Later," I promise. "Get Zay inside and look after him."

She nods, unable to argue with that, before tucking him into her side and guiding her toward the house.

I don't hear the car door shut, so when Luciana steps beside me and takes my hand in hers, I startle.

"Let's get you inside," she says softly.

Allowing her to take charge, I force my legs to move.

"Which room?" she asks once we're upstairs.

Blake's soft voice comes from the room Zay had been staying in, and confident that they're okay, I release Luciana's hand and walk toward Alex's room.

She chuckles behind me as she follows. "Typical boy, huh?"

"Trust me, there's nothing typical about Alex," I say with a smile. "He's... one of a kind."

My eyes land on the photographs, focusing on his smile and the happiness in his eyes.

Fuck, I could really do with seeing that sparkle in real life about now.

Dropping to the edge of the bed, I wrap my arms around myself and hang my head.

Silence fills the room, and I love that Luciana doesn't feel the need to fill it with words.

After a few seconds, movement makes me look up, and I see her disappear into the bathroom before the sound of running water hits my ears.

I almost sob in relief at the thought of washing today—their touch—from my body.

As I laid there with their hands all over me, all I could think about was the promise Damien made me before I left his office.

You might not be able to hear us, but we can hear you.

We'll get you out before it goes too far.

Logically, I knew he was right. But the small, almost invisible device they planted in my ear before allowing me on my mission felt huge and obvious. I knew if they spotted it that it would all be over.

All I had to do was trust them.

And am I glad they followed through on their promise?

Just another two minutes and Alex and Zay would have

witnessed—I would have experienced—something neither of us wanted.

I shake my head, remembering all too vividly how rough and demanding their touches were, the heat burning in their eyes.

Lying there between them, I felt small and stupid.

I should have guessed it was someone I knew behind it all.

Grant, yeah, maybe I'd have picked his name out if someone made me guess who was involved. He'd been nothing but a creep since the first moment I laid eyes on him.

But Pete...

He was always so sweet, so caring and considerate.

What a fucking idiot I am, because I fell for all of it.

"None of this is your fault, Evie," Luciana says as if she can hear my thoughts. "Your father did this, not you."

"I-I know I just... it's been a long day."

"Trust me, I understand."

When she holds her hand out for me, I slip mine into it and allow her to guide me to the bathroom.

The tub is almost full and already overflowing with bubbles.

"You okay alone or—"

"Don't go," I blurt, terrified of being left with nothing but my thoughts again.

"Okay," she agrees softly.

Standing me in front of the bath, she slides her jacket from my shoulders and encourages me to get in.

Before I do, I glance over my shoulder to see she's turned her back to hang up her jacket and give me some privacy.

The hot water burns in the best way as I sink beneath

the bubbles and wrap my arms around my legs, ignoring the sting of the grazes on my knees.

Luciana sits on the closed toilet seat, something I can't imagine she does all that often.

I take a few moments to study her. Her black dress is uncreased, her hair still falls over her shoulders in perfect waves, and her make-up is flawless. If you didn't know she'd shot more than a few men dead only an hour or so ago, then you'd never guess from how she looks.

Where the hem of her dress has ridden up, it exposes the holster, gun and knife that are hidden there.

She's fearless. Beautiful. Everything I could only ever dream of being. And she's sitting here with me as if she cares.

"You can ask me, Evie. Anything."

Her eyes are soft and open, unlike when I first met her in Damien's office. She was in boss mode then, but now, now it's almost like she's an entirely different person.

It makes me wonder how many people have ever met this side of her.

"You said... you said that you understood. H-have you been..." I trail off, unsure if I actually want her to answer this question or not.

"Sold?" she confirms. "Yes."

My breath catches at her honesty.

"I was a little younger than you, but one day I was just plucked from my life and planted into a new one where I was expected to do all these things I'd never really thought about before with a man I didn't know, who I didn't really like, in a place that never felt like home."

I stare at her, trying to grasp a thought that's nagging at the back of my head.

"You're... you're not American, are you?"

She smiles. "I never did totally leave my British-ness behind. Even if they never liked it, I clung onto my accent with everything I had." With each word she says, she sounds less and less American.

"I was the youngest of five sisters. At the beginning, I never questioned their disappearance. Dad always told me they'd gone off to start their own lives. And I guess in a way, he was right. But I was too young to ever question it.

"It wasn't until it was my time to embark on my new life that the pieces of the puzzle I knew I was missing began slotting into place."

"All your sisters had been sold too," I whisper.

She nods sadly.

"Have you ever found them?" I ask, assuming from her position now that she'd have the power to get whatever she wants.

She hangs her head, her shoulders dropping. It's all the answer I need.

"I'm so sorry."

"I'd given up hope of finding any connection to my past once I discovered that they'd all gone, and I focused on taking down the men who were still allowing all this to happen.

"In doing so, I managed to find more than I ever could have expected."

"They're not really gone?" I ask hopefully, utterly sucked into this tale.

"They are. But I discovered who purchased my eldest sister and discovered that she had three kids before she died. Unlike the others, she wasn't killed. It seemed she might have actually lived a somewhat normal life."

I blink, studying her as she confesses her story.

"It's you, Evie."

"Me?" I ask, confused. "I'm what?"

"You were one of her children. You're my niece."

My chin drops in shock.

"I-I-I'm…"

Dropping to her knees, she rests her elbows on the bathtub and reaches for my hand.

"Your mum was my older sister. I was only a child when she left our family. I have very few memories of her. But she was purchased for your father."

"My dad? My dad has never had any money," I explain, my brows pinched tightly.

"No, but your grandparents did."

"Who were they?"

She shakes her head. "No one important that I can find. Your grandfather was a businessman with connections in all the right places and dreams of things far beyond his reach. He tried to rule over anyone he could, your father included.

"From what I've found, your father's choices were… questionable. Your grandfather thought he was doing him a favour by buying him a wife. But it didn't make any difference. He still defied the rules.

"I've spoken to your father." My breath catches at her confession. "Deep, deep down, I don't think he's a bad person." I shake my head, refusing to accept that.

"I'm not saying he's good either, Evie. I'm just saying that he's a product of his upbringing. His young life was hard, and he took every ounce of bitterness and hatred and allowed it to carve out the rest of his life. I think your mum might have been his only bit of light."

My lips open and close as I try to figure out what to ask first.

"My grandparents?"

"Dead. With thanks to your father. I'm sure you don't

need me to tell you that your dad and Derek were involved with bad people."

"But he sold me, was going to sell Blakely if she hadn't lost her virginity so young. Why, why would he do that if—"

She sighs sadly. "I don't know. He refused to talk about it. At best, maybe he was hoping you might find a better life. At worst, he didn't have a choice. It could be a whole host of things. He's... he's not well, Evie. I don't think he has been for a very long time."

"He's been a terrible father to all of us," I state. "I don't know why they've kept him alive."

"He doesn't have to be," she says coldly. "Say the word, and I'll take care of it."

I stare at her, beyond overwhelmed by all of this. But as I look into her eyes, that comfort I found in her in the car, and even before that... How she relaxed me with just her presence in Damien's office... It makes so much sense.

Mum had that aura about her too.

"I can see it now," I whisper. "You have her eyes."

She hangs her head, cutting off my inspection of her, but not before I catch the emotion etched onto her face.

"You did it, Luciana. You found them, and you took them to the ground."

She glances at her watch. "By now, they should have done that literally as well."

18

ALEX

I wake with a start, and the second my surroundings clear, the confusion sets in.

I blink a couple of times, trying to figure out if my brain is tricking me, or if I'm really in my bedroom at Dad's.

My head is hazy. And really fucking numb. The kind of numbness that comes courtesy of seriously strong painkillers.

Images flicker through my mind.

The church.

The cross.

The men.

Evie.

My eyes dart to the left, the side she prefers to sleep on, but I don't find her beside me. Instead, I find the floor, and the second I look up, my eyes fall on exactly the person I need curled up on the chair right beside me.

"Evie," I croak. Just that one word is like knives down my throat, but thankfully, it's all she needs.

Her lashes flicker before she drags them open, and the second she finds me staring back at her, her eyes widen.

"Alex, you're awake," she whispers, shuffling to the edge of the chair.

Silence falls between us and I hate it. I hate that she's so far away, that I don't know what she's thinking.

"W-why are you over there?" I force out.

A soft smile pulls at her lips. "Because someone insisted on taking my spot."

My brows pinch as she looks over my shoulder.

Following her lead, I do the same, my heart shattering when I find who's curled up fast asleep on the other side of my bed.

Zayden.

"I-is he o-okay?" I croak.

"Physically, nothing more than a black eye and a couple of scratches. Mentally?" She shakes her head. "He refused to sleep unless he was with you."

My mouth opens, but I have no words to respond to that.

"I'm so sorry," I whisper eventually. "I tried to protect him. I really did b-but—" My voice cracks and I cut myself off when the bed dips beside me and a warm hand slides into mine.

Gently, she cups my cheek and gazes down at me.

"I know you did. And I'm so grateful. We all are. Here," she says, holding a straw to my lips.

I want to talk, but I'm unable to deny the relief to my wrecked throat.

"It wasn't enough though. What he saw, what he—"

"Alex, stop," she begs, her eyes pleading with me to do as I'm told. "Do you know why he wanted to be in here with you?" I don't respond and she continues after a few seconds. "Because he knows that you'll protect him. You're his hero."

A massive fucking lump crawls up my throat, and the backs of my eyes burn with red-hot tears.

"No, Evie. I can't—"

"Shh," she whispers, placing two fingers gently over my lips. "Take the title, you deserve it."

"I didn't do anything. I was stuck watching as they... fuck." I reach for her, realising my mistake instantly when pain shoots up my arm. Gritting my teeth, I fight to keep my reaction under wraps. After everything Evie has been through, the last thing she needs is to know that I'm suffering. "Are you okay?" I ask, focusing back on her.

"I am now I've got you both back," she says honestly.

"Fuck," I breathe, closing my eyes and taking a deep, calming breath.

"I need to know everything, baby."

"Not right now. When you're stronger, I'll tell you everything about the past few days. But now, you need to rest."

"I need you," I confess.

"And I'm right here," I assure him.

"Sitting in that chair isn't good enough, Vixen. We've been apart too long for that shit." She stares at me hesitantly. "What?"

Her entire expression softens. "I'm so sorry, Alex. All that stuff I said in the cabin. I didn't mean any of it. I was angry and... that's never going to be a good enough excuse. I'm so ashamed of what—"

"It's okay, baby. I get it. Everything about our stay there was intense. The situation was... bizarre. Things were always going to blow up eventually, especially when I was keeping things hidden that you should have known."

"You were trying to protect me. I get that, Alex. And I appreciate everything you did more than you could know."

I don't respond. I don't have words worthy of a reply to that comment. Instead, I put all my energy into shifting to the side to give her a little more space to lie down with me.

The pain is unbelievable, and as I wiggle about, achieving very little, I refuse to let it get the better of me.

Zay doesn't so much as twitch as I move.

"Alex, you don't need—"

"Please," I beg like a pussy.

Unable to argue with me, she gently lies down beside me, careful not to touch me any more than she needs to.

Resting her hand over my heart, I turn my head to the side to study her. What I really want to do is roll on my side and give her all of me, but I can't, and it fucking kills me.

"I'm right here," she whispers.

With the warmth of her palm warming me from the outside in, I allow my eyes to fall closed once more.

I'm tired. Exhausted. More so than I think I've ever been in my life. I want to defy the odds and stay in the present with my girl, but the darkness is trying to drag me back under already.

Now I know she's here, that she's okay, as much as she can be, I can relax fully.

I'm safe at Dad's. No one can hurt any of us here.

Dad and Daemon will fight until death to protect us, I already know that. And something tells me that the others aren't too far away either.

Just before I drift off again, a thought slams into me.

"You rescued us, didn't you, Vixen?"

She doesn't respond for a beat, and I start to think she's not going to. But then, her whispered words float around as I finally fall under.

"Just doing what I needed to do for those I love. And I'd do it again."

When I wake again, the first thing I do is reach for her, and my heart drops into my feet when I discover she's not there.

"Evie," I croak.

"Hey, I'm right here," she says, softly, laying her hand on my chest once more.

Turning to the other side, I find her there, lying on her side watching me, protecting me.

"Where's Zay?" I ask, a bolt of unnecessary panic shooting through me at his absence.

"He's okay. He's downstairs with Blake eating. He woke up starving."

At her mention of food, my stomach growls obnoxiously, making her laugh.

"Looks like he's not the only one."

"Can't say we were served up five-star luxury meals in there, baby."

Guilt flickers across her face at my words.

"No, don't do that. None of this is your fault. And just like you said, I'd do it all over again if it meant keeping you safe." She nods in agreement, but I'm not entirely sure she accepts my words.

"What do you need?" she asks, focusing on the physical stuff that's a little easier to process.

"I could really use a piss, and then whatever food you can get your hands on."

"Well, lucky for you, you've got a small army downstairs who will make you—or order you—whatever your heart desires."

"You," I state simply.

She laughs. "You can't eat me," she says before her

cheeks heat.

"Too fucking right I can," I say confidently, despite the fact I'm unsure if I can get off the bed right now, let alone do anything else.

"Alex," she breathes, shaking her head before her tone turns more serious. "Can you walk, or do I need to call your mum to catheterise you?"

My eyes widen, and I'm pretty sure my cock shrivels up at the thought alone.

"I can walk. There's no need for any of that shit."

"You should know, I almost told her just to do it," she confesses with a smirk.

"What? Why?"

"Payback. Ideally, it would have been my parents, but seeing as I'm out of luck with them, yours will have to do."

"Mum's seen it all before," I say flippantly. "She'd probably be proud of what a fine specimen she produced."

She laughs. "You're something else."

"That's why everyone loves me."

She stills beside me.

"Alex," she says, her voice suddenly more sombre than before. "You know that's not the only reason everyone loves you, right? Yeah, you're funny and a bit of an idiot, but there's so much more to you than that." I shrug, uncomfortable with where this conversation is going.

"You've been talking to Calli," I surmise.

"Yeah, but I've been talking to the others too. You don't need to hide, not from them. They're your family. They love you."

"And you?" I ask, happily deflecting.

"I... uh... I love you too." She holds my eyes as she says it, and I feel the words right down to the tips of my toes.

"You're my family too?"

"I hope so, because you're a big part of mine."

Reaching over, I ignore the pain and take her hand.

"There are so many things I want to say," I tell her, "but I'm afraid that if I do, I'll piss myself."

"I guess the talking can wait a little while."

Throwing her legs off the bed, she walks around to my side wearing nothing but one of my shirts.

"Damn, you look hot," I mutter, taking in her insane legs and the way her nipples press against the fabric.

"Don't be getting any ideas, playboy. Your mother gave you a blood transfusion while you were out. You need every ounce of it in every inch of your body. Not just your dick."

"Peeing with a hard-on is no joke," I mutter.

"I can only imagine. Now, how do you want to do this?" she asks as she pulls the sheets back, revealing the true extent of this shitshow.

Both of my arms are wrapped up like I'm pretending to be a mummy, and when I look down, I find that my chest isn't much better.

And while my legs might have got off lightly, they're still littered with bandages, permanent reminders of what all of this resulted in.

"Do you want me to go and get the guys? They're stronger than me and—"

"No. I've got this."

"Alex, you really don't need to—"

I silence her with a look. One of pure determination. Although, she'd probably call it stubbornness.

"Come on then," she concedes.

With her help and every drop of energy I have, I manage to get to my feet.

The room spins, making me feel dizzy as fuck, but thankfully, it settles after a few seconds of standing still.

"Okay?" Evie asks, her hands on my waist as if she'll be able to hold my weight should I stack it.

Once I'm a little more confident that my answer is a yes, I shuffle forward.

Pain lashes at my body, making my teeth grind and my eyes water, but fuck being stuck in that bed and having anyone carry me to take a piss.

By the time I get to the bathroom and shove my boxers down, I practically collapse onto the toilet.

Evie hovers, not knowing what to do for the best. But unlike her, I don't have an issue with her watching me pee and I let go, finding a little relief in all of this, even if it is only my bladder.

Once I'm done, she helps me to the basin so I can brush my teeth. But before I do anything, my eyes fall on my reflection.

"Shit," I gasp, hanging my head, unable to look.

"These won't last forever. Your mum said that—"

"The scars will," I whisper.

She swallows thickly but doesn't say anything. What can she say? We both know it's a fact. I'm going to be left with more than a handful of physical reminders of what happened, which in turn, is going to remind her.

From behind me, she wraps her arms around my waist, gently pressing her palms to my abs before resting her head on my shoulder blade. I know I've got wounds back there too from that whip. I've no idea if they've healed or if they're bandaged too right now.

"One day at a time, yeah? And anyway, they might make you even hotter than you already are and I'll be fighting the girls off with a bat."

"I wouldn't even see them, Vixen. I only have eyes for you."

"I love you, Alex. The real you, not just the fun playboy you show the rest of the world. Scars don't scare me. Pain doesn't scare me. The only thing that does right now is losing you."

"Not going to happen," I say fiercely, wishing I could look into her eyes as I say it so she can see how sincere my words are.

19

EVIE

By the time Alex is done, my SOS message has been answered and a soft knock fills the bathroom.

"Come in," I call as Alex side-eyes me.

I know he said he doesn't want anyone's help besides mine, but he's crashing harder than he'd ever admit, and there is no way I'm taking his weight to get him back to bed.

Daemon's head pokes around the door, and I have to give myself a second to remember that there are two of them.

"Hey, how's the patient doing?"

"Stubborn, as you'd probably imagine," I tease as Alex groans.

"Ready to get back to bed, Bro?"

"I can do it," he grunts, shuffling back from the basin.

"Sure you can," Daemon mutters, pushing the door wide to allow him through. But predictably, he only makes it four steps before his knees give out.

I gasp in horror as he starts to plummet, but Daemon is right there, stopping him from hitting the floor.

"You good?" Daemon asks not even bothering to hide the smugness in his tone.

Alex mumbles some kind of agreement before the two of them move out of the bathroom together.

"I don't ever remember being this hard work when I was out of action."

"That's because you had a head injury and you don't remember," Alex groans in agony as Daemon lowers him to the bed.

"Nah, I remember my nurse perfectly fine" Daemon counters. "Perfect fucking angel," he muses.

"Ew, dude, don't get those sappy sex eyes when you're talking about Mum," Alex jokes.

"Fuck off."

Daemon drops into the chair beside the bed with a soft smile playing on his lips. Something I'm not sure happens all that often. His relief to have his twin back is palpable. Hell, I feel it just as keenly.

"Seriously, Bro. How are you feeling?"

"Like I've been locked up, tortured, and hung from a fucking cross. How are you feeling?"

I cringe at hearing the truth laid out quite so brutally.

"Pretty happy. Did you see that perfect shot I had on that cunt?"

"The one whose brain matter you sprayed all over me?" I ask, continuing to cringe.

"The one and only. Thank me anytime." Daemon winks.

"You really do enjoy killing people, don't you?" I ask, utterly bamboozled by the whole thing. Until a few weeks ago, I hadn't even wished anyone dead. Now here I am, having experienced what we just have and discussing this as easily as if we're talking about the weather.

"Bad people who deserve it, yes. And that cunt more than deserved it."

"You got them all, right?" Alex asks. "Derek?"

"He was there?" I ask, realising for the first time that I didn't see him.

"Not that I knew."

"That would be because he was locked up in the room next to yours," Daemon explains.

"What? Why? He did this. He—" I cut myself off as I remember what I've learned recently.

"Yeah, he might have been involved in the whole thing, but selling you wasn't something he wanted to do."

"He told you that?" I ask Daemon.

"Not me personally, no."

"Where is he now?"

"Dead."

"Oh."

I'm not sure what I was expecting to feel, learning that. I hated Derek and the things he got women involved in. He was the one who helped Blakely get into the life she did way too young. And clearly, he's been a part of this human trafficking ring that everyone's been trying to take down. But I've still known him all my life. I guess I wasn't expecting to feel nothing.

I'm not glad, sad, or even disgusted. There's just nothing.

Alex's fingers thread through mine, squeezing as tight as he can.

"You okay?" Glancing over at him, I smile. He's here. He's right beside me, and Zay is safe and downstairs, filling his face.

Everything is okay.

"Yeah." Gently, I rest my head on his shoulder and close my eyes, taking a moment to appreciate his presence.

Daemon's attention makes my skin tingle with awareness, but he doesn't say anything. Nor do we. All of us are just trying to make sense of everything we've been through and process what the next few days might bring.

Voices and feet pounding up the stairs are the first clues that our peace is about to end, and not three seconds later, there's a knock on the door, and it's thrown open to reveal the rest of Alex's friends.

Seb, Theo and Calli are the first to burst into the room, quickly followed by everyone else. Taking up the rear, Emmie and Stella carry two trays full of coffee, and Bri has a tower of very familiar boxes stacked on her hand.

"Is that Betties?" Alex asks, ignoring all his friends in favour of the pastries.

"Sure is."

"Hell yeah. Maybe this was all worth it after all."

A ripple of emotion goes around the room before Jodie pulls the lid off the top box and passes it over to Alex.

He takes a second to appreciate the goodies laid out before him, making his selection and stuffing it into his mouth like an animal.

"So good," he mumbles, crumbs falling from his lips to his abs.

My eyes follow and my mouth waters.

"It's okay, Evie. We won't judge you if you lick them off," Stella says.

"Uh... I think I just need one of these." Reaching my hand into the box to snag a pastry, I don't even look to see what it is.

"Hey," Alex complains with a frown. "They're mine."

"Evie deserves them just as much as you," Ant says, appearing last through the door with armfuls of water.

"Yeah," Alex says, finally swallowing his mouthful. "About that." Turning to look at me, he lifts his brow. "Whose arse do I need to kick for allowing you in that place when you were nice and safe here?"

"Umm," I hesitate as Ant stands firm at the end of the bed.

"She stood before Damien, Matteo, Reid, and Luciana, and she demanded to play her part. It was fucking bad-arse, bro," Ant explains.

"So I'm assuming you're the mug she convinced to put her in that position in the first place?" Alex growls.

"She's a hard woman to say no to."

"That's what Isla said," Nico coughs.

"Dude," Ant sighs. "Seriously?"

Nico shrugs before stealing a kiss and a pastry from his wife.

"He's got a point. How is our lovely Isla?" Alex asks.

"Jesus, you lot are a pain in the arse," Ant grumbles before resting back against the chest of drawers.

"How are you feeling?" Calli asks, who's sitting on the edge of the bed on the other side of Alex with her hand resting on the duvet covering his legs.

"Yeah, you know. Like I always do after a solid impression of Jesus."

She rolls her eyes at him.

"Good to know your stellar personality is still intact, bro," Seb says.

"Pfft, you'd miss it and you know it."

"Fucking hardly. You're not even funny," Theo quips.

"Funnier than you."

"He's got you there, Boss," Emmie teases.

"So," Alex says, his tone entirely different from a few moments ago. "What happened after I passed out?"

"Oh mate, it was so fucking beautiful. I can't believe you missed it," Seb says, grinning like an idiot.

"What happened?"

"We blew that place to kingdom fucking come. Don't worry, we recorded it for you."

Shimmying between us, Seb holds his phone so we can both see.

Seeing the church again makes me shudder as an intense wave of fear washes through me.

Alex glances over, sensing my unease. Pain flickers in his eyes that he can't comfort me with Seb between us.

"Are you fucking watching or not?" he barks, dragging both our attention back to his screen.

Something flashes inside the building.

"Was that—"

"Wait," he barks like a pissed-off parent scolding an impatient toddler.

There's another flash, and then a fireball finally explodes out of the windows, instantly engulfing the building.

"Holy shit," I breathe as the screen glows with the heat of the fire, anyone inside burning to a crisp.

"We really are going to hell, aren't we?" Alex murmurs, his eyes glued to the video.

"We already had one-way tickets, Bro," Daemon states. "Blowing up a church is just the cherry on the top."

"So it's over?" Alex confirms.

"It is. Reid's already booked his plane ticket home. Pussy is missing his family," Seb scoffs.

"Dude, you have three hours away from Stella and you start pining; you're hardly one to speak," Theo points out.

"Yeah, well, her pussy is just that good."

"Maybe Reid's girl's is, too."

"You seen a photo of her?" Nico asks. "She's banging. Ow, fuck," he complains when Bri punches him in the stomach. "Not as banging as you, obviously," he backtracks.

"It's all downhill from the day you say 'I do', isn't that right?" Toby asks, tugging Jodie into his side as he baits his best friend.

"I dunno, it's been pretty fucking epic this far. Current situation aside, of course."

"Sorry for getting in the way of all the marital fucking," Seb scoffs as he climbs from the bed. "Feel free to fuck off and make better use of your time."

"Do they ever stop?" I whisper to Alex while everyone continues to bicker around us.

"Never," Alex and Calli say simultaneously. "Just be glad you don't have to listen to your older sibling talk about sex twenty-four seven," Calli adds.

"Don't worry, I'd heard enough," I confess, thinking about some of the wilder stories my sister has returned home with over the years.

"Oh, I bet she's got some crazy tales to tell," Jodie says, also ignoring the guys' banter.

"Yep. Although most I think she's tried to forget. There have been so many less-than-desirable clients over the years."

"She's just a dancer though, right?" Calli asks innocently, making Daemon's interest spike a little.

"Um… officially, yeah but it's not always all she does." Calli's eyes widen. "Blakely's amazing. She's been the mum both Zay and I needed after we lost ours. She's done what was necessary to keep a roof over our heads. She's not always been proud of what she's had to do to ensure we're fed and clothed, but it is what it is. I'm proud of her, no matter what. I can't imagine what would have happened to us if she didn't step up."

"She's pretty awesome," Calli admits. "I'd love to have her as an older sister instead of that pig." He points at Nico, who hears her and narrows his eyes.

"I heard that."

"You were meant to."

The banter continues around us, the sound of Alex's friends'—our friends'—voices and laughter filling the room. It's incredible. To know that we're surrounded by such a fierce group of people who would literally kill for each other is mind-blowing.

I'm honoured to have been welcomed into the group without question. I'll be forever grateful.

I've no idea how much time passes as I sit with Alex, just enjoying everyone's company, but eventually, he begins to slip lower in the bed, his lids getting heavy, no doubt helped along with the painkillers Daemon insisted he took after he finished stuffing his face with pastry, as per his mother's orders.

"We should head out. Someone looks like they need a nap," Stella points out as Alex begins dozing with his head resting on my shoulder.

The volume around the room decreases as they all notice him sleeping before they slip out, leaving only Ant behind. He stands at the end of the bed with a deep frown lining his brow and dark rings around his eyes.

"You okay?" I whisper.

He shakes his head and rubs the back of his neck.

"What I let you do, Evie... It was foolish and reckless and—"

"It worked, didn't it?" I interrupt.

His eyes dart to Alex. "Yeah, it did. But if it didn't..."

"Do you usually worry about the what-ifs of jobs you do?" I ask, assuming none of the men—and women—I've just been surrounded by second-guess many things in life. They're all so confident and sure of their actions.

"No. Never. It's just... this was different. It was Alex and—"

"You care."

"Yeah," he agrees before his eyes widen. "But not like that," he says in a rush. "I don't—"

"Hey, it's okay. What happened between you, it doesn't need to change your friendship or make you question caring about him."

"Yeah, I know. I dunno what's going on. Before... that... I never... Shit. I should go."

He backs away from the bed looking even more defeated than before.

"No, don't."

"I'm sorry. I can't."

He's gone before I can argue any more, pulling the door closed quietly behind him.

"I might want to hurt him for whatever he did that resulted in you being inside that church, but I'm glad he was here for you," Alex says sleepily.

"They all were. You have the best friends in the world."

"Yeah," he agrees. "I do."

20

―――

ALEX

I wake with a fright but no memory of what I was dreaming about, although it doesn't take an expert to guess. The cold sweat that covers my skin, the way my heart races and the need to fight that burns through my veins give it away.

But the second I look to the side, I find Evie sleeping beside me, and everything settles in an instant.

She's here. It's over.

Sucking in a deep breath, I force myself to focus on the future instead of what's behind us.

Yes, we've got a long way to go yet. We have a lot to talk about and things to figure out. But with her here, knowing what she did—or at least the very basics of what she did—gives me confidence that we have a future beyond everything we've been through.

I was meant to meet Evie that night at my Dad's. And not just to help but figure out this whole human trafficking ring, but to be the other half of me I was searching for. Everything we've been through, our time together... It's been beyond intense and fast and all the things that most normal people probably wouldn't understand. But for us, it's perfect. Or at least, I think it is.

As gently as I can, I roll out of bed and press my feet to the soft carpet, determined to get to take a piss without any help this time.

The sun might have set, but it's still light enough to see where I'm going. Not that I really need to. I know every inch of this room like the back of my hand. I could navigate it with my eyes closed.

Thankfully, my legs cooperate this time, and I get there and back without too much drama.

I'm halfway across the room, heading back to bed when the door opens and a head pokes into the room.

Zay immediately looks at the bed, his eyes widening when he finds only Evie in it before panic takes over.

"Hey," I whisper. "I'm right here, bud."

Relief floods his features before he practically runs at me.

I try to keep my grunt of pain in when we collide, but I don't manage it. Thankfully, or not, I'm not entirely sure, he's too lost in his own head to hear it.

His arms wrap around me as he rests his head against my chest. He doesn't say anything. He doesn't need to. I feel it. His pain, his desperation.

Soft footsteps move closer and the door is pushed open a little more, revealing Blakely.

Her eyes soften at the sight of us, her own pain over this whole situation reflected back at me before she glances at Evie curled up on the bed.

'You okay?' she mouths, not wanting to interrupt.

I nod. After a few seconds, she takes a step back, leaving Zay with me.

"Every time I close my eyes, I see you on that cross," he confesses after the longest time.

"I'm okay, Zay. Evie saved us." He nods, sending pain shooting down my body. "We're all okay. It's okay."

"Will I ever forget?"

He moves, his big blue watery eyes staring up at me, making my heart clench in my chest.

Keeping the promise I made when I first woke and found he was in that hellhole with me, I tell the truth.

"Probably not, bud, no. What we went through... it was massive, horrific, and potentially life-changing. You'll probably always remember it, although the details will fade. What you need to do is focus on harnessing it in a positive way."

"What do you mean?"

"Focus on the good that came out of it. Focus on how much you love Blake and Evie. Find ways to show them how important they are. To the other important people in your life too."

"Don't take them for granted?" he asks wisely.

"Exactly. On days when you're feeling weak, or if you're at school struggling with something, remember how bloody strong you were. You survived that, Zay. You held your head high and made it through. If you can do that, you can smash any algebra equation or pass any test."

"I wasn't strong. I cried a lot."

"Crying doesn't make you weak, Zayden. It makes you human. It shows you have a big heart, that you care about the people who love you. You fought to be back here just as hard as I did. You—"

"They didn't hurt me," he counters. "Not really."

"Pain doesn't have to result in blood. It comes in so many other forms." *Just ask Daemon*, I think. Thankfully, keeping the thought inside. Probably not what fragile Zay needs right now.

"Everything we go through, whether it be as awful as that, or something incredible, shapes you in ways you don't even realise. Do whatever it takes to ensure it makes you a better person."

He nods, agreeing with me, although I'm pretty sure he has no idea how to make that happen right now. Honestly, nor do I really, but it sounded smart as shit, so I'm rolling with it.

"You want to come to lie with me and Evie?" I offer, unsure of what else to say.

He nods, and I can't help but sigh in relief when he releases his grip on me.

He hovers at the side of the bed, watching through concerned eyes as I climb on and shuffle as gently as I can into the middle so I don't wake Evie. Then, he slots his smaller body beside me.

"Thank you," he whispers, blinking up at me, making my heart ache once more.

"Nothing to thank me for, bud. Get some rest, yeah?"

He watches me watch him for a few minutes before he finally closes his eyes.

It takes only seconds for his breathing to even out and for his small body to relax.

Unfortunately, I don't follow.

Instead, I stare up at the ceiling, my head spinning with everything that happened and all the things I still don't know about it.

Yes, I know it's over and that they're all dead. I know that thanks to Ant, Evie put herself in a seriously dangerous situation, but I don't know the details.

I probably should be pissed at Ant, but listening to him

and Evie talk earlier, yesterday, whenever it was, made me realise that he cares way more than he'll ever admit. He did what he had to do, and I fully appreciate that she won't have given him much choice. And to have stood in front of Damien, Matteo, Reid, and Luciana... Damn, I wish I could have seen that. I bet she was fierce.

The soft creak of my bedroom door drags my eyelids open. I used to fucking hate that noise. During the day, it was nothing, but come sneaking out at night when I wasn't meant to and it was loud as shit.

I find Mum looking at me with a soft smile playing on her lips.

"Hey," I whisper.

"It's good to see you awake," she says, walking in. "You ready for more pills?"

I shake my head. "I'm fine."

Her eyes narrow in a way I remember all too well from when we were kids.

"Alex, just these last two. For me?"

"Guilt trip, really?"

"They've worn off. That's why you're lying here awake while these two sleep. Just have these, and then I'll leave you to it. Suffer as much as you want."

"Is that what you say to all your patients?" I tease, pushing myself up enough to take the bottle of water and pills she hands over.

"Not usually. Thankfully, they're not often as stubborn as you are."

"Aw, you love me really," I tease.

"More than you could ever understand," she confesses quietly.

"Sorry for giving you a few more grey hairs."

"Oh shush, there isn't one single grey hair on my head," she counters.

"Your colourist made sure of it, huh?"

"You little shit," she laughs.

"Tell me I'm wrong?"

She shakes her head, still smiling with relief filling her eyes.

"You've really made an impression on this young man. He's holding you at godlike status right now," she says, looking at Zay beside me.

"I didn't do anything."

"To him, you did everything." She smiles fondly again.

"I just hope it was enough. I know how much shit like that can fuck a kid up."

Dark shadows pass through her eyes. Her pain is palpable for what we suffered without her knowledge.

"You both turned into incredible men, Alex. I couldn't be prouder of either of you."

"Pfft, don't lie. D's about to give you a grandbaby. You know you like him more right now."

She chuckles but doesn't argue. "Your time will come. You've found yourself quite a girl there that you need to hold onto."

"I intend to."

"Good, now rest."

She backs away from the bed but stops at the door when I call for her.

"How bad is it? Honestly?"

She hangs her head for a beat and my stomach bottoms out.

"Some of the cuts were really deep. They're going to scar. Others were a little more superficial."

I nod, accepting her words.

"I guess they'll just make D and I more identical again, huh?"

Those dark shadows return to her eyes but the second she blinks, they're gone again.

"I love you. Sleep."

"Love you too, Mum," I whisper as she disappears.

"You're too cute," Evie croaks sleepily.

"I'm a long way from cute right now, baby."

"Fine. You're a cute bad-arse."

"That isn't much better."

"Is Zay okay?" she asks, peeking over at him.

I breathe out slowly, trying to find the right words.

"He will be. Surrounded by people he loves, he'll get through it. I'm going to talk to my dad about getting him into Knight's Ridge College," I blurt.

"W-what? No. We can't ask that. The fees are—"

Rolling onto my side is painful as fuck, but for her, I'll do anything.

Pressing my fingers against her lips, I cut off her argument.

"I love you, Evie. I love you so fucking much. And that extends to him too. He deserves to have every opportunity available to him. And Knight's Ridge will give him that."

"But—"

My lips curl into a smile as I pinch her lips together this time.

"We'll talk about the logistics later. For now, just know that it's happening. I'll fight until the death for both of you, I thought I'd already proved that. Let me do this. Let me, let us, give all three of you the kind of life you've all been working toward. You all deserve it."

"Ale—" Leaning forward, I swallow down the pain and do what I've been desperate to do since I woke and saw her sitting in that chair watching me. I press my lips against hers.

I don't move to deepen the kiss, and nor does she. But it's perfect.

It's everything.

"We're going home today," Alex whispers in my ear as I stand at his basin with a towel wrapped around my body and my just-washed hair limp around my shoulders.

"Is that right?" I ask, my eyes finding his in the mirror.

He spent almost all of the first three days here asleep. I couldn't really blame him after what he went through, and I was so fucking relieved to have him there beside me. But despite his presence, I still missed him terribly. The few times he was awake and allowed me glimpses of the boy I fell in love with weren't enough. I needed to see that sparkle in his eyes and his cheeky smirk.

By day four, Gianna had reduced his pain meds enough that he wasn't knocked on his arse by them quite so much, and he was able to get up and about. He was still slow, and obviously in pain, but progress was being made, and I couldn't have been happier. Well, actually, that's not entirely true, because I was craving some one-on-one time with my man more than I thought possible. He was right there beside me, but there was always someone else too.

It was selfish of me to want him all to myself when everyone else had been as scared for him as I was. The guys seemed to have a rota for their visits so that someone was always with him. It warmed my heart to see just how tight their friendship, and their family were again.

And if it weren't his friends, then it was Zay. Watching the two of them together melted my heart every single time. I hated begrudging my little brother because of the attention he was getting from my boyfriend, but I haven't been able to stop myself.

"It is. It's time I got my girl all to myself for a while."

His lips find the sensitive skin of my neck, and he trails kisses down my skin until he's at my shoulder.

Butterflies flutter wildly in my stomach at the thought of it being just the two of us.

"I want to take my time with this body and be confident that no one—namely your little brother—isn't going to storm in and catch me with my face between your thighs. That kid has already seen more than he ever should. That might just tip him over the edge."

Sadness and concern wash through me for my little brother. As the days have passed, he's gotten stronger, shown signs that he's going to be able to put everything he and Alex went through behind him. But it's still early days. And he's still very attached to Alex, which makes this sudden decision to leave, no matter how much I might want to, hard.

"He's not going to like you leaving."

"No, I know. But Mum and Blake think it's probably for the best before he gets too attached."

When his eyes meet mine in the mirror once more, I find the same unease over this situation swimming within them.

"We can come back tomorrow to see him. But a night to ourselves is long overdue."

I nod, because there's no way I'm arguing. We need some privacy, and more than anything, we need some time to talk.

He still has questions about what happened—I see them swirling in his grey depths whenever I look at him—and we have plenty to discuss for the future, starting with the bomb he dropped on me the other day about Zay going to Knight's Ridge. Obviously, I want him to. Attending that school could open up so many doors for a bright kid like Zay. But at the same time, I don't want Alex, Stefanos, or anyone to offer up some charity just because Zay got tangled up in their dark underworld. Maybe it's deserved after what he went through, but accepting something so huge isn't something I'm used to, and I know Blakely isn't going to take too kindly to it either.

We work for every penny we have. It's how we've been forced to live for years. It's why everything feels so up in the air right now.

With all this over, do we just go back to our old flat and return to our old life? Or do we need to pull up our big girl knickers and accept that we've landed on our feet here and accept all the offers of help we can get?

I gasp when he tugs the bottom of my towel, making it fall from my body, leaving me standing naked before him.

"So beautiful, Vixen."

Closing the space between us, he cups my breasts as I rest my head back against his shoulder, watching us in the mirror.

"So fucking hot."

With just his hands on my breasts, my chest begins

heaving in only a few short moments, heat blooming between my thighs.

"Alex," I moan.

Nuzzling my neck, he rolls his hips, grinding his erection against my arse.

"Sounds like my girl might have missed me," he groans.

"You've no idea."

I don't hear the warning—I'm too focused on Alex's hand as he begins descending my body—so I shriek in fright when someone starts knocking on the door.

"Alex?" Zay shouts. The sound of his voice is akin to someone throwing a bucket of ice water over us.

"See. Time to go home," Alex says as I rush to wrap my towel back around my body in case my little brother decides to barge in.

Alex attempts to rearrange his hard-on in his sweats, but it doesn't do much good.

"Yeah, bud. I'll meet you downstairs in a few, yeah?"

"Yeah, okay. You good?" he shouts back.

"Yeah, man. I'm good. Promise." Soft footsteps move away from the door as our eyes hold. "I love you, Evie. But I kinda love that kid too."

My heart shatters in my chest at his confession.

"I sincerely hope you like Blakely too, because we kind of come as a package deal."

"Yeah, I guess she's okay. Hot," he says teasingly. "Who doesn't want a hot sister-in-law."

"You're a knob," I mutter, pulling the door open and going in search of some clothes.

"She is though," he calls after me. "Hottest housekeeper Dad has ever had. And let me tell you, he's had some fucking good ones. There was this one when we were almost sixteen. Damn, the tits on that woman."

When I look back, he's resting against the doorframe with a smirk on his face.

"Tell me you haven't fucked any of your dad's housekeepers before," I demand, refusing to comment on anything else he just said.

He pauses, and it's all I need.

"I don't want to know."

"I didn't go after her, if that's what you think. My grandfather planted her to help... train me."

A shudder rips through me.

"If your mother hadn't already offed him, I'd be at the front of the line to do it myself," I spit as anger at the old man gets the better of me.

"Oh don't worry— wait... what?"

"Umm..."

"Mum killed him?" His eyes are so wide as he asks that question I'm sure they're about to pop out.

The air crackles between us as I try to come up with something to say, but I can't. Gianna told me... she... shit. What did she say? All I can remember is being sure that she was confessing to it. I wasn't exactly in the best headspace to be taking on those kinds of revelations.

Before I figure anything out, Alex has blown out of the room, leaving me standing naked with a pair of knickers in my hand.

"Oh shit," I gasp, rushing to get dressed so I can chase after him.

He's still slow, so there's every chance I'll get to him before he accuses his own mother of being a murderer.

The moment I'm decent, I dart from the room. But Alex is long gone.

"Fucking hell." I skid around the bannister at the

bottom of the stairs and follow the laughter, just as Alex marches into the room.

"Alex?" Gianna says, her eyes locked on him as he closes the space between them.

"Is it true?" he demands, his voice deep and harrowing.

I come to a stop in the doorway, but my movement catches Gianna's eye and she nods.

"Did you... did you... *kill him?*" he whispers because Zay is in the room.

"Zay, shall we go out and have a kick about?" Blake asks, climbing from the sofa they're sitting on.

He's wary. His eyes are glued to Alex as he reluctantly follows her out. It seems that he might be just as overprotective of Alex as Alex is him.

I scruff up his hair as he passes, which he hates, but the only sound that spills from his lips is laughter. It's so good to hear after all the crying in the past few days.

The second they're gone, their voices fading into nothing, Alex repeats his previous question.

"Did you kill him?"

Gianna holds his eyes firm, unwavering for a few seconds before she nods her head once.

Alex deflates, his shoulders slumping, and I dart forward, expecting his knees to buckle, but he doesn't go down. Instead, he launches himself at Gianna, wrapping his arms around her and holding her so tight I'm not sure she can breathe.

He's so much taller than her that I can only just see the top of her head, but I sure hear her sniffle.

Not wanting to encroach on what is obviously a very personal moment, I start to back away. But sensing my distance, Alex turns to look at me.

"Don't," he warns, his voice rough with emotion before he releases one arm and holds his hand out for me.

Unable to deny him, I walk over and join their embrace.

Dropping his lips to the top of Gianna's head, he whispers a very broken 'thank you', which makes her sob harder.

And that's exactly how Stefanos finds us a few minutes later.

He clears his throat and Alex reluctantly releases his hold on us.

"Everything okay?" he asks, his brows pinching as he looks between his son and ex-wife.

"Y-yeah," Gianna says, wiping the tears from her eyes.

"Mum just confessed to being the one to kill Grandad," Alex announces without second thought.

Stefanos, a man I've only ever seen as strong and confident, crumbles in front of us.

First, it's anger at the mention of the man no longer walking this earth, and then it morphs into nothing but undiluted pain. But not the pain of loss—the pain of years and years of suffering.

"What?" he breathes, total disbelief shining in his eyes.

Gianna, however, stands tall and squares her shoulders.

"You knew I discovered the truth, Stefanos. Did you really think I was going to allow it to continue? You were too weak, too broken down by that monster of a man to do anything about it. But I wasn't. He was hurting my boys, and I'd take on anyone who dare to lay a single finger on either of them, let alone the horrific things he did," she spits, sounding like an entirely different person to the sweet, caring mother I know.

"H-how? He had a heart— You drugged him. How didn't I know this?"

"Because, dear husband, I learned a lot over my years in this house, and covering up indiscretions was at the very top of the list. I learned from the best, after all."

Stefanos's mouth opens and closes like a fish as he tries to come up with a response. Instead, he just rubs the back of his neck, looking utterly lost.

"Why didn't you tell me?" he finally says.

Gianna shrugs. "You loved that man as much as you hated him. He was gone and no longer able to hurt any of you, and that was good enough for me."

"Mum," Alex says with a grin. "You're a fucking bad-arse, and we never even knew."

She chuckles. "Don't go getting any crazy ideas. I'm not joining the Family. I just... I did what I needed to do to protect my own, and I'll stand by that until the day I die."

"Fuck. I really should have bought you a bigger bunch of flowers for Mother's Day," Alex mutters, pulling her in for another hug.

"There's always next year. And Christmas."

"Her birthday is first," Stefanos adds, letting everyone know that he hasn't forgotten his time as her husband.

"True," Gianna laughs.

A moment of silence passes between everyone as they all try and process what's just been revealed before Alex breaks it.

"Evie and I are heading home."

I have to bite on the inside of my cheek to stop from arguing about where my home is.

"Okay," Stefanos says.

"What about Blakely and Zay?" I ask, focusing on Alex's dad.

His jaw tics, but otherwise his reaction over what his ex-wife did to his father and the man who abused him and his sons has been put behind him.

"They're welcome to stay as long as they need. Blakely is doing a good job. I don't welcome the idea of trying to find someone new already."

I can't help but laugh. "I appreciate the sentiment, but I think we both know she's the worst housekeeper you've ever had."

"She has her benefits," he confesses with a wink to Alex. In that moment, I see exactly where his cheeky side might have come from. I also don't miss the way Gianna tenses at the comment before rolling her eyes as if it's some big joke.

"Dad," he growls. "You promised."

"What is it you kids say?" he asks lightly before walking into the kitchen and pulling the fridge open. "Rules are made to be broken."

"Dad, I swear to God, if you've—"

"Leave it," I say, pressing my hands to Alex's chest lightly. "He's baiting you. And it's working."

"You're a prick."

"Love you too, kid," he says before disappearing from the room with a bottle of water and slipping into his office down the hallway.

"Right, well, if you're heading home, I guess my time here is over once more." Gianna moves toward the door. "I should probably go and find Daemon and confess my sins before you do it for me."

"He's going to be pissed you got in there first, I hope you know that."

Gianna chuckles lightly, but she doesn't argue.

Leaving them to have a moment, I head out through the wall of sliding doors to find Blake and Zay to tell them we're leaving. Not something I'm looking forward to.

22

ALEX

With my heart in my throat, I give my mum one last squeeze before she walks toward her car.

I'll see her tomorrow when she comes to change my dressings as promised, but after the bomb that was just dropped, her going home alone just seems wrong.

Pulling her driver's door open, she looks back up at me. Love and pride shine in her eyes, making the emotion I'd battling with burn hotter.

She killed him. She found out the truth and took him out like a fucking bad-arse.

And none of us had any idea.

I remember the night Dad got the call that he'd had a heart attack and paramedics were unable to revive him. Mum was there, but I don't remember her reaction. I was too busy celebrating the death of the devil to notice. D was too. Pretty sure he even smiled that night. And Dad... I just remember him blowing out of the room and then the house in a rage. But knowing what I know now, I'm pretty sure it was relief even more potent than ours. We'd had a few years dealing with our grandfather's abuse. He'd had a lifetime and was forced to watch history repeat itself with us.

The need to talk to Dad open and honestly burns through me, and before Mum's disappeared from the driveway, I dart back into the house, pausing to knock on Dad's office door.

"Come in," he calls, and when I push the door open, I don't find him sitting behind his desk but standing at the windows staring out at the back garden.

"You okay?" I ask, unease rocking through me as I realise that the two of us have never had a conversation about the hard stuff.

"Shouldn't I be asking you that?" he counters, glancing over his shoulder for a beat.

"Just a few cuts and bruises. Nothing I can't handle."

"Alex," he whispers, his voice full of pain.

"Seriously, I'm good. What Mum just said—"

He shakes his head, focusing on whatever is holding his attention outside.

"I'm sorry," he says after what feels like the world's longest silence. "I should have been the one to do that a long time before she ever had the chance."

"Yeah, probably. But we understand why you didn't. Why you couldn't. Same reason we didn't."

Ripping his eyes from outside, he hangs his head. Regrets and anguish pour off him in waves.

"Life under his control is all I've ever known. Your mother... she gave me such relief from it all. I never should have been selfish enough to drag her into my life. But I can't regret it, because she gave me both of you. I might have fucked up, Son. Many, many times. But you are the most important things in my life. Everything I do, I do for you both. To help build you a future to—"

"I'm not doing any more jobs, Dad," I blurt, cutting him off.

He sucks in a deep breath, his shoulders lowering.

"I know," he agrees. "Have you always hated it?" he asks, finally turning to look at me.

My lips part to say yes, but I quickly realise that would be a lie.

"No, not always. It's taught me a lot about myself, allowed me to learn what I really want."

"Evie," he says.

"Evie."

A smile twitches at his lips as he thinks about my girl, and no matter how hard I try, I can't stop jealousy from bubbling up inside me. It's ridiculous. He's my father, and I'm pretty sure he'd never go there, but my possessive tendencies over my girl know no bounds.

"She's really quite incredible. There aren't many women who would stand in front of us like she did and lay her life on the line."

His words are like a bat to the chest.

"Just so you know, before she got involved, I point-blank refused for it to be an option."

"Good."

"If I'd known she was eavesdropping and then begging Anthony for help, then..."

"It's over, Dad. It doesn't matter what anyone did or should have done."

He nods, his eyes moving back to the window.

My curiosity has me crossing the room to see what's captured his attention, but I'm pretty sure I already know.

"Dad," I warn when I find that he has the perfect view of Evie, Blakely and Zayden playing football together.

"He's a good kid," he says, ignoring my warning. "He reminds me a lot of you two when you were his age."

"He's pretty awesome. Did you—"

"He's enrolled from September, full ride."

My heart swells as I watch Zay run carefree around the garden, both Evie and Blake trying to get the ball from him.

"He has skills too. The team is going to need fresh blood, after all."

"Pretty sure Atlas and his massive ego has it more than covered for next season."

Dad barks a laugh at my comment but says nothing more as he watches them.

My warning about Blakely and him teeters right on the tip of my tongue, but I swallow it back down.

"He deserves it. He's got a bright future ahead of him."

"They all do."

We stand shoulder to shoulder, watching them, my eyes locked on Evie, his on... I think I'd rather not know.

"Promise me something," I mutter.

He doesn't respond, so I continue.

"Don't make their lives any harder than they need to be. If cutting them free now will save any more pain, you need to do it."

I glance over just in time to see Dad close his eyes tightly.

"I won't do anything to hurt them. You have my word."

Silence falls once more with that promise. All I can do is accept it and pray that he keeps it.

"I'm taking Evie home," I state.

"Blakely and Zayden will be safe here."

I nod. "I'm only a phone call away if he needs me."

He nods in agreement, and I move back toward the door.

"Alex," he growls.

"Yeah."

"One day, you're going to be an incredible father. I hope you know that."

A somewhat nervous laugh spills from my lips, and I make the mistake of lifting my arm to rub the back of my neck.

Pain shoots off in all directions, and I quickly give up on the idea.

"We'll see."

"Go and spend some time with Evie. Heal. We'll talk soon."

I leave his office with a little more hope than I walked in with. I didn't really know what I was expecting him to say when I told him I was no longer going to run jobs, but 'I know' wasn't it.

Laughter floats into the kitchen a few seconds before the three of them emerge, all red-faced with wide, happy smiles spread across their lips.

My heart tumbles in my chest when Evie's eyes light up —even more the second she sees me and comes rushing over. After reaching up to brush a quick kiss on my lips, she gently tucks herself into my side.

"Do you really have to go?" Zay asks, letting me know that Evie has already explained our plans.

"Sorry, little dude. I don't actually live here anymore."

"You could move back," he says, his previous happiness dying.

"Zay," Blake warns. "Alex has his own life now. He's heading to uni in September, just like Evie."

"I know," he whispers.

"Let us get settled and you can come to visit. I've got a better X-box than the one here, and a bigger TV."

That makes his eyes light up a little.

"And you've got Atlas coming to hang out, so you won't even notice they're gone," Blakely says, trying to soften the blow.

"I guess," he mutters.

With the tension suffocating us all, Blakely announces that it's ice cream time and directs Zay deeper into the kitchen while Evie and I go upstairs to pack.

"I know we're doing the right thing," she says softly as she zips up her bag, "but I hate seeing him sad."

"I know. But he needs this. To return to some kind of normal life."

Her lips part to say something, but she second-guesses herself.

"What is it?"

"What about school? He can't go back—"

"There's time for those discussions. It's almost summer; he can make up for whatever he misses." Stepping up to her, I wrap my arms around her upper arms. "He's got a place at Knight's Ridge College, but the decision is between the three of you as to whether he takes it or not."

"Alex," she breathes. "How is that fair? You can't offer up something so incredible, something that could change his life, and then ask us to discuss it and possibly turn it down."

"Knight's Ridge is an incredible school, Evie. But it's not for everyone. Yes, it will open up avenues that Lovell Academy wouldn't, but that's not to say he won't carve the same path for himself."

"I know, I just—"

"Stop, Evie," I beg. "Let all of this die down a little, and then you and Blakely can talk to him. Let him decide. He's a smart kid. Trust him to make the right decision for him. If it's Lovell, then you can bet your arse I'll support him all the way too."

"You're an amazing brother," she says, slowly sliding her hands up my chest and looping them around my neck.

"Dad reckons I'll be a good father someday," I blurt, unaware that those words were going to spill free.

"Oh yeah? You want that?"

"One day, yeah. You?"

"A month or so ago, I'd have said no. But now, yeah, I guess I do."

I take her lips in a bruising kiss, my need to have her to myself all-consuming.

"Let's get out of here," she whispers into our kiss.

"You want to get me alone, Vixen?" I growl, unable to think about anything but getting her naked and remembering just how her body feels against mine.

"I do."

"Then what the fuck are we waiting for?" I release her in a heartbeat and grab both of her bags, ignoring the pain that shoots up my arms.

"Alex, no," she cries, trying to wrestle the bags off me.

"I'm taking my woman home. Now let's go," I demand, marching from the room.

"Stubborn prick," she mutters behind me.

After a quick round of goodbyes with teary-eyed Blake and Zay, I finally drag Evie away and through the front door.

"Did someone order a taxi?" Theo asks, climbing out of the driver's seat at the same time Atlas bolts from the car, making a beeline for Zay.

"Dude, you got taken captive. That's so cool. Tell me everything," Atlas demands.

"Atlas," Theo growls. "What did we just talk about?"

Atlas waves his big brother off as if he isn't one of the most terrifying men in the city before the two of them go tearing into the house.

Blakely looks at Theo and the two of them shrug.

"Anyway, have fun with them, Blakely. We've got places to be going and things to be doing."

"I bet you have," she scoffs as I tug Evie toward Theo's car.

He takes the bags from me but not before giving me the evil eye for carrying them in the first place.

Pulling the back door open, I gesture for Evie to slide inside.

"Such a gentleman," she murmurs.

"You probably won't be saying that in a few hours."

"Alex," Theo barks. "Sit in the fucking front."

"I love you, man. But there's no chance in hell of that happening."

I slide in after Evie and don't stop until I'm right up against her.

"Be good," she warns with a smirk as Theo drops into the driver's seat.

"Where's the fun in that?" I mutter before gripping her chin and slamming my lips down on hers.

"I guess I should be grateful you're still too injured to fuck her back there," Theo scoffs, making Evie laugh.

"Bit rich, considering what you did right next to us in the back of Seb's car not so long ago."

"Fuck that motherfucker. He's screwed Stella on every surface I own. He deserves it."

"So his spunk was here first... interesting."

"It's been fully valeted since they were back there. Fucker paid for it too."

"Your friends are crazy," Evie says lightly. "I love them."

"Shh, don't let them hear you say that, it'll go to their heads."

"Too late," Theo confirms. "And you're right, they're all crazy. Aren't you glad the sane one stopped by to bring you home?"

"Sane my fucking arse. Did you know Theo has OCD?" I ask Evie.

"I do fucking not."

"Ask him how many packets of anti-bac wipes he has in this car right now," I encourage.

"The fuck, dude?"

"How many?" Evie asks, happily playing along.

Theo sighs. "One in the glove box and another in the boot."

"Liar."

"No, I'm not. That's it."

"Alex is right," Evie says, leaning forward and plucking a pack out of the pocket in the back of his seat. "Here's another."

"Three is not ridiculous. Especially when you have sex-obsessed friends like we do."

"Takes one to know one, bro. Now, all this chit-chat is fun and all but..." Twisting my fingers in my girl's hair, I give her little choice but to turn toward me so I can claim her lips once again.

I lick into her mouth hungrily, claiming her, possessing her, making her mine all over again without the secrets and lies hanging between us.

It's us now.

Just us.

Fucking perfect.

23

———

EVIE

"Fuck, I've missed you," Alex groans, slamming me back against his closed front door the second we're inside.

His hands slide up my body, squeezing my breasts before coming to rest on each side of my face, holding me exactly where he wants me as his blazing eyes burn into mine.

He's still in pain—I can see it in his grey depths. He's not going to be able to do this like he wants, like he craves, but he's going to give it his best shot regardless.

"Alex, you're meant to be resting," I argue between my heaving breaths. Just the look of unfiltered desire on his face has my temperature soaring.

"We can do this in bed. I might even let you do some of the work."

"Not exactly what—"

"Don't care," he mumbles, slamming his lips down on mine.

Just like in the back of Theo's car, I melt for him.

Wrapping my arms gently around his waist, I pull his weight against me.

"Evie," he groans, rolling his hips so I've little choice but to feel how much he needs me.

"Bedroom," I whisper.

"Fuck. Yeah. Okay,"

Without breaking our kiss, he drags me from the door and blindly guides me down toward his room. Thankfully, he knows his space well enough that I don't end up on my arse.

We spill through the door and before I know it, I'm on my back on his bed with him looming over me.

He looks as beautiful as ever, even with the lingering bruises around his eyes and darkening his jaw. They just show the depth of his strength.

"I love you," I whisper, searching his eyes.

"I love you too, Vixen." He tucks his fingers beneath the waistband of my leggings and tugs them down. "I'm going to make you scream, then make you mine, and then..." His words trail off as he stares at me, spreading my legs wide. He licks his lips, then swallows roughly. "Then we're talking."

I nod, unable to speak as desire runs red hot through my veins, my clit pulsating with need.

I should tell him no, force him to rest more. But he needs this as much as I do. After the way our last time ended, and the stress of the days which followed, we need this.

We need to connect, to remind ourselves of why we ended up here in the first place.

"Okay," I breathe as his hands slide up the inside of my tank, pushing the fabric up until he's cupping my breasts once more.

"Off," he growls before ripping it from my body, quickly followed by my bra.

He stills, staring down at me with nothing but awe and love in his eyes.

"Fuck, baby. So perfect."

"Please," I beg, needing more than just his eyes on me. "I need you."

He begins to descend the bed, but I don't miss the way his teeth grind and his jaw tics.

"Alex, you're in pain."

"I don't give a fuck," he groans. "I need—"

"Switch. Lie on the bed."

"Evie," he growls. "I need—"

"To do as you're fucking told?" His eyes widen at the strength in my tone.

"Shit. Okay."

I roll out of his way, and he flops onto his back, his eyes closing for a beat as he battles with his pain.

"You need pills?" I ask, already aware that he's going to refuse.

"No, they make everything numb. I don't want to be numb. I want to feel. Everything."

Heat floods my core, but it's not enough to be able to push his pain aside.

"Where are you going?" he asks when I climb to my feet and walk toward the door.

"I'm naked, Alex. I'm hardly leaving," I tease.

I don't need to look back to know his eyes are eating up every inch of me; my skin burns red hot with his attention.

Before I change my mind and launch myself at him, I rush from the room, rummaging through my bags for the pills Gianna gave me.

After getting him a glass of water, I return with both in my hands.

"Evie, I said no. I don't—"

"They're not the strong ones. Just standard. They'll help take the edge off but won't make you sleepy."

He studies me for a beat before his eyes drop to the box.

"See, they even have caffeine in them," I say, holding it closer.

"Fine, okay."

When he holds his hand out, I pop two pills into his palm and wait for him to swallow them.

"Are you done? Can you climb up here and sit on my face now?"

Everything south of my waist clenches as my mind conjures up the image of me doing just that.

"You're wet for me already, aren't you?"

I saunter closer, my cheeks burning.

There was a moment when both Pete and Grant had their hands on me when I feared it would be all Alex would see whenever he looked at me again. But the second he came to and looked into my eyes, I knew it wasn't going to affect us.

Maybe if Daemon hadn't got involved and put an abrupt end to it all, then things might have been different.

But right now, thoughts of what happened in that church are far from Alex's mind as he stares at me impatiently and rubs himself through the fabric of his sweats.

"I can already see you're ready for me," I taunt, my eyes on the more-than-obvious tenting of the fabric. "Fancy giving me a better view?"

"Not until you give me what I want," he growls. "Now

get the fuck up here and let me eat you until you're screaming for mercy."

Unable to hold back any longer, I step up to the bed and crawl on.

"Hurry," he growls, his impatience getting the better of him.

But while I might need this badly as he does, I'm not ready to rush.

I spent so long not knowing what was happening, where he was, if he was alive or dead. Now, I need to savour this—having him here, his warm skin under my fingers and his addictive lips against mine.

Throwing my leg over his waist, I dip low, taking his mouth in a filthy kiss that promises of all the things to come.

His hands are everywhere. It's as if he doesn't know which part of me to touch first. My thighs, my arse, my waist, my tits, my hair. Every single one makes me burn up for him, my nerve endings tingling with desire.

We kiss until we're both breathless, and then finally, with his hands locked around my waist, I cave and crawl up his body, resting my knees on either side of his head.

"Fucking dreamed of this while I was gone. Thoughts of you kept me going, baby. Nothing would have stopped me from getting back to you."

"Enough," I complain, not wanting to go there right now.

The time for talking, for confessing a few more of our sins is coming. Right now, it's about pleasure. And hopefully, a lot of it.

After all, I think we both deserve it after what we've been through.

With another frustrated growl, Alex wraps his hands

around my hips, his fingers digging into my skin as he drags me down.

"Want to fucking suffocate on you, Vixen," he confesses before his words are cut off, replaced by my loud moan of pleasure as his tongue licks up the length of me.

"Fuck, I missed you," I cry, grinding down on his face shamelessly.

He says something in response, but I can only make out the vibration of his deep voice as he works me like a pro.

In only minutes, I'm shattering into a million pieces with my fingernails digging into the hardwood of Alex's headboard.

He holds me up as my muscles turn to mush before he moves me lower in favour of my mouth.

His kiss is wicked as he lets me taste myself on his tongue.

"You're a filthy boy, Alexander," I moan into his kiss.

"You fucking love it," he counters.

I moan in agreement as he sucks on my bottom lip.

"Now get down there and get my dick out. I want to see your lips wrapped around it before you ride me like the dirty girl you are."

"You want me to—"

"Too late to be shy now, Vixen. I'm too injured to take charge, remember?"

"Yeah," I mutter, shimmying down his body. "When it suits."

"Right now," he says, tucking his hands behind his head, his eyes glued on me as I begin tugging his sweats down his legs, "it suits me just fine."

The majority of the cuts on his legs have scabbed over now and are healing nicely. Unlike his arms. Only a couple needed stitching and wrapping, but even those are looking good as I peel his sweats away.

Lowering my lips to the worst one across his thigh, I press a soft kiss to the edge of it, my eyes locked on his.

"Evie," he groans as I move, peppering kisses to the wound that until this morning was hidden from the world.

"I love you," I whisper. "Every inch of you."

His eyes close for a beat. Despite not really having a chance to talk about it properly, I know he's struggling with this, his scars. The physical evidence he's going to be left with.

I hate that it's my fault. If it weren't for meeting me, then he never would have found himself in that situation. But the thought of not having him in my life is so much worse.

"Look at me," I demand, just like he has to me so many times before. "I'm right here and there's nowhere else in the world I want to be," I promise him, kissing higher up his thigh until I hit the hem of his boxers.

His dick strains against the fabric and my mouth waters, more than ready for a taste of him.

I keep my eyes on his as I drag them down his thighs, and then I lean forward and lick up the entire length of him.

His hips thrust up the second I make contact, and his eyes blaze with barely restrained fire.

"Shit," he hisses, untucking his hands from his head in favour of twisting his fingers in my hair. "More. Evie. Fuck."

Unable to deny him anything, I wrap my fingers around his shaft and lick him like a lollipop.

His eyes practically roll back in his head. His grip on my hair tightens, but at no point does he try to force me lower.

"Fucking love you, Vixen," he gasps when I finally take pity on him and sink down on this length. "Fuuuuuck." My core clenches with need as his growl fills the room.

His lids lower, but he never breaks our eye contact as he gently helps me bob up and down on his length.

"Jesus, I could watch you do this forever," he confesses, biting down on his bottom lip.

I work him with both my mouth and my hand until he's thickening, getting ready to blow.

And just before I'm convinced that he's about to come down my throat, his fingers tighten on my hair and he drags me off him.

"What are you—"

"Not coming in your mouth this time, Vixen. Ride me."

My body flies in to action long before my brain catches up with me, and he chuckles as I eagerly follow orders.

As he holds himself up for me, I grind down on him, coating him in my juices before sinking lower.

"Oh fuck," he grunts as I cry out.

It doesn't hurt anywhere near as much as it did that first time, but hell, it's a tight fit.

"Oh, Jesus. You have no fucking idea how good that feels."

His grip on my hips is bruising as he helps hold me up, but I love it. I'll happily walk around every day with his marks all over me.

It takes a few seconds for me to fully seat myself on him.

"You okay?" he asks, staring up at me in awe.

I nod. I'm pretty sure I'm more okay than I ever have been in my life.

Every part of me is so full of everything this man has shown me, given me, and opened me up to.

"More," I beg, tucking my fingers under the hem of his long-sleeved shirt, desperate for more inches of skin.

But before I get any further, he releases my hips and stops me from exposing him.

"No. I don't... Let's just pretend for a few minutes that it never happened. Please," he begs.

My heart shatters right down the middle at the vulnerability in his eyes.

Leaning over him, I plant one hand beside his head and the other cups his jaw.

"Anything. But I love you, Alex. Every single inch of you, and nothing will ever change that."

Finally, he closes his eyes, severing our connection as he tries to absorb the truth in my words.

"It's going to take a bit of time to believe that, baby."

"We've got all the time in the world," I whisper, peppering kisses over his face before settling at his lips.

His eyes flutter open, and I find nothing but love and devotion staring back at me.

"Hell, yeah, we have."

Taking my hips in his hands once more, he encourages me to rock over him.

"Oh, oh, oh," I chant as he hits some magical spot deep inside me.

"Fuck me, baby. I want to feel you coming all over my co—"

I steal his lips before he finishes that demand and kiss him until my lungs are burning and my body is screaming for more.

"Oh shit," he groans when I sit up, allowing him to hit me at a whole new, mind-blowing angle. "So fucking hot, Evie. Fuck," he barks as I start fucking him harder. "Yes, just like that. Let me watch those tits bounce."

My eyes close as my head falls back, focusing on the sensations zapping through my body.

"Play with your clit. I need you coming before I ruin your pretty little pussy."

"Your mouth is filthy, Alexander Deimos," I force out through heaving breaths.

"Don't even pretend you don't love it. Your pussy practically strangles my dick every time I mention you being my dirty girl. See?" He smirks.

My gasp rips through the air as my fingers collide with my sensitive flesh.

"That's it, baby. Show me how you do it. Use me. Get yourself off. Let me hear you scream."

I swear it only takes five seconds with that added pressure before I do as I'm told and scream out his name.

"Fuck, Evie. Fuuuuck," he groans, his dick twitching violently inside me as he fills me up.

Carefully, I fall onto his chest, a sweaty, sated mess.

Still semi-hard and happily inside me, Alex wraps his arms around me and kisses the top of my head.

"I love you so much."

"I love you too," I whisper as stupid tears burn the backs of my eyes.

I could have lost him. If I didn't do what I did, when I did, he might have died up there on that cross and I never would have had this again.

24

―――

ALEX

It might have hurt, but I wanted to keep Evie's weight pressing down on me for as long as I could. Also having my semi still inside her was a definite benefit for the position as well, but predictably, she rolled off me after a few minutes, too scared of hurting me.

I didn't voice the words, but I've discovered after everything I went through that the only thing that could truly hurt me now would be her figuring out I'm not worth it and turning her back on me.

I'm not the guy she first met. I don't need to look at the bandages littering both my arms to know that. She keeps saying all the right words, but under all my bravado and confidence, even I admit I'm scared.

And my concerns only multiply when I look over and find tears streaked down her rosy cheeks.

"Evie, what's wrong?" I ask, my heart in my throat.

I swear to God, if she tells me that all of this, coming back here, having sex with me was a mistake, then I'm not entirely sure how I'm going to move past it.

Thankfully, that's not what happens.

Instead, a shy smile tugs at her lips as she shakes her head.

"Nothing. I just... I got a little bit overwhelmed with everything a-and—" she stutters, lifting her hand to wipe her cheeks. "All these stupid thoughts hit me about what could have been, and I'm so fucking happy they never happened, that you're here."

Her tiny hand lands on my jaw and she stretches up to give me a slow, sensual, relief-filled kiss.

The saltiness of her tears coats my tongue, making me wish I could steal them all straight from her eyes and take the pain away.

The intensity of the kiss never increases, and after a few minutes, she pulls away, resting her head on the pillow beside me.

Rolling onto my side, I ignore the pain in my arm beneath me and reach the other out, tugging her closer.

"Talk to me, Evie. I want to know everything from the minute I left for my exam."

She closes her eyes for a beat, and I start to think she's going to refuse, but then they open again, her lips part, and she starts talking.

"I thought I was being a rebel by going outside to do yoga. I needed to relax after everything that had happened, all the awful things I said to you. I knew it was a risk being out there alone, but as it turns out it might have just saved my life. It gave me the head start I needed when they descended on the cabin."

"That never should have happened, but they were on to us. They'd mapped out our security's schedule and knew the best time to strike. I'm so sorry."

She searches my eyes, her face serious. "It's not your fault. It was inevitable."

"It shouldn't have been though. I promised to protect you."

"I'm here, aren't I?" she says with a smile. "A dog called Murphy saved me."

I can't help but mirror her grin.

"A dog called Murphy?" I question.

"Yep," she says happily before explaining everything from how she ran from the deck to begging a random woman to drop her at Dad's house, promising her that they'd take care of her.

She tells me about her time there and how the guys were out almost every hour of the day, trying to put a plan together. How wrecked my dad looked with me missing and about a little middle-of-the-night bonding session they had. And then to her eavesdropping on his office.

"I hope you realise that listening in to sensitive information can come with a death sentence," I warn in a low, deadly voice.

She swallows nervously.

"D and I got caught when we were like... I dunno, six, maybe. I've never seen my dad lose his shit quite like he did that day."

"What were they talking about?" she whispers as if it's still the Family's biggest secret.

"That's the worst bit. We had no idea. We couldn't have told anyone even if we were stupid enough to share."

"Jesus."

"We learned, though. Never even slowed our pace when we passed his office after that."

"I guess I should be lucky he didn't catch me then."

"Something tells me my dad's got a bit of a soft spot for you. He'd have probably let you off scot-free."

"Helps that I saved his son, huh?"

"Yeah, about that... how badly do I need to hurt Ant when I'm recovered?"

She chuckles. "You don't. You should be thanking him that he listened to me. If he didn't and I never..." She trails off, not wanting to say the words filling her head.

"So he listened and took you to The Empire," I say, recollecting what I do know about this. "And shy little Evie Moore stood with her head held high in front of the city's most dangerous men."

"And woman," she corrects, her eyes flashing with something I can't read.

"Ah yes, Luciana. There's a story there too, isn't there?"

She bites down on her lip and nods.

"Go on then."

Pride washes through me as she explains about standing in front of Damien's desk and demanding that they accept the trade.

My fists curl in anger that they were even willing to put her in that position. But fuck, am I glad they did.

If they refused... well, I'd probably still be hanging on that cross right now.

"So they bundled me in a van, and whoever drove me there made a show of dragging me out and throwing me at their feet."

"When were they going to deliver me and Zay back home?" I ask.

"No idea. I left them all to plan that. Not that it really mattered, because they had every intention of storming the place once the coast was clear."

Leaning forward, I bump my nose against hers. "I'm in fucking awe of you, Evie. There aren't many people in the world who would have had the strength to do what you did."

"What is it they say?" she asks lightly. "Love makes you crazy."

With a smile, I put all my effort into looming over her.

"I can live with being crazy."

Her smile spreads across her face, making my heart flip over in my chest.

Dipping lower, I focus on taking her lips, but just before I close the space between us, she lets out a confession that rocks through every inch of me.

"Luciana is my aunt."

All the air bursts out of my lungs as if someone just swung a bat at my back.

"W-what?"

"My... our mum was Luciana's older sister."

I sit back and stare down at her.

"Holy fuck, Evie. That's... huge."

Pushing up, she tucks her legs under the covers and tugs them up to her chest.

"Dad's parents... they... they bought Mum for him, apparently."

"Fuck."

"And Luciana was sold to the Riveras years later. There were five of them. Only Luciana has survived."

I stare at her dumbfounded and scrub my hand down my face.

"She discovered what happened and went on a mission to take the ring down and discover the truth about her family. She found us because of all this. Because of you, and Brianna, Reid."

"Holy fuck," I blurt again, apparently unable to come up with anything more eloquent. "Did you know she had sisters?"

I shake my head.

"Wow. Have you told Blake?"

"Of course. She looked about as stunned as you do right now."

"Understandable."

"We did DNA tests while you were out of it just to check."

"And they're positive?" I ask, although I don't need to. Firstly, she wouldn't be telling me all this if they came back any other way, and secondly, looking into her eyes now, I can see it. "Fuck. Evie, that woman, she's—"

"Beautiful, fierce, terrifying."

I can't help but laugh. "Yeah, all those things and so many more. So your mum was purchased for your father. And then all these years later, he turned around and put you up for sale. Why?"

She shakes her head. "We don't know."

"You can ask him, though, right?"

Again, she shakes her head.

"What am I missing?"

She lets out a pained sigh. "They found him dead in the cell he was in a few days ago."

"WHAT?" I roar. The level of injustice in that slams into me so hard I've no doubt I'd topple over if I weren't already sitting. "Fuck, Evie. I'm so sorry."

She waves me off. "Doesn't matter. It's not like he deserved to live to tell his tale," she says without even a tremor of doubt in her words.

"You mean that?"

"Yeah, I really do. Am I pissed that I don't get answers? Yeah, I am. But am I sad he's no longer in my life? Nope. I'm surrounded by incredible people, and I have a new aunt that would probably burn down the world to keep me safe and a boyfriend who would be standing right beside her. What more could I need?"

"Baby," I breathe, falling even deeper in love with her with every word she says.

"Now it's your turn. I know it's not going to be easy, but will you tell me what happened? Help me understand what you've been through so that I can do everything I can to help you through this?"

"You sure that's really what you want?"

"I want everything, Alex. Always. No matter how hard or painful or ugly, I want everything with you. Of course, that's if you want—"

"Everything with you too?" I finish for her. Holding her chin between my thumb and forefinger, I lean forward and nudge her nose with mine. "There's nothing I want more. I'll tell you anything you want. No more secrets."

"No more secrets," she promises, sealing it with the gentlest of kisses.

25

EVIE

By the time Alex finished shredding my heart to pieces by giving me a play-by-play of his and Zay's time as prisoners, he could barely keep his eyes open.

We lie with our arms and legs intertwined, him seeking comfort, me just holding on for dear life as the reality to how close I came to losing both of them settling within me.

He was up on that cross long before I turned up at the front door.

If I hadn't... what might have happened?

Would they have got him down eventually so they didn't lose their new playmate, or would they have left him up there to bleed to death?

A violent shudder rips through me, my muscles tingling with my need to do something, to hurt someone for what they did to them. But it's over. There's nothing left.

I played my part. I helped to bring them down.

That should be enough. But listening to his confession, looking at him with his shirt still hiding his arms... It hurts more than I ever thought possible. It would be easier to deal with if I were the one who was suffering.

Leaning forward, I press a gentle kiss on the tip of his nose. He doesn't so much as flinch.

After a few more moments watching him, I untwist myself from him and climb from the bed as softly as I can.

Grabbing one of his shirts as I pass his chest of drawers, I slip into the bathroom and close the door behind me.

The shower at Stefanos's house might have been as good, as powerful as this one here. But it didn't have the memories that make a smile pull at my lips as I step under the spray that this one does.

Closing my eyes, I allow myself to get lost in thoughts of my first time here. I was so concerned that night about Alex taking his attack on Grant too far. But knowing what I do now, maybe another hit or two might have changed everything.

With a pained sigh, I reach for his shampoo, just like I did at Stefanos's despite Blakely ensuring I had my own brand waiting for me. The lure of his scent, of being surrounded by memories of him was just too much to deny.

Alex is still sleeping soundly when I emerge, and I cave to my need to do something. Marching into his kitchen, I take a punt on where I'll find everything I need and drag open the cupboard beneath the sink.

"Bingo," I whisper, pulling the bucket of cleaning supplies out.

Despite being confident they have a cleaner—I mean, no one has lived here since before Alex went to Vegas and it's still spotless—I set to work, burning off my need to go and set the remains of that church on fire all over again myself with every scrub of the kitchen counter and swipe on a window.

I scrub with such ferocity that I quickly work up a sweat, but I don't slow down. I need this.

As I work, anger bubbles up within me as I repeat what Alex described from inside that church. Hatred like I've never known surges through my veins, quickly poisoning me from inside out. My movements become erratic as tears burn red hot, making my nose tingle and a sob threaten to break free.

When I can no longer see through the tears flooding my eyes, I spin around, crashing back against the wall. The cloth in my hand drops to the floor as I drop my head into my hands, allowing my emotions to erupt.

My knees buckle with the weight of the last couple of weeks and I drop, landing like a lead weight on my arse. But I don't feel it. I don't feel anything but the soul-deep ache of knowing that people I love have suffered, are suffering, and that there's nothing I can do about it.

And that's exactly where Alex finds me sometime later.

"Evie," he cries, rushing to my side, dropping to his knees and pulling me into his arms. "Baby, I'm here. It's okay. Everything is okay." His voice is rough from sleep and cracked with emotions.

"I-I know. I'm s-s-sorry."

"Hey, shush now. It's okay," he whispers into my hair, clutching me as tight as he can to hold me together.

Silence falls between us as my sobs continue and my body trembles against his.

Long minutes pass before I manage to get myself under control and pull my face from his chest. His shirt is soaked through from my tears. My face is probably red and blotchy, my eyes swollen and bloodshot, but he stares down at me as if I'm the most beautiful girl in the world. My heart flips over and a fresh round of tears threatens.

But before I crumble again, he tucks me against his side and guides me back toward his bedroom.

He gets us into bed without releasing me and curls his large body around mine.

"It's over, baby. I'm not going to let anyone touch you again."

I nuzzle against his chest, praying that I'm not hurting him and just breathe him in, soaking up his strength, promises, and love. It's a heady feeling and I drift off to sleep feeling lighter than I have in a while. Emotional breakdown aside, things are good, and he's right; it's over, and we're all going to be okay.

———

The heat of Alex's hand slipping under my shirt wakes me a second before his fingers tickle over my ribs.

My nipples pucker, waking up rapidly with the rest of my body. I arch my back, offering myself up to him while grinding against his morning wood.

"Could wake up like this every morning," I whisper when he finally cups one of my boobs and pinches my nipple.

"You can," he whispers, peppering kisses across my neck, sending goosebumps racing over my skin. "Every. Single. Day. I can wake you with kisses."

I moan in delight, my entire body sinking into the mattress. "More."

"As if I'd stop," he laughs, rolling his hips against my arse, letting me know how much he loves waking up with me too. "I'll never get enough of you, Evie. Never."

"Same," I gasp as he sucks on the sensitive skin beneath my ear until it hurts in the best kind of way.

"You sore?" he asks, being the caring guy I remember all too well from before.

"Not enough to worry about," I say, reaching over my head so I can twist my fingers in his hair.

"Can't promise you won't be saying that in about thirty minutes."

"Thirty minutes, huh?"

"I had a really, really good sleep," he growls in my ear. "I have some energy to burn off before Mum turns up to torture me."

"She's looking after her boy, making sure you heal properly," I argue.

"I think she secretly loves dishing out the pain for all the grey hairs I've given her over the years."

"Can't argue with that."

"Thing is, I don't think I've been quite bad enough."

I moan in frustration when his hand slips from under my shirt, leaving my skin cold and desperate for his touch. But then he shifts about a little behind me, and the burning heat of his cock brushes between my thighs.

"Lift your leg and push back a little farther," he demands.

Something tells me he hates the fact he can't just drag me into position himself, but it won't be long until he's got full use of his arms again.

"Good girl," he praises when I shift into position.

He pushes the tip inside me and groans, teasing me by not giving me any more.

"I've barely touched you and you're soaked for me, Vixen."

"Need you."

"Fuck, yeah, you do."

His grip on my hip tightens before his entire body locks up behind me, and he thrusts his hips forward. I cry out as he fills me.

"I hope you know that any day now, I'm going to be able to move more freely, and I'm going to fuck you so hard and for so fucking long that you're not going to be able to walk for a week."

"Big promises," I gasp as he thrusts again, hitting a spot inside me that makes my eyes cross.

Oh, I have so many new things to discover with him now.

"Oh God, Alex," I cry when he hits it again.

"Good?" he asks, his tone smug and arrogant.

"You know it is," I counter.

"Good to know all those years of training weren't for nothing."

My stomach knots even with the briefest insight as to what he's been through. He hasn't been forthcoming with any information about what his 'training' entailed, but I have a pretty good imagination. Hopefully, one day, when he's ready, he'll be able to talk about it openly with me. But there's no rush. He can deal with all that in his own time. We both can. I'm certainly not going anywhere.

"You're amazing. And not just in bed," I add quickly. "I fell in love with you long before I knew just how skilled your dick was," I blurt like an idiot.

"Good to know. But..."

Thrust.

Cry.

"How about I make you fall even harder with those skills?"

"Not possible."

He chuckles, his fingers digging into my hip bone once more as he ups his pace, chasing both of our releases.

"Clit, baby. Let me feel you coming on my dick."

Without questioning his demand like I once would, my hand immediately jumps into action.

"Fuck, yeah. You feel so fucking good."

"Alex," I cry, my release racing forward.

"Let everyone hear you, baby. Everyone in this fucking city needs to know that Alexander Deimos can't be taken down that easily."

I want to laugh, to tell him that he's the world's biggest idiot with the planet's largest ego, but I don't get a chance to do any of those things because he pushes me over the edge and I scream out my release as it barrels into me.

"Evie. Fuck. Vixen. I love you. I love you," he chants before he falls, his body locking up behind me.

Our heaving breaths fill the air around us as we come down from our simultaneous highs.

"Best morning ever," I whisper.

"I dunno," he confesses, making my brows pinch. "Give me a few days, a week at worst, and I reckon I can beat it."

I giggle, the endorphins from my release making me all light and floaty.

He moans in frustration when I roll away, forcing him out of my body before I flip over.

"Morning, boyfriend," I whisper, smiling happily at him.

"Mmm, I can get used to that, girlfriend."

Pushing up onto his elbow, he looms over me and steals a wet and dirty kiss, not giving a single shit about our morning breath.

We just get into the groove of it when his alarm begins blaring.

"Nooo," he complains into our kiss.

"We can come straight back here after your mum checks you over," I offer. "Spend all day in bed."

"As fucking amazing as that sounds, we promised to go see Zay."

"Oh shit, Zay," I gasp, sitting up so fast I almost headbutt Alex. "I didn't call him last night."

"I did," Alex announces proudly.

"W-what?"

"I FaceTimed him while you were sleeping."

My entire body softens in relief.

"You're too perfect, you know that?"

Briefly, so fucking briefly, his eyes flick to his still-covered arms.

I wish there was something I could do to make him understand that it doesn't matter. But I know that only time will heal those wounds, like those littering his body.

"I need to shower. I'm pretty sure my mother doesn't want to come anywhere near me while I smell like sex with my girl."

Internally, I cringe hard.

"She told you to wait, your bandag—"

"She's literally about to turn up to replace them. Plus, I'm going to tell her it's your fault."

"Oh? How'd you figure that?" I ask as he climbs out of bed before holding his hand out to pull me to my feet.

He immediately drags his shirt from my body, leaving me naked before him, and then he turns me and shoves me toward the bathroom.

"What are you doing?" I laugh when he doesn't say a word.

I'm manhandled into the shower, and before I get a

chance to jump aside, he turns the dial, spraying me with ice-cold water.

A shriek rips from my throat before I get what I was craving yesterday when I rode him. Slowly, he peels his own shirt from his body, revealing inches upon inches of tanned skin and ripped muscles.

My mouth waters as he fights with his arms. If I were a little less distracted, I'd probably offer my help, but as it is, I'm too far gone in my ogling.

Throwing the shirt aside, he steps closer.

"My girl screamed in the shower, and I had little choice but to be her knight in shining armour," he says, stepping under the now warm spray, soaking all his bandages that aren't meant to get wet.

"How can I ever thank you for saving me, kind sir?" I ask, batting my lashes at him.

His eyes twinkle with mischief.

"We have an hour until she's meant to be here. I'm sure you can find multiple ways."

Evie stares up at me with her big blue eyes, and my heart seems to beat even faster.

Standing here with only bandages covering my body, I've never felt so self-conscious.

It's stupid. I know she doesn't care. I shouldn't, either.

If someone would have told me that I'd have ended up like this, I'd have been adamant I wouldn't care about the scars or damage done to my body. It's just a fucking body, for fuck's sake. A machine. But the moment I woke and saw the state of me, my arms especially, my unease over it started to grow.

It's their fault, and it probably all stems from being locked in that room with Zay. And I'm sure a good therapist will fix me, because it's bullshit. I know it is. And yet, the fear of Evie taking one look at my fucked-up arms and turning away from me is so fucking real it rocks me to my very core.

Stupid fucking irrational fears.

I was forced to face my fear of my own blood in the

most brutal way, and it seems to have been replaced with another bullshit one that has no place in my head.

Proving me right, at the sight of my body, Evie doesn't turn away or look disgusted in any way. Instead, her eyes darken as she bites down on her bottom lip, studying me with more than just a little interest.

"An hour, you say?" she whispers seductively, taking a step closer, lifting her hand and tracing one finger over the ridge of my collarbone. "That sure is a long time."

"It is. And yet, you seem to be wasting it," I tease, focusing on us and her instead of the shit in my head.

My skin erupts with goosebumps as she drags her finger over one of the bandages still on my chest until she circles my nipple, making my entire body shudder.

Her other hand lands on my waist, her thumb grazing down the V that will direct her straight to my dick like a three-dimensional map, and I flinch.

Her eyes widen in shock, but I don't get a chance to tell her that is was desire, not fear.

"None of this scares me, Alex. Whatever is hiding under these bandages, it won't stop me loving you, wanting you. You're as beautiful to me as you've ever been. You always will be."

A massive, messy lump of emotion crawls up my throat as I stare down at her, stopping me from saying even the simplest of words.

Leaning forward, Evie presses a soft kiss to my pec before another and then another.

I watch her every move and she heads toward my shoulder.

I know what she's going to do—I can practically see her intentions written in her eyes—but it doesn't stop me from gasping when her lips touch the corner of the first bandage that wraps around my upper arm.

I swallow thickly as she continues kissing over the healing wound hiding beneath. Her eyes never stray from mine as she silently tells me how much she loves me.

'Evie,' I mouth, my voice apparently broken as she kisses a trail down my arm, ensuring she makes contact with every bandage, every cut. Her hand mimics her actions on the other side, ensuring my entire body is covered in goosebumps, and my cock is rock fucking hard.

When she can't reach any lower, she drops to her knees, continuing down my forearm. When she gets to my hand, she lifts it and presses a kiss to the centre of my palm.

'I love you,' she mouths, her hands landing on my thighs, her fingers gently brushing my almost healed cuts there.

I can't move. I can barely fucking think as she slowly moves closer to where my dick bobs in front of her, desperately seeking action.

Just as gently as her previous touches, she presses a kiss to the side of my shaft.

That one kiss rocks through me with the power of a fucking tsunami.

"Evie," I growl, cupping the back of her head.

My chest heaves and my head spins with everything she's giving me.

I'll never be worthy of this woman. Never.

But I'm going to fucking try, because she's everything.

My fingers twist in her hair, and it takes every ounce of my self-restraint not to push her forward, choking her on my dick. But instead, I encourage her to stand.

"No," she argues, swatting my arm away.

When her eyes meet mine, they're full of fire and

determination that make any argument I had vanish in an instant.

"Let me take care of you."

Leaning forward once more, she licks a line up the length of my dick before swirling it around the tip, collecting the precum that's beading there and savouring it as if it's something special.

"Fucking hell," I moan when she sinks down on me so fucking slowly I swear my head is going to pop right off my body.

She works me with precision. Every single one of her movements is meticulously planned until she has me right on the edge of release.

Then, she pulls away.

I cry out at the loss, and she smirks up at me with a sinful twinkle in her eyes.

Oh, my girl is playing dirty.

Well, two can play that game.

My fingers find themselves at home in her hair again, and this time when she parts her lips to take me, I steal control, thrusting into her mouth as my grip tightens.

Her eyes widen and the corners of her lips twitch.

"Did I last longer than you expected?" She nods, her eyes shining with happiness as she swallows and submits to me as I flip our roles. "Ready?"

"Always," she mumbles around my shaft.

I take her roughly, unable to hold back. Saliva spills from the corners of her lips as she swallows me down.

I fucking love every second of it. And I know she does too.

But still, I don't finish in her throat.

I need to be inside her again too badly for that.

"Get up," I growl, pulling her from my dick with a pop.

"Get up, bend over and place your hands on the tiles. Oh, and brace yourself."

She smiles at me teasingly as she does exactly as she's told, and the second she's in position, I thrust inside her.

She cries out at the intrusion, her pussy probably still sensitive from round one.

"Alex. Yes. Fuck. Oh shit."

Her fingers curl against the tiles as pleasure rocks through her.

With one hand still twisted in her wet locks, I curl the other around her hip and fuck her like I've been craving since I first met her. Like a fucking savage.

She comes first—I am a fucking gentleman, after all—before I roar out my own release.

Time ceases to exist as the warm, powerful water rains down on us. Our hands and lips are everywhere as we continue to remind ourselves that it's over, that we're together again.

"I mean it, Alex. I'm so sorry about all those things I said that morning. I didn't mean—"

"You were right. Everything you said was true," I murmur into the soft skin of her neck.

She tenses, her hands immediately finding the rough skin of my cheeks as she pulls me away so she can look into my eyes.

"You're not a whore, Alex. What you do, it doesn't make—"

"Did," I correct. "What I did."

Her eyes search mine for a beat, but she doesn't respond.

"I told Dad that I'm done. No more jobs."

A frown forms between her brows.

"But that's your job. That's how you earn—"

"Are you going to cam again?" I ask.

"Hell no. Theo has already deleted the evidence that I was ever there."

I told myself that I would be cool about it if she wanted to continue. And I would have been. I'd never, ever stop my girl from doing something she loved. The fear that would come with it after what we've just lived through would be all-consuming. But I still wouldn't stop her.

"Are you going to dance?"

She shakes her head.

"Well look at us, all unemployed," I tease. It's not true; I have other jobs. That one was just my most useful, and I guess exciting, one. Working security doesn't really stack up in the thrills department, even if getting near another woman or guy sounds about as appealing as sticking a steak knife into my eye right now.

"I'll find something," she says in a rush, her eyes wide as realisation dawns. "I'll talk to Jodie about—"

Pressing my fingers to her lips, I cut her off.

"Not necessary. There's no rush to figure all this out. I have a job with the Family no matter what. It might just be nights doing security at one of our venues. And even if I don't, I have money."

"I don't want your—"

"Evie," I growl. "I love you. I love every single inch of your skin and hair on your body. Everything I am, everything I have is yours. Not out of obligation or charity, but because you are the other half of my soul. The Ben to my Jerry, the Bonnie to my Clyde. From here on out, we're an us, if you'll have me."

Tears swim in her eyes as she stares back at me, her bottom lip trembling.

"Move in with me, Evie. I want you to be here with me.

I want you to be the last person I see before I fall asleep at night and the first one I see in the morning. I want midnight kisses, early morning fucking, and everything in between."

"Alex," she whimpers.

"I mean it, Evie. I want you here. I want to start a life with you."

"It's crazy. We barely know each other."

"That might be true, but I know everything I need to to know that I want you, that I never want to let you go. That you're mine."

"What if we drive each other crazy?"

"Baby, I think that's pretty much guaranteed," I laugh.

"But what if—"

"It's amazing?" I ask, my heart thundering in my chest at the thought of her refusing and insisting on going to stay with Blakely and Zay at my dad's.

"Are you sure you want that? Me invading your space with my sketchbook and pencil collections?"

"I want it. All of it. I want to come home from work and find you sketching on the sofa. I want to teach you how to make croissants. I want to embark on uni together and spend our Sundays studying naked."

"Naked, huh?" she asks with a twinkle of naughtiness in her eyes.

"Anything. I'll give you anything you want."

She blinks, her large eyes gazing up at me with so many emotions shining in them.

"I just want you," she whispers.

"Same, Vixen. Same," I growl before slamming my lips down on hers, pinning her back against the wall and wrapping her leg around my hip.

Before long, I'm unable to deny the temptation before me and I thrust back inside her.

"Say yes, baby," I groan in her ear as I move, making her head fall back against the wall.

"Not fair," she whispers, her muscles rippling around my dick.

"Didn't you know? None of us play fair when it comes to getting what we want."

A smile twitches at her lips before she whispers, "Yes, Alex."

"Fuck, you're amazing."

With our lips locked and our bodies entwined, the rest of the world falls away.

EVIE

"Ah, how nice of you both to join me," Gianna says from her spot on Alex's sofa.

"Oh my God," I mutter, spinning around to hide my burning face in Alex's chest.

"Mum. Hi," Alex stutters. "What time is it?"

"Twenty minutes after I told you I'd be here." Her tone is teasing, and it makes my cheeks get even hotter.

"Sorry, we got distracted," Alex says without a hint of embarrassment. "Did you want a coffee?"

"There is something very wrong with you," I whisper, making him bark out a laugh.

"Sure, I'll have another. The one I made myself is long gone."

"You want one, baby?" he asks, dropping a kiss on the top of my head.

After agreeing, I have little choice but to find a seat and face Gianna.

"Morning," I whisper, still mortified that she was sitting out here waiting while we were... Jesus Christ.

"Good morning, sweetheart. When Stefanos and I were seventeen, he took me out on the most romantic picnic," she says, throwing me for a loop. "It was perfect until the clouds descended and one of the worst rainstorms I can remember took hold.

"He drove us back to his parents; and pulled into the garage. The second the sound of the pounding rain faded, he slid his chair back and dragged me onto his lap."

"Mum," Alex groans from the kitchen.

"Oh shush, boy. We were soaked through, and the car had long steamed up on the inside and that helped us both forget where we were. Reality sure came crashing back down fast when his mother knocked on the window, letting us know she was aware we'd returned home and that she knew exactly what we were doing.

"To this day, I've no idea how much those fogged-up windows hid from view. All I know is that her face was pretty clear on the other side."

"If you tell me that was the night D and I were conceived, I'm done," Alex warns.

Gianna laughs. "No. That wasn't the night. That night we—"

"And that's the end of storytime, thank you very much," Alex announces, placing Gianna's fresh coffee in front of her. "Did you do anything useful like bringing breakfast?"

"Breakfast? It's lunchtime, Alexander."

"I'm healing and allowed a lie in."

"Oh, so you two managed to get some sleep then."

"Are you here to cause me pain or embarrass my girl?"

"I'm here for neither," she says with a smile.

"Could have fooled me," Alex mutters, returning to the kitchen for our coffees.

"How are you feeling?" Gianna asks him. "I see you

took my advice about not getting those wet," she says, eyeing the soaked bandages that cover most of his arms.

"When have you ever known me to follow the rules?"

She shakes her head, watching him with nothing but love in her eyes.

"Evie's moving in," he informs her.

"You say that like I didn't see it coming," she deadpans, and I swear her eyes drop to my left hand.

"Not yet," Alex says, clearly seeing the same thing. "But I will," he promises, making my breath catch.

"Are you two trying to age me before my time? I'm not old enough to be a mother of the bride or a grandmother."

"Then I guess it's a good job you only need to worry about one of those for a while, Granny."

"Pfft, I am not a granny and you know it."

"Grams? Nanna?" he teases.

"What did you say earlier about me coming here to hurt you?" she asks darkly.

"Shall we get it over with before I give you any more ammunition?" Alex asks, pushing from where he was perched on the arm of the sofa I'm sitting on.

"Let's see how much damage you've done then," she says, joining him on his feet and gesturing toward his bedroom.

"Evie, if I scream, call social services."

"You're eighteen, kid. They don't care anymore," Gianna warns as she grabs her supply bag and takes off ahead of him.

"Good luck," I say, accepting his kiss before he disappears.

I sip my coffee as their voices float down to me, and I can't help but smile as their teasing continues.

There was a moment in the shower when I thought

Alex was going to lose the fight with his insecurities over his arms.

I can't imagine how he's feeling. He's barely seen the damage beneath the bandages. Most of the times Gianna has changed them, he was out of it. I'm pretty sure she did that for his benefit, aware of his fears.

"Evie, help me," he calls with a laugh.

Unable to sit here just listening, I take my mug and wander toward the bedroom.

"Aw, is Mummy hurting my baby?" I tease, resting my hip against the doorframe as I watch them.

Alex sits on the edge of the bed, Gianna resting on one knee beside him, inspecting his cuts.

"She's mean."

"You're a baby, Alexander. If this were Daemon, he wouldn't have made a sound."

"You're nicer to him."

Gianna rolls her eyes.

Alex smiles at me before looking at the wound Gianna is focusing on. My eyes follow and I swallow roughly at the sight of the angry marks littering his arms. They're better, so much better than the last time I saw them.

They might be angry and a permanent reminder of what he went through, but they're not ugly. The only thing I see when I look at them is his strength. I remember the way he looked at me, the fire that burned so bright in his eyes with his need to rescue me, to protect me. If I ever doubted how he felt about me, it was clear as day in those moments. He'd have destroyed the entire world for me if it was what was necessary to keep me safe. He still would. All we can hope is that there won't be another reason for him to even think it.

"Changing your mind yet?" he asks me anxiously.

"Wash your mouth out with soap, Alexander Stefanos Deimos. It's going to take more than the evidence of your strength to turn me away," I say fiercely.

"Listen to your girl. Scars are hot. Right, Evie?"

"For the love of God, do not start telling me about any Dad has that you traced with your tongue or some shit."

Gianna shakes her head. "You're not fun."

"And you need a new bloke. You spend too long reminiscing about your youth. Anyone would think you no longer have any fun."

"Oh, I have plenty of fun. In fact, I had a date about a month ago, and he—"

Behind me, the front door slams closed, footsteps moving closer.

"Thank fuck for that," Alex mutters before Daemon and Calli appear in the living room.

"D, get your arse down here. If I have to listen to tales about Mum's love life then so do you," Alex calls.

The way Daemon's face screws up makes me bark out a laugh.

"Oh, Gianna, give us all the dirty details," Calli giggles.

"Angel, she doesn't need any kind of encouragement. I'm still trying to forget the story she told us about sex positions while pregnant."

"She's a nurse. It was purely factual information." The second Calli's eyes meet mine, she winks.

"Whatever you say," Daemon mutters, striding toward me. "Where is the ugly motherfucker, anyway?"

"Bit rich, seeing as we look even more alike than ever before these days," Alex says as Daemon walks into the bedroom, assessing his arms closely.

"Speak for yourself. Fuck man, they did a number on your ink," he says, resting his arse back against the chest of drawers.

Alex's eyes drop to his forearm, and he frowns.

"Shit."

"You can get it fixed," Gianna says softly. "Just wait until your scars are healed first, unlike someone else." She shoots a glare at her other son, who immediately pushes the sleeve of his t-shirt up to reveal a matching tattoo to the one currently being discussed.

"Looks perfectly fine to me," he argues.

"Do you have to look so smug about it?" Alex scoffs, making Daemon's smirk widen.

Calli comes to a stop beside me in the doorway, watching them with a soft smile playing on her lips.

"Once I get the approval from my tyrant of a nurse, I might go for full sleeves. Get something bad-arse."

"You don't need to pull anymore, so you can do what you really want and cover your arms with tats of cute puppies."

"Fuck off," Alex barks before wincing in pain as Gianna does something.

"If you want a tyrant, I'm sure Janice would be up for a home visit."

"Hell no. If I never have to see that woman again, it'll be too soon."

"Who's Janice?" I whisper to Calli.

"Come on," she says, taking my hand and tugging me back to the kitchen. As we go, Gianna's warning voice rings out. "No ink until I've announced you're fully healed, you got that?"

"Yes, Mother," Alex teases.

"Janice is a nurse on the Cirillo wing of the hospital. She has a special kind of love for the guys."

"Don't tell me, they're terrible patients?" I deadpan.

Calli turns around from where she's stopped at the coffee machine. "How did you know?"

"Do they ever follow the rules?"

"Only if they're set by us. And even then, it's probably fifty-fifty."

"I can't imagine Stella and Emmie take too well to being ignored."

"Girl, you've already experienced what they're like when it comes to driving their boys wild."

"This is true."

With a mug of steaming coffee, she hops up on the stool next to me.

"Shouldn't you be on decaf?" I ask in concern.

"Oh, it is. I forced Alex to buy me a box."

I can't help but smile. "I love how close you all are. How much you care for each other."

She returns my smile before her expression turns serious again.

"How's he doing really? I know the jokes and smiles are a cover."

"He's..." I sigh, struggling to find the words. "Finding it all hard to get his head around, I think. His arms are bothering him more than he wants them to."

"Before me, Daemon hadn't shown his scars to anyone but Alex. And even showing me took time."

"What did you do to help him accept them?"

She shrugs. "Nothing really. Just proved how much I love him. All of him. This world we live in might be thrilling and exciting, but we can't forget the danger. We've all got scars; some are just better hidden than others."

I nod, taking a sip of my coffee.

"Did Gianna talk to Daemon yesterday?" I ask.

"She did," Calli confirms. "I've got to be honest, that was not what I was expecting to come out of her mouth when she said she needed to talk."

"Can't say I was expecting the confession either. She's so sweet."

"Appearances can be deceiving," Calli whispers.

"Don't I know it," I mutter, sipping my coffee again.

"You never could have predicted any of this," she assures me, resting her hand on my forearm and squeezing gently.

"No, I know that. Doesn't stop me feeling guilty though."

"You've nothing to feel guilty about. If it weren't for you, then they might still be nowhere near finding who was running that trafficking ring. Because of you, they're all dead. They're not going to hurt anyone else. Reid found peace, and a sister. Luciana completed her mission and can begin terrifying someone else. And we, hopefully, get to have a nice calm summer before exam results and you guys all start at uni."

"Here's hoping."

"I'm ordering lunch from Burnt Coals. Did you want to choose?" Calli asks, sliding her phone over. When my brows pinch, she continues with, "It's the best burger place in the city, and this one," she says, rubbing her small bump, "is demanding one. Or five."

"Fair enough. What does Alex have?"

"Their spicy burger. It's already in the basket."

Of course it is.

After a quick scroll through the options, I make my selection and pass it back.

"I've got some money in my purse. I'll get it when they've—"

"Evie," Calli says, an edge to her tone that I'm not sure I've heard before. "That's not how things work around here. "Alex will pay next time.'

"But—"

"You're one of us now. Better start getting used to it."

With a smile, I park my argument for another day. I might have a decent stash of money from camming and dancing, but it's not going to last me forever. Especially once I start uni. I'll need to find a job at some point.

We continue chatting for a few more minutes, keeping the conversation light before the rumbling voices from down the hall begin to get louder.

"Look out, here comes trouble," Calli says under her breath before Alex and Daemon appear, standing side by side.

"Jesus," I mutter. "I bet they used to cause people hell trying to tell them apart when they were kids."

"Oh, they've got stories," she confirms.

"Right, my time here is done. Where are my girls?" Gianna says with a wide smile as she steps around Alex.

The second she steps up to us, she wraps an arm around each of our shoulders, pulling us in tight.

"Look after my boys," she whispers. "I know they like to act all tough, but we all know they're teddy bears really."

"Mother," Alex warns. "What secrets are you spilling now?"

"Oh, nothing they don't already know. Call me if you need me, any of you." She pins us all with a look before grabbing her handbag from the sofa and throwing the strap over her shoulder. "Just not after eight tonight. I have another date with that guy I was telling you—"

"Mum," Daemon warns.

"What? He's taking me to see a show. It's not like we're going to Hades or anything." She rolls her eyes dramatically.

"A little warning if you do start spending your evenings there. We'd hate to bump into you and make your date awkward."

"Enough, Alexander. Be good, all of you," she instructs before disappearing from our sight, the front door slamming behind her a few seconds later.

"She doesn't really go to Hades, does she?" Calli asks.

Daemon rubs the back of his neck, looking equally as intrigued by Gianna's confession as he does disturbed.

"I really fucking hope not. I have every intention of taking Evie once I'm fully functioning again, and I do not need to find my mother within twenty feet of that place."

"Prude," I tease.

"Baby, I think we all know that's not the case. But I draw the line at fucking in the same room as the woman who pushed me out of her vag."

"Ew," Daemon complains. "Did you have to go there?"

Tugging Calli from the stool she was sitting on, he pulls her onto his lap on the sofa before the two of them get comfortable.

"Staying, I assume?" Alex quips, wrapping his freshly bandaged arms around me from behind.

"I've ordered burgers. They'll be here in about thirty minutes."

"Mmm," Alex groans against the curve of my neck. "Thirty minutes you say. What could we do to pass the time?"

"Don't even think about it," Daemon warns.

"Behave, Alexander."

"It's only because I know you need a rest that you're not already on your back on my kitchen counter," he whispers in my ear, although it's nowhere near quiet enough for our guests not to hear.

"Don't start a game you won't win, Deimos," Calli warns. "You might flaunt your skills, but I gotta tell you, Daemon also knows what he's doing."

"You're trouble. All of you."

"Yep, and I think you love it."

"I love you," I say, tilting my head back so I can find his lips.

"I love you too."

"Everything okay with your arms?"

"Yep, healing perfectly. Now I just need to talk to Emmie about what she's going to cover them all up with."

"Mum said a year at least," Daemon points out.

Dropping his head to my shoulder, Alex groans.

"You know, I think I preferred it when you were single and grumpy."

"You just can't handle the competition for the funniest twin."

"Pfft, what the fuck ever," Alex counters.

And that's pretty much how the four of us spend the rest of the afternoon—Alex and Daemon shooting insults back and forth at each other while Calli and I roll our eyes and laugh at their expense. It's pretty perfect.

Being with Alex and moving in here with him might mean distancing myself from Blake and Zay a little, but it also means gaining a whole new kind of family that I never could have imagined for myself.

I smile to myself as I sit in Stefanos's back garden later that evening as the sun sinks behind the trees and the scent of barbecue fills the air surrounded by my family, and remember what Jodie said to me back in the cabin.

"Blood just makes people think they have a right to fuck with you. You get to choose the water for yourself. They're what's really important."

And fuck was she right.

"**I**f Theo is a neat freak, why does he host all the parties?" I ask as Alex leads me toward Theo and Emmie's front door on the floor above our flat.

Our flat...

What is this life?

It's been two weeks since he asked me to move in with him in his shower. Two weeks of laughter and happiness and more pleasure than I thought existed.

I can't help the wide smile that spreads across my lips as I think about our time together.

Every day, at least one of us has dropped in to see Zay. And while he might not be getting over his ordeal as fast as Alex seems to be, every time I look into his eyes, I see a little more of the happy-go-lucky boy I know and love.

One day last week, Blake and I sat down with him to discuss what he wants to do in September, and unsurprisingly, the second she mentioned the possibility of attending Knight's Ridge with Atlas, he jumped at the chance.

I can't really blame him. His and Atlas's friendship is

getting stronger by the day, and quite frankly, who actually wants to go to Lovell Academy? We sure didn't.

He's already nagging us to go uniform shopping, something that Stefanos has agreed to help with, seeing as the cost of everything he's going to need is almost as expensive as the tuition.

Accepting all this help doesn't sit easy with either of us, but at the same time, we figured it's okay to let those who care about us help. And Stefanos sure seems to have a soft spot for our little brother.

Although, I'm pretty sure it's not just Zay who's stolen his attention. Blakely somehow manages to deflect the conversation every time I try and bring it up. But I see the way her body language changes when he walks into the room. And I sure as shit notice the way he watches her when he thinks no one is paying attention.

I know Alex has warned his father multiple times to stay away from her, but honestly, would it really be such a bad thing? He seems like a decent guy, and he's treating Zay as if he's his own. Both of them could do a hell of a lot worse than Stefanos. I'll leave whatever is going on under that roof to them. I've had more than enough drama to deal with myself. I'm happily enjoying my easy life with my incredible boyfriend.

"It's the biggest," Alex says simply, reminding me that I asked him a question.

"Of course."

Tonight, we're celebrating. And not just that the last single guy in their friendship group finally has a girl, but everyone has finished their exams.

Stella, Emmie, and Brianna still have a couple of weeks of classes left, but the stress of uni and what happens next is over for a while. The results are out of everyone's hands now. We just have to wait for fate to decide our futures at the end of the summer.

"You ready for this?" Alex asks with a laugh.

"I really, really don't think I am. What happened the last time you guys partied?"

"Well, last time we were in Nico's place, and I left on my search for you. The last one in Theo's was probably the night I also found you."

"After hooking up with Ant?" I ask with a teasing smirk.

"You're never going to let me forget that, are you?" he asks, rolling his eyes.

"Why the hell would I want to forget it? It's hot as hell."

"Vixen," he growls, pulling me in front of him and nuzzling my neck. "You're wicked."

"You won't be complaining later when you're reaping the benefits."

"I sure as hell wasn't an hour ago in the shower, either. Can't get enough of you, baby."

"The feeling is entirely mutual," I confess.

As we close in on the door, the music filters down to us.

"Sounds like the party has already started."

"You have met Stella and Emmie, right? The party will have started the second they got out of class earlier."

"And there's something wrong with that?" I ask, looking back at him with a teasing smile.

"Oh, how we've corrupted you."

I can't help but laugh. It's true. I'd never been to a party before finding myself in the middle of this group. First a Wolves party, and now this more intimate one with their inner circle.

It gives me whiplash if I think about how quickly my life has changed in only a few short weeks.

"While you're fantasising about me and Ant, do you remember what I told you my fantasy was?"

My cheeks burn red hot as he spins me around and presses me against Theo's front door.

I swallow nervously, realising that I may have made a mistake wearing a skirt to this little shindig.

"Your cheeks are telling me that you do," he breathes, dipping his head to brush his lips against mine.

"Alex," I warn when he pulls back, refusing to kiss me like I want.

"There's plenty of time for all that."

"When you told me we were going to a party at Theo's, you should have just been honest and told me that we were going to an orgy."

He chuckles, still keeping his lips just out of touch.

"It goes without saying if Seb and Stella are in attendance, baby. Now," he says, pressing his hand to the scanner. "Are you ready to party?"

Wrapping his arm around my waist, he holds me against him as he swings the door wide open.

"Let's party?" He bellows over the music.

"Ah look who finally decided to join us," Emmie calls back. "They're even later than Seb and Stella."

Alex leads me around the corner and into Theo's massive open-plan living area with the most spectacular views of the city sprawled out behind the floor-to-ceiling windows.

"Pipe down, Cirillo. We've got a lot of ground to make up for. You've all had months on us," Alex muses.

"Not how it works, dude," Toby says.

"Pfft, how would any of you know, anyway? Drink, baby?"

"Yeah, I think I'm going to need one."

"Evie," Stella shouts happily from her position next to Emmie in the kitchen as she mixes cocktails. "Do you want a screaming orgasm or a slippery nipple?"

"Oh my God," I mutter.

"She'll have both to match what she's already had twice today," Alex announces way too loudly.

"Yes, girl. Get that boy's skills working for you."

Abandoning me, he pulls the fridge open and grabs a beer.

"She certainly doesn't have any complaints," he says proudly.

"Oh yeah?" Emmie teases. "For all you know, she's been faking it every time."

"I can assure you, she hasn't. I can spot a fake from a mile away."

"Oh Alexander, I do sense a challenge of some kind there."

"Sebastian, put a lead on your girl," I call out.

"Don't worry, she wouldn't know how to fake it even if she tried."

"Arrogant much," Stella scoffs.

"Have you ever had to fake it with me, Hellion?"

She grins at him. "Don't worry, I'm fully aware of how to fake it when necessary."

"Stella," he growls, prowling closer. "Don't you even try to pretend that I've ever left you high and dry." She pins him with a deadly look. "Not on purpose," he corrects. "Withholding doesn't count here."

"Fine," she concedes, "I've never faked it with you. But remember, I wasn't a blushing virgin before I met you and your magic dick."

"What have we said about those small-dicked boys of your past?"

Stella smirks at him and begins reciting something as if she's heard it about a million times.

"The boys of my past no longer exist. I have no memory of any dick other than the one that brings me pleasure multiple times a day."

"Jesus Christ, I need new friends," Theo mutters, having joined us for that little nugget of information none of us needed.

"Now say it like you mean it," Seb demands.

Everyone groans when he backs her up against the counter before lifting her onto it and stepping between her spread thighs.

"You'd better be wearing underwear, Doukas," Theo growls, his fists clenching.

"My sister is a whore," Toby calls out jokingly before downing his beer as if it'll help the situation.

"Jodie," Stella calls. "Come distract your man so he doesn't have to watch this."

"He doesn't have to watch either way," she jokes back.

"Fuck my life. Fuck my life," he mutters, turning his back on his sister in favour of joining Jodie, Brianna and Nico on Theo's massive sofa.

"I'll finish the drinks then, shall I?" Emmie asks as Seb practically devours Stella's face.

"You ordered more Dettol when you did the shopping, right?" Theo asks her.

"Dude," Alex says, clapping him on the shoulder. "You have fucking issues. There's no way you haven't fucked your wife on your kitchen counter."

"Of course I have. That's different though, she's my fucking wife."

"And one day, Stella will be mine," Seb says when he comes up for air, proving he can multitask.

"Fuck, Seb," she cries.

From where we're all standing, we can't see what he's doing, but it doesn't take a genius to work out.

"I'm going to stop inviting you to hang out here," Theo warns.

"No you fucking won't. You're about five minutes away from grabbing your wife and fucking her into the wall yourself right now."

"Ignore him," Emmie says, finishing off my cocktails and sliding them over. "You know he's only jealous because yours is bigger."

Seb flips Emmie off with his free hand before we all turn our backs on the shameless couple.

"So, Evie. How's it going, living with this muppet? Regretting it yet?" Theo asks.

"He has his good moments."

"Damn fucking right I do. It's not just those two living their best lives," Alex says, pointing over his shoulder.

The front door opens, and a few seconds later, Daemon and Calli walk in.

"Come and sit down, baby momma," Alex says, shifting closer to me to give her some space.

"Never thought I'd prefer baby C for a nickname," she mutters, sitting onto Daemon's lap when he steals the space first.

"How's bump?" I ask seeing as they disappeared earlier for a midwife appointment.

"We heard the heartbeat," Daemon says with a smile splitting his face.

"It was incredible," Calli breathes. "I know we've seen her—"

"Him," Nico corrects.

"But to hear her heart," she continues as if he never spoke. "It was so incredible."

Nico and Bri share a look that instantly gets my attention. And it seems I'm not the only one.

"Got something to tell us, cuz?" Theo asks.

But the second Brianna's shoulders drop, I realise we weren't meant to notice that exchange.

"No, we don't," Bri says, swallowing down what I can only assume is a little disappointment. "We thought maybe, but no."

"We're still young, babe," Nico says before kissing her head.

"I know. It's silly. I'm not even ready. The not knowing just fucks with your head."

"Can you imagine how crazy life will be if we all have kids at the same time?" Jodie says.

"Nah, our little prince will be the oldest and will keep them all in line," Daemon says confidently.

"That's why he is going to be a she. No man could control all of your womb goblins," Calli says, somehow managing to keep a serious face.

"Womb goblins?" I chuckle.

"Well, what would you call them? Seems like Seb and Stella are getting a little more practise in, ready to make one of their own."

"Practising is the best bit," Seb calls before Stella cries out his name.

"I feel sorry for their future kids already. No one needs to catch their parents fucking as much as they will."

"Builds character and promotes a healthy sex life," Seb argues before tugging Stella off the counter and pushing her to her knees.

"Jodie has a point though," Nico says. "Just think of the

shit we got up to over the years. The bullshit we pulled on our parents. I'm not sure any of us are ready for that."

"It's a good job some of us were good kids who followed the rules then, hey, big bro? If all our offspring follow the females then—"

"Seb, you beast," Stella calls.

"Okay, forget it. We're fucked. We're all utterly fucked," Calli concedes.

Our laughter covers what's happening in the kitchen, and as I finish my first drink, Theo turns the music up and Alex takes my hand.

"Let's dance, baby."

Unable to argue with anything that will ensure I have his hands on me, I get to my feet and press my body against him.

The others continue chatting—or more shouting now, with the volume of the music to drown out the sex pests—but as Alex's lips descend on mine, they all vanish. Everything around us fades away, leaving just the two of us.

One hand rests on the back of my neck and the other grips my arse so tightly, there isn't an inch between us.

I don't hear the front door; nor do I notice we're joined by others until an unfamiliar female voice fills the air.

"I found some strays out in the hallway. I assume they belong to you lot."

Alex and I pull apart just as Theo growls angrily behind me.

"Rhea, what the fuck are you doing here?"

I blink when my eyes land on what looks like a younger version of Emmie.

Just how strong was that cocktail?

She's dressed head to toe in black—ripped denim shorts,

fishnets, biker boots, and a black tank that shows off way more cleavage than I'm sure she should be, seeing as she's Theo's little sister.

"I heard there was a party, so here I am."

"I don't remember extending an invitation to my underage sister," he snaps, stepping up to her. There's a muscle in his temple pulsating as he glares.

"But it's okay to invite Miss Andr— Sorry. Mrs. Cirillo?"

"Brianna was our friend before she was a teacher at— what am I doing? I don't need to answer to you, kid."

"No, you're right, you don't. Just give me a drink and I'll jump straight to enjoying myself."

"Oh, no. You are not—"

"Dude. Chill, yeah?" A blonde girl I've never seen before says, stepping up to Rhea and throwing her arms around her shoulder.

The second the boy in my arms speaks, I get a clue as to who she is.

"Did anyone ask for your opinion, Pest?"

"Fuck you, Deimos. Her surname is all the invite she needs. Come on, Rhea, let's go make cocktails."

"Oh no, I don't think—"

"Theodore," Isla sighs, stepping right into his space. "How old were you when we all got wasted in my parents' garden after some party?"

Theo's jaw tics.

"Exactly. Younger and way fucking dumber than Rhea. Wouldn't you rather she do it here than out there where any motherfucker could take advantage of her?" she says, gesturing to the city beyond the windows.

"Daemon," Theo growls, his eyes still locked on Isla's. "Rein in your best friend. She's a pain in the arse."

"Fuck that," Daemon scoffs while Alex laughs. "There ain't no motherfucker who can tame that."

"I knew turning up was a bad idea," another voice says, capturing my attention.

Ant smiles at me in greeting, and my own lips curl up.

"Evie," Alex growls in my ear. "I can practically hear your thoughts."

"What?" I ask innocently. "I've no idea what you're talking about. I do think we need more drinks, though."

"Behave," he warns before releasing me so I can hug Ant.

"Ah, so you're the magical unicorn who's got that buffoon wrapped around her little finger. I need some tips," Isla says, immediately adopting me.

"Evie, don't you dare tell her anything she can use against me," Alex calls after us.

"Me?" I ask innocently. "As if I would."

"Oooh, I like you already," Isla says. "And don't worry. He's totally not as big a prick as I make him out to be. What's so funny?" she asks when I just laugh at her confession.

"Nothing. It's nothing."

Her eyes narrow in suspicion.

"What has he told you about me?"

"Not much, actually, unless it's details from the last party you all attended here."

Her eyes widen so much I'm half expecting them to pop out and roll around at my feet.

She leans in. "He told you about that?"

"Yeah. I made him."

"And you're still standing here talking to me?"

"Why shouldn't I? Were you looking for a repeat with him?"

"Hell no. I can't even bear to look at him."

"Sure."

We both look back, finding Alex and Ant deep in conversation.

"Was it hot?" I ask, still beyond curious about the whole thing. Many women would probably be jealous standing here, talking to a woman who's slept with her boyfriend fairly recently. But there's no doubt in my mind about how Alex feels about me, and I don't feel the slightest bit threatened. It's a really good place to be after spending most of my life feeling like I don't really belong.

"Oh hell, yeah. Just… don't tell them that. Their egos are already big enough."

A squeal rips through the room as Rhea darts around the back of the sofa. On the other side of it, Theo glares pure death at her. Not that she's fazed.

"What did she do?" I ask.

"Knowing Rhea, it could be anything. She's epic. I love her."

I watch Emmie laugh at the two of them. "I don't think you're the only one."

"Theo loves it really."

"Not so sure about that."

I gasp when a large pair of hands lands on my hips, but I soon relax when a set of lips brush down the side of my neck.

"You two had better not be comparing notes."

Isla scoffs. "Hardly. I have nothing good to say."

"You're in a delightful mood tonight, Pest," Alex points out, keeping all his attention on me. "What did we do to deserve your presence?"

"This might shock you, but I didn't come here for you."

"That means she's here for me," Ant teases, throwing his arm around her shoulder. "You missed me?"

"Meh," Isla says, doing a really bad job of pretending.

Finally, Theo manages to relax. And while everyone might have Rhea pegged as the wild child, she's actually very well behaved and doesn't overdo the alcohol, unlike Stella and Emmie, whose cocktails only get stronger with every one they make.

I'm once again lost in Alex's arms, his lips on mine and our tongues twisted together, when someone demands the music be cut.

The room is immediately plunged into silence as I look around to see what's going on.

In the entrance to the kitchen, Jodie stands with her phone pressed to her ear and all the blood drained from her face.

"What's going on?" I whisper, terrified to break the silence.

"No idea, but whatever it is doesn't look good."

"NO," she cries, backing away from where Toby is standing before her, desperate to find out what's going on. "NO. No. She won't have done that, she won't—"

"Shit," I hiss, my heart sinking despite not knowing what's being said on the other end of the phone.

Bri jumps to her feet and rushes over, crowding her with Toby.

"NO. No," she cries, tears flooding down her cheeks.

Her phone slips from her hand, landing on the floor with a soft thud. Her knees buckle, but long before she goes down, Toby is there and has her in his arms.

Her cries are harrowing, and they rock me to my very core.

Alex's arms tighten around me as both Toby and Brianna hold Jodie up.

I don't need to ask what's happened. I've heard enough about what's been going on in Jodie's life to guess.

Emotion burns up my throat, tears stinging the backs of my eyes as I watch the two of them try to console her.

No one speaks bar their whispers, the atmosphere in the room turning sombre. It's a far cry from the happiness and laughter we've been experiencing all night.

"Jessie," Jodie suddenly cries. "We need to go to Jessie."

She fights her way out of Toby and Bri's arms and rushes across the room for her shoes.

"We need to go now. Call an Uber to Lovell; we've all had too much to drink."

Brianna looks across the room at Nico, who's hovering in front of the sofa, not knowing what to do.

"I'm on it," he agrees, pulling his phone from his pocket and rushing across the room. "It's five minutes away," he says after confirming the ride. "You two go; we're right behind you," he says, pushing his feet into his own shoes as Jodie and Toby flee the flat.

Bri looks back at everyone, her own cheeks wet with tears.

"Sara, she..." Widening her shoulders, she pulls herself together, being strong for her best friend. "She took a load of pills. By the time her parents found her, it was too late."

"What can we do?" Rhea asks in a rush, showing a side to her that I'm not sure most people know exists.

Brianna swipes her tears from her cheeks.

"I'm not sure there's anything that can be done."

"Babe, we need to go if you want—"

"Yeah."

"We'll message. Let you know what's going on," Nico promises before they disappear from sight.

Taking my hand, Alex leads me to the sofa where the others are all sitting, dumbfounded by the tragic turn of events.

I've no idea how long it is before Emmie speaks, but when she does, it only rips another piece from my heart.

"Jessie isn't going to deal with this after everything else."

I don't know Jessie personally, but I know of him from life in Lovell. From what I've heard, he's a decent guy. And if Emmie vouches for him, I've no reason to believe otherwise.

"Archer and the guys will be there for him, Em. They won't let him break," Theo says softly.

Silence falls once more before heavy footsteps move closer.

When I look up, I find a familiar face scanning the room, although he's not the one who speaks.

"Uh... I thought there was a party."

"Yeah, there was," Ant says, getting up to join Matteo and the other guy. "Jodie just got some bad news and—"

"What can we do?" Matteo offers.

"Any chance you could take Rhea home?" Theo asks. "We're all wasted and—"

"Theo," Rhea whines.

"Rhe, please. Em wants to go to Lovell, and we all need to be there for Jodie. Please can you just—"

She nods, accepting her fate.

Solemnly, she gets to her feet, but she doesn't leave until she's downed what's left of her drink.

"It should go without saying," Theo starts as she walks toward their Italian counterparts, "that no one so much as looks at my little sister the wrong way. I'm not opposed to restarting that war."

"Bro, she's a kid," Matteo states.

"Oh goodie," Rhea pipes up, her voice a little slurred. "This is going to be about as fun as riding with Dad."

"Exactly as it should be. Behave, Rhea Cirillo."

With a quick goodbye from Ant, he disappears with his boys and Rhea.

"Go get changed, Hellcat. I'll sort a car for us."

Emmie rushes down to their room as the rest of us stand.

"You need us, call, yeah?" Alex says. "We'll be right there."

He shakes his head. "Go and try to enjoy the rest of your night."

Tucked under Alex's arm, we follow Seb, Stella, Daemon, and Calli down to our floor. With quiet goodbyes, we break off to our flats and lock ourselves away.

"Well, that wasn't quite how I thought the night would end," Alex confesses, kicking off his shoes and dumping his phone and wallet on the kitchen counter.

"Life is so fucking unfair sometimes," I muse.

"Yeah," he agrees. "But other times, it gives you all the luck in the world and lands you exactly where you're meant to be, gives you everything you've ever dreamed of."

After tucking my loose hair behind my ears, he cups my face in his giant hands.

"I truly believe that we were meant to meet, Evie Moore. You were meant to be mine. And sometimes, life needs to be a little bit shit so that we can really appreciate just how fucking epic it can be when everything is right."

"You're incredible, Alexander Deimos."

"Not as incredible as you, Vixen. I was right that first night, you know."

"Oh?"

"You were a thief."

I rear back in surprise.

"Only you weren't stealing my watch. Without me knowing, you were in the process of stealing my heart."

"Oh, smooth. So freaking smooth."

"You fucking know it. Now, let me show you what other moves I've got."

"I'm yours, Alexander. Do your absolute worst."

29

———

EVIE

"What's this?" I ask as Stella and Brianna pass out envelopes around our group.

Despite it being summer, we're all hanging out at Theo's place because it hasn't stopped raining for three freaking days.

We've spent way too many days indoors recently. So much for the epic summer plans.

"A surprise," Stella says with a wide-arse grin on her face.

I glance around at the others. Most of them look as perplexed as I feel. Even Jodie has a twinkle of excitement in her eyes, something that's been absent since she got that phone call almost four weeks ago about her childhood best friend.

That news certainly put the dampeners on the beginning of our summer. But as I'm quickly learning with this incredible group of friends, they all rallied around her—Jessie too—And supported them both through it.

The funeral was both agonising and beautiful at the same time.

Sara's parents continued on their path to try and remove Jessie and his way of life from their daughter's and demanded they didn't attend.

As you can imagine, that didn't go down very well with the Wolves or us. And as a group, we descended on the small chapel they'd chosen for what they thought was going to be an intimate ceremony.

I didn't know Sara, but Jessie and Jodie did. Better than anyone. Even better than her parents. And they were adamant that she'd have wanted them to gatecrash. So that's exactly what we did.

With their closest friends by their sides, both Jodie and Jessie said goodbye to one of the most important people in their lives.

Jodie has hardly heard anything from Jessie since. She's worried, rightly so. But Archer and the guys keep her updated. All we can do is hope that time helps heal the wounds the loss of his girlfriend left behind.

"Hurry," Stella says, barely keeping her excitement contained.

Simultaneously, we all rip into the envelopes and pull out a single slip of paper.

"Oh fuck, yeah," Nico barks excitedly before everyone else joins in on the excitement.

"What? I don't under—"

Alex leans over, his breath rushing down my neck, instantly causing goosebumps to erupt.

"We're going to Florida, baby," he whispers while the others' chatter fills the room.

"Florida? As in America?"

Alex chuckles. "Yeah, as in America. It's where Stella used to live, and where Reid is."

I stare back down at the paper in my hand, reading the letters.

LWG to MCO.

"Tonight?" I blurt, checking the date and time.

"Hell, yeah. Come tomorrow, we're going to be sitting in the sun next to a pool. You better get those bikinis ready," Stella practically shouts.

I swallow nervously despite how incredible the image she just painted sounds.

"Um," I say, speaking a little louder than before. "I don't want to burst anyone's bubble or anything, but... I don't actually have a passport." The confession makes me wince. I'm surrounded by these incredible people who have more money than I could ever imagine. I bet they've jet set all over the world already. Hell, it was only a few weeks ago really that they were in Las Vegas.

"Evie," Theo sighs, a smirk appearing on his lips. "How you underestimate us."

Alex shifts beside me, pulling a second envelope from his back pocket.

"What's this?" Stupid question, I know. But they've totally blindsided me with this.

"Vixen," Alex laughs.

Ripping it open, I find my very first passport staring back at me.

"Visas are sorted. All that's left to do is pack and we're out of here, bitches," Stella announces. "The cars will be here in two hours."

In an instant, everyone jumps to their feet and disappears from Theo's living room to do as they're told. All the while, I remain sitting exactly where I am in total disbelief.

"Is this really happening?" I ask absently.

"It really, really is," Emmie says, a beaming smile playing on her lips.

Excitement explodes in my belly. It might be a little delayed compared to the others, but I figure that they're all used to this last-minute, pull-the-rug-from-right-under-your-feet shit.

"Well," I say, jumping to my feet and staring down at Alex, who's watching me with amusement. "What the hell are we waiting for? Let's go pack."

Grabbing his hand, I drag him from the sofa and toward the door.

"See you in a bit," Emmie calls before the door slams behind us.

"I'm going on an aeroplane," I say in a rush as we wait for the lift.

Reaching up, he tucks a lock of hair behind my ear and stares down into my eyes in a way that makes my heart rate pick up and my temperature soar.

"I love you, Evie," he whispers, making my heart explode.

All these weeks on, it's still hard to believe that this boy is mine. That I get to keep him.

Sliding my hands up his chest, I lock them behind his neck and reach up on my toes, brushing my lips over his.

"I love you too," I whisper before deepening the kiss.

He accepts happily, his lips parting to allow my tongue entry.

By the time the lift dings, announcing its arrival, he's consumed me to the point I barely hear it.

Without breaking our kiss, he tugs me inside and presses me up against the wall as he blindly searches for the button for the floor beneath us.

"Realistically," I mutter into his kiss, "how long do you think it'll take to pack?"

"Ten minutes," he says before diving back into our kiss.

The journey might only be short, but my chest is heaving and my body burning up with need by the time the doors open once more.

Ripping his lips from mine, he takes my hand and pulls me from the lift.

He doesn't stop until we're in our bedroom.

"What the—" I blurt, seeing a whole set of new suitcases waiting for me. "How long have you known?"

He laughs. "Long enough to ensure you have everything you're going to need. Open them."

Dropping to my knees, I lie the cases down and unzip each one.

Inside, I find more bikinis than I can count. Cover-ups, sun cream, two hats, multiple sets of sunglasses. A beach towel, a waterproof phone case thing and a whole heap of brand new lingerie and summer clothes. All with the tags removed so I can't see the prices. Naughty, naughty boy.

"Alex, this is—"

"Everything you could possibly need for our first holiday together?"

"I was going to say too much, but yes, that too."

"Nothing, and I literally mean nothing, could ever be too much for you, baby. I'd give you the world if you asked for it."

"I guess it's a good job all I want is you then, huh?"

Climbing to my feet, I wrap my arms around him once more.

"You're incredible."

He shakes his head, refusing to accept my words.

"Without you, I'm nothing."

"So we've already used what... ten minutes? Plus another ten to finish packing. That leaves us with—"

"Enough time for multiple orgasms between us," he says, bending down to grip my thighs and lifting me from the floor.

I squeal as I land on my back in the middle of the bed, but it's soon cut off when Alex pulls his shirt over his head, revealing his incredible body to me.

His scars still bother him. I've caught him studying them with disgust curled at his lips more than once in the last few weeks. But thankfully, he's learning to embrace them a little more as the days go on.

He might have been wearing long sleeves most days, but on the rare occasion we've actually had a summer's day, he's braved short sleeves. I was so fucking proud of him the first day he stepped outside to meet the guys for a kick about wearing a t-shirt.

His jeans and boxers go next, leaving him bare for me to ogle for a few seconds before he pounces on me.

His lips devour mine as he rids me of my clothes, and before I know what's happening, he has my legs spread and his tongue is on my clit.

"Alex," I scream as he works me, pushing two fingers inside me and curling them against my G-spot.

"I want three before you get my dick. Then, I'm dragging another two out of you. That should tide me over until we're on the plane."

"On the— Oh fuck," I gasp, my lust-addled brain finally catching up.

"Joining the mile-high club, baby," he growls against me.

"Oh God," I moan, twisting my fingers in his hair, as if he could possibly get any closer.

"Nah, not God, Vixen. Just Alexander motherfucking Deimos."

If I weren't on the brink of my first Alex-induced orgasm, I'd tease him for the size of his ego. But I'm too far gone.

Just as he promised, he sends me crashing into three mind-blowing releases before he sits up and wipes his mouth with the back of his hand.

"Up you go," he mutters with his hands clamped around my hips, flipping me over and dragging me onto my hands and knees. "Ready?" he asks, but before I get a chance to respond, his palm collides with my arse, making me moan like a whore.

"Fucking perfect," he groans, lining himself up at my entrance.

My core aches to feel him inside me, my muscles clenching around nothing.

"Please," I whimper. "I need you."

"Fucking love it when you beg for me."

"Please, Alex. Fuck me. I need— yes," I cry out when he caves to his desire and thrusts forward."

The growl of pleasure that rips from his throat is almost enough to send me head first into another release.

Releasing one of my hips, he slides his hand up my spine and grabs my ponytail, tugging my head back and making my back arch.

"Yes," I cry as he hits me impossibly deep.

His pace increases until he's fucking me like a savage.

The sounds of our skin slapping and our combined groans and cries of pleasure fill the room until he fucks me into my next release.

"One more," Alex grunts, releasing my hair in favour of my neck.

His fingers tighten on my throat in warning before he lifts me until my back is against his chest.

Wrapping my fingers around his forearm, I hold tight as he continues to rut into me.

His other hand slips from my hip in favour of my clit.

I cry out when his fingers collide with my sensitive skin.

"Fuck, I'm not going to last," he says into the sweaty skin of my neck.

Reaching back, I thread my fingers through his hair.

"I'm right there. I'm right—" He pinches my clit and I fall. He follows me with an animalistic roar only a few seconds later.

We crash to the bed, still locked together in a heap of sweaty limbs.

"Think you'll sleep through the flight now?" he whispers breathlessly in my ear.

"How long is it?"

"Dunno, about seven hours I think."

"Can Seb and Stella go that long without fucking?" I ask seriously.

"Nope. Last time they did a long haul, Nico organised a private jet and they basically spent the whole way there molesting each other."

"In front of you?"

"Of course. They have zero shame. And Nico and Bri got the bedroom. I was too fucking miserable over leaving you to care. I just put my AirPods in and drowned them out."

"Aw, my poor baby," I coo.

"Flying commercial could be entertaining though. They'll be so fucking obvious that the rest of us should get away with it easily."

"Interesting theory," I murmur.

"I'm not getting off that flight until I've dragged at least two orgasms from you."

"I thought I was sleeping through the entire thing?"

"I'll wake you for it, don't worry," he assures me, finally taking his weight from my body and climbing from the bed.

Lifting my head, I run my eyes down his body before they pause on his semi, standing proud from his body.

Licking my lips, I continue staring at him.

"How long do we have?"

"Long enough." Reaching out, he effortlessly lifts me into his body and carries me into the bathroom, placing me on my feet in my second favourite place in this flat beside the bed—the shower.

30

ALEX

By the time Evie and I appeared after our little impending holiday fuck fest, everyone was sitting in the back of the limo Stella and Brianna had organised, getting impatient.

They pretty much ribbed the both of us the entire drive to Gatwick Airport. Not that I gave a fuck. It was about time I was the one making them all late while I was busy getting some action.

Since the moment Evie opened that envelope, her eyes have been wide with shock. And as we make our way through Gatwick and to a bar for drinks, the awe in her expression only continues to grow.

"Enjoying yourself?" I ask as she watches the other travellers in fascination.

"It's just so crazy to think that all these people are going to be getting on aeroplanes in the next few hours and heading around the world."

"Yeah, and what's the betting that out of all these people, that family over there with the two screaming kids will be on our flight?" Emmie complains.

"Well, based on the fact both kids have Disney suitcases, I'd say the possibility is fairly high," Jodie points out.

"Not only that, but the dad's been forced to wear a 'Family vacation' t-shirt. I hope his wife's pussy is good enough to make up for that," Nico snorts.

Bri rears back. "You mean you're not going to wear the 'Cirillo Family does Disney' t-shirt I had printed for everyone especially?"

Silence ripples around the group.

"I'll happily wear it," I pipe up to piss off the rest of the guys.

"Seb will too, won't you, baby?" Stella coos as if she's talking to one of those screaming kids.

He blinks at her. "Uh…"

"Wow, would you look at that? There is something that Seb would risk not getting any pussy for," Theo jokes.

"Nah, fuck it. I'll wear whatever you want me to wear, Hellion. Mickey ears, a fucking tutu. Bring it on, as long as I get to indulge in you whenever the hell I want."

"You're assuming I'd be willing," Stella teases.

"When the fuck aren't you willing?" Calli asks seriously.

"Whore," Brianna coughs.

"Loud and proud, baby. Just like you." Stella lifts her cocktail glass and Brianna immediately clinks it.

"This is nice," Evie says, snuggling into my side.

"What? Listening to my best friends' girls debate who's the biggest whore?"

Evie snorts. "Is there even a debate? Stella hands down."

"I heard that," the girl in question teases.

"You were meant to," Evie quips back.

Stella, Emmie, Brianna and Calli fall into conversation about where we're going, and my attention turns to Jodie and Toby, who are sitting quietly beside us.

"How's our girl doing?" I whisper to Toby.

"Yeah, you know," he says sadly.

Combing my fingers through my hair, I glance at Jodie once more. She's lost in her own little world, looking sad.

"I just wish I could do something to help. I'm hoping this break will give her something else to think about."

Hera has been great in giving Jodie the time she needs to deal with her grief. But that meant she's had no focus other than the pain and Jessie detaching himself from life.

I can't help but wonder if she'd have been better off working to help distract her.

"It's going to be epic. And she'll get there. You'll get your girl back."

"I know." Wrapping his arm around Jodie's shoulders, he presses a kiss to her temple.

"You okay?" she asks him.

"Of course, Demon. We're going to fucking Florida."

She smiles. To anyone who doesn't know her as well as us, they might think she's okay. But there are shadows in her eyes.

"Are you going to show me where we're staying yet?" Evie sulks.

The whole ride here, Stella has teased us all about where we're going once we arrive, but apparently, Brianna is the only one in on that secret. Not even Theo knows. Or if he does, he's just playing along.

"Nope. It's a surprise."

"And the others are meeting us there?" Calli asks.

"Yep."

"Everyone?" I ask.

"Harley and Kyle, Poppy and Zayn and Ruby and Ash."

"What about Reid?" Jodie asks, proving that she's actually listening.

"We're going to meet up while we're there. He's got too much scary gang shit to deal with to have a holiday," Brianna says, rolling her eyes.

By the time our gate appears on the big screens above the bar, the girls have had one too many cocktails and our beers have been going down a little too well.

"I'm so fucking glad you got us first class, princess," Seb slurs. "Can't wait for a nap."

"As if that's what you're going to be doing in your little cubby," Daemon snorts, grabbing both his and Calli's carry-ons.

"I feel sorry for the flight attendants, that's all I'm going to say," Theo adds.

Taking Evie's hand, we follow behind Calli and Daemon as the twelve of us leave the bar.

"I'm so excited," she whispers beside me.

"Me too."

"You've flown before. It's not the same."

"I've never flown with you," I counter. "Everything I do with you is exciting. Even if it's grocery shopping."

"Aw."

"Sounds like someone else is going for their fully fledged members card for the mile-high club," Nico barks from behind us.

"Fuck off. Some of us can do romance without the need for an orgasm at the end of it," I scoff.

"Such bullshit," Nico mutters, earning himself a slap from Brianna.

"Ignore him, I think you're cute."

"Vixen, we've been over this. I am not cute," I argue. "I am a mean and dangerous Cirillo soldier."

"Nope, you're my cute puppy dog, and I won't have it any other way."

With a sigh, I nuzzle her neck. "I'll be whatever you want me to be, just... don't tell the others."

"Too late," Nico says. "We've already heard it all."

"Prick," I mutter, picking up speed as we march toward our departure gate.

When we get there, Evie pulls me straight to the huge windows so she can watch the planes outside and the staff who are loading the suitcases on.

"Is this ours?"

I glance at our gate and where the tunnel we're going to be walking down goes.

"Good chance."

"Oh, maybe we'll see our cases."

"Fuck. I love you," I blurt.

"You don't think I'm immature and stupid?"

Wrapping my hand around the back of her neck, I turn her to face me.

We're sitting on our knees while everyone surrounding us—bar the children—are sitting like adults, not-so-patiently waiting to get on a plane while my girl lives her best life experiencing all these new things.

"No, Evie. I love that I get to experience all of this with you. I think you're incredible, and I can't wait to spend the rest of my life figuring out all the reasons you are."

"Alex," she breathes, leaning into my touch as I move my hand to cup her cheek.

"I've never been to Florida before. We get to have that first together."

"You're going to make me go on all the roller coasters, aren't you?"

"Hell yeah, I am. I can't fucking wait."

"Would now be a good time to tell you that I have a mild fear of heights?"

"Doesn't matter if you do; you know that I'll keep you safe no matter what."

"My hero," she muses as the announcement comes through that first-class travellers for our flight can begin boarding.

"Ready to embark on your first flight?"

"Hell yes. Just... tell me we're not sitting next to Seb and Stella."

I bark out a laugh as I climb down from the seat and grab our bags.

"Here's hoping."

With her tucked into my side, we follow the others as they have their passports and boarding passes checked.

"Can't believe I get to fly first class for my first ever flight."

"Stick with me, baby. I know how to treat you right."

"Um... excuse me, Alexander Deimos," Stella snaps. "Who exactly booked these flights?"

"Oh pipe down, Doukas. Doesn't Seb need his dick sucking or something?"

"Probably," she laughs. "I told him we have to wait until the seat belt sign is off to get freaky."

"I should probably go warn the attendants." I pretend to take off down the aisle, but I don't make it more than a step before her fingers wrap around my upper arm.

"Did you want to keep your balls attached to your body?" she growls.

"Yes, please," Evie answers for me. "I kind of like them."

"Then I suggest you watch your mouth, Alexander. It's not too late to change my mind and send you back home."

"Like you would," I tease, staring her dead in the eyes.

"Okay, Hellion," Seb says, tugging her away. "How about we don't piss off the attendants before they've even closed the doors."

I'm still laughing when he all but throws her into her seat and silences her with a kiss.

"Her friends in Rosewood... are they as insane as you lot?"

"Is that even possible?"

"Fuck knows. I'm just trying to prepare for what's to come."

"What's to come," I tell her honestly, "is the best few weeks of our lives."

Evie listened intently—probably the only one on the plane who did—to the safety demonstration. She read every single word of the safety card tucked into the pocket of her cubby, and then she scrolled through every option available to her on the in-flight entertainment.

I, however, didn't so much as turn my screen on, content with watching the happiness on her face with every new thing she found.

"Blake and Zay are going to hate me for this," she mused at one point. And the second I pointed out that we had Wi-Fi, she immediately started messaging Blake photographs. And when my phone buzzed in my pocket, I found Zay's name staring back at me, wishing us a good holiday and telling me to look after his sister.

Man, that boy is beyond cool. I fucking love him something fierce.

With Evie happy watching a movie and everyone else around us distracted, I lowered my chair, pulled a blanket over me and closed my eyes.

Fuck, I had the best friends in the entire fucking world.

"Alex. Alex. Alex."

"Just whack him between the legs. That'll wake him up faster."

Lifting my hand from the blanket, I flip Seb off.

"Alex, we're going to be landing soon," Evie says, making my eyes pop open in surprise.

"Dude, you slept the whole flight. You've no idea the entertainment you've missed," Theo says from behind. "They actually threatened to land and kick Seb and Stella off when they caught them fucking in the toilet for the second time."

"No, they didn't. Stop exaggerating," Seb sighs.

"Dude, they totally did."

My eyes find Evie, and the amusement I find lets me know that Theo isn't actually lying.

"I'd have thrown you out from a great height if I knew you were threatening to ruin our holiday."

"They were overreacting. Everything is good now, right, Hellion?"

"I don't know. I'm pretty sure I've pulled something in my back," she confesses.

"Nothing a good massage won't fix later."

Seb is ushered into his seat for landing. and I quickly

put my chair upright and tidy everything up, but I pause at the sound of Evie's voice beside me.

"You owe me."

"Oh yeah? How'd you figure that?"

"You promised me two orgasms while in the air. I only had one, and I had to do it myself."

My chin drops as she delivers the words smoothly.

"Vixen, you didn't?"

She shrugs, a sinful smile playing on her lips.

"I guess you'll never know."

Reaching out, I wrap my fingers around her wrist and bring her fingers to my nose.

"Alex," she gasps, her cheeks burning.

"Mmmm," I murmur. "You have been a naughty girl, haven't you, Vixen? I do hope you filmed it for me."

Her grin widens, and my cock swells.

"That's my girl."

"**O**h my God, that's huge," I gasp as the house Stella has rented for us comes into view.

"That's what Stella said," Seb quips, earning a round of groans from the entire group.

"Enough, Sebastian. We're sick of anything that has to do with your dick," Toby mutters.

"Speak for yourself," Stella argues.

"Says the one who's walking funny because of it."

"Exactly, because it's huge."

"Bro, you're forgetting that we've seen your dick almost more than we've seen our own. We're all aware of how many—or not—inches you're rocking," Nico teases.

They continue to rib Seb, but I tune them all out. I'm too enthralled with everything I've seen on the journey here. The bright, cloudless blue sky, the sparkling ocean, the houses, the size of the roads, the trucks. Everything. I want to see it all and experience even more.

Alex's hand tightens on mine, letting me know that he's watching me.

At the airport, I was embarrassed, but now, all of that is gone. I'm too fascinated.

The second the limo pulls to a stop, the front door of the house opens and six people spill out. The three girls run full speed toward the car.

Stella launches herself toward the door, and the second we pull to a stop, she jumps out and straight into their arms.

One by one, we climb out and I'm introduced to Stella's friends. The girls pull me into hugs, telling me how nice it is to meet me, making me realise that they know a hell of a lot more about me than I do them.

The guys are all a little less excitable as they greet each other, and before long we're walking into the house, towing our cases behind us.

"Oh my God," I breathe the second we're in the entrance. "It's like something off the TV."

"Ten bedrooms, twelve bathrooms, a games room, a movie room. A pool and hot tub outside along with basketball and tennis courts."

"What, no gym?" I ask, jokingly.

"Yeah, there's one of those too."

"Of course there is."

"We've put Post-it notes on your rooms. All of them have been converted into doubles but—" Harley's words morph into a laugh when most of our group dart toward the stairs.

With Alex and I the only Brits left behind, Harley, Poppy, and Ruby smile at us.

"We've given you two the nicest room. It's got the best view."

My chin drops in shock.

"You didn't have to do that. I'd have been happy with—"

"It doesn't matter what you'd be happy with. You've got the best view. Jodie and Toby have the quietest, and we've put Seb and Stella right at the end between two bathrooms for—"

"Understandable reasons," Alex finishes for her.

"Yeah."

"Trust me, you might have heard how bad they are. But there's no way you can appreciate the truth of it until you really experience it."

"Great," Poppy says sarcastically.

"We can hardly wait," Ruby adds.

"Anyway, the refrigerators are fully stocked; everything you could possibly need is here. All you've got to do is sit back and relax."

"Sounds like heaven," I breathe.

"We'll be out on the deck if you want to join us."

"Thank you," I say before Alex tugs me toward the stairs to go and find our room.

Despite my arguing, he carries both our huge cases up the stairs, leaving me with the small ones. But that's soon forgotten when we step into our bedroom and the floor-to-ceiling windows reveal the incredible view of the ocean beyond.

"Wow. There's even a balcony."

"Perfect," Alex murmurs. When I look back, he's got a dark look in his eyes that makes my core clench.

Pulling the sliding doors open, he encourages me to step out. The warmth of the evening hits me, the sun making my skin tingle with the need to strip down to a bikini and soak up every ounce of it, as voices and laughter float up from above.

He pushes me right up against the railing and leans into me, allowing me to feel just how ready for me he is.

"Do you think you can be quiet?" he whispers in my ear.

"Alex," I breathe. "They're right down there."

"Yep. One moan or cry from you and they'll know exactly what we're doing."

I gasp as he shoves his hand down the back of my leggings, finding me wet and waiting for him.

"That gets you hot, doesn't it? The thought of them knowing exactly what's going on up here."

"Alex," I moan quietly when he spears two fingers inside me, teasing me in the most delicious way.

His lips tickle up my neck before he nibbles on my earlobe.

"I'm going to fuck you right here. Then, we're going to go down there and hang out as if your pussy isn't dripping with my cum. And then, when it's bedtime, I'm going to do it all over again with the stars staring down at us."

"Holy shit," I gasp when he thrusts harder inside me.

"Shhh. Don't give the game away yet. I'm not even inside you."

By the time we get to the deck, everyone else is already there. And true to his word, I'm full of the evidence of what we did upstairs and my knees are more than a little weak.

"Late to join twice in one day. Keep using it that much, bro, and it'll fall off," Nico teases.

"I think Seb's testament to the fact that isn't true," I counter.

The man in question flips me off, but he doesn't

comment. Probably because his girl is sitting on his lap, distracting him.

"You like your room?" Harley asks innocently while everyone else stares at us with knowing smirks on their lips.

"Love it. The view is insane. And it's so peaceful."

"Wasn't down here," Theo coughs.

"Fuck you all," Alex says happily, grabbing two beers from the cooler and pulling me down onto an empty lounger. "So, what's the plan? When are we hanging out with Mickey?"

They begin laying out our plans for the next two weeks, but I quickly realise that I don't really care and drown them out. I mean, of course I care; I want this holiday to be as incredible as everyone else. But I'm not ready to start mapping out the days. I want to just live for now, not already be thinking about next week.

But despite wanting to savour every moment, I'm pretty sure I blink and we're two days away from going home.

"Ready to head out?" Toby asks when we join the others who are hanging out around the pool.

After almost two weeks of theme parks and pool days, we're finally heading to spend the day at the beach. And I am so ready for a lazy day to finish off our holiday before we head back to reality.

Part of me is more than ready. I've never been away from Blake and Zay for this long before; I'm missing them like crazy. We've talked every day and video called more often than not so I could give them a tour of the house, making them green with envy over what I'm experiencing without them.

"Yep, good to go."

No one even comments now on the fact that we're last to join the group. It's a position we seem to have taken from

Seb and Stella, and honestly, I can't say I'm all too bothered.

With my beach bag over my shoulder, I take Alex's hand and lead the way toward the front door and the cars that are waiting for us. We might not have picked them up at the airport, seeing as Stella had a limo waiting for us, but we've had rentals delivered since, giving everyone—bar me —a chance to drive.

As with every day that we've been here, the sky is cloudless and beautiful and excitement for the day ahead flutters in my belly.

Lifting our conjoined hands, Alex presses a kiss to my knuckles as he stares out of the window at the clear blue ocean growing before us.

With a contented sigh, I rest my head on his shoulder while the others chat around us.

I had no idea life with another person could be this easy, this effortless. But that's exactly how it is with us. I'm one hundred percent me, and he's unashamedly him. I trust him more than I do myself, and how secure I feel as a couple in only a short number of weeks would be terrifying if it weren't for the incredible way he makes me feel.

He's told his Dad he's finished taking jobs, but I'm pretty sure that if he decided that he missed it—and I don't mean the sex part; we get more than enough of that—the thrill of breaking someone down and extracting intel, then I don't think I'd have a problem if he decided to start again. Hell, the whole thing almost sounds thrilling enough for me to suggest embarking on it with him.

I remember the fear, the excitement as I talked my way into letting the leaders of the city trade me for my boys. There was a definite buzz there that I'm scared he'll miss.

He keeps telling me it's fine, but I'm desperate for him

to understand that I'll support him no matter what. I know he'd do the same for me too. Not that I'm ever going back to camming. Dancing, maybe. With the Cirillos—or more so Stefanos and Blake—taking over from Derek and Vincent, giving the girls jobs and ensuring all their venues have the best dancers and servers, I'm confident that they're being looked after properly.

Kyle brings the car to a stop and puts an end to my thoughts about life when we return to London.

"Come on, baby," Alex murmurs, throwing the door open and tugging me out.

I suck in a deep breath of ocean air and savour the moment.

This place is incredible. I can understand why Stella has missed it so much. Her friends are amazing too.

With the woman in question taking up the lead, we all follow her to what appears to be the end of the beach, but she doesn't stop. Instead, she marches straight into the water and begins making her way around the huge rock.

"So I guess we're going around that then," Alex teases.

"Looks that way."

We follow, splashing through the warm waves as they lap at our legs. For a girl who'd never left London before this, it's heaven.

"Oh wow," I breathe when we finally round the rock and find a small section of beach.

Ashton and Zayn lower a cooler of food and drink while everyone else begins laying out towels and stripping down to their swimwear.

"Yeah, it's... not exactly what we can find in London," Alex says, dragging me from the water and finding us a spot next to Calli and Daemon.

"I have good memories of beaches with you two," Calli

says happily. She looks stunning in her pink bikini with her cute bump.

"Ah, hiding our girls from enemies. Good times," Alex muses. "And if I remember rightly, you two had waaaay more fun on that beach than I ever did."

"Don't think I haven't forgotten that she kissed you," Daemon sulks.

"Dude, you need to get over that. It was dark; I snuck in. She thought I was you."

"She still put her lips on yours."

"Oh my God, is he pouting?" I laugh, unable to believe what I'm seeing.

"Fuck off," Daemon grunts, crossing his arms over his chest.

Like Alex, he's spent our time here embracing his scars. None of the others batted an eye when he first peeled his shirt off, but we all knew just how much of a big deal it was for him. Calli gazed at him with so much love and pride in her eyes, it was almost too intimate to watch. And I felt the same whenever Alex stripped down.

"Want me to make it even?" I offer lightly. "I barely remember our first."

"Vixen," Alex warns, jealousy burning in his eyes.

"What? It only seems fair. Calli knows which one of you kisses better, so I should too."

"Their lips barely brushed. She has no idea what a bad kisser Alex is."

"Should we be concerned about the fact that you clearly do?" Calli asks with a smirk. "Something you two aren't telling us?"

"Jesus Christ. I didn't sign up for this shit," Daemon mutters while Alex chuckles.

"Pretty sure the last time I kissed you was when we

were like five or some shit. I hadn't perfected my skills at that point."

"You're a fucking moron."

Alex shrugs, not fazed by his brother's teasing in the slightest.

"Well, as far as I can see, there's only one thing for it." I get to my feet despite Alex's complaints.

Dropping my knees to the edge of Daemon's towel, I move faster than he's expecting and lean forward to steal a chaste kiss before he has a chance to back away.

Calli cracks up laughing at the horrified look on Daemon's face, while Alex just watches intrigued. And possibly a little bit turned on.

"Huh, you're right. It really is hard to tell from just that. I guess I'd better..."

This time when I lean forward, Daemon is ready for me. His hand wraps around my throat, shoving me back. Although way more gently than I know he's capable of.

"Get your hands off my girl, you big brute," Alex barks while I get to my feet and stalk over to him.

Straddling his waist, I loom over him until my lips are right next to his ear.

"Complain all you want, that got you hot and you know it."

His breath catches before he speaks, totally giving him away. "These lips are mine, Vixen."

"Of course. Every inch of me is yours. Forever."

When I pull back, his eyes are dark, and when I rock over him, I find that he's more than ready for a little sex on the beach action.

That is until Stella yells, "Girls, let's go," and she, Emmie, Harley, and Ruby run full steam toward the water.

"Yes, come on." Grabbing Calli's hand, I drag her up, leaving Alex wanting and tenting his shorts.

"Fucking tease," he barks, and when I look back he's got his hand in his shorts, attempting to rearrange himself.

Jodie, Brianna, and Poppy join us a few seconds later.

"Look at them," Calli muses when we come to a stop and look back at our boys laying out in the sun, their eyes locked on us.

"Yeah," I sigh. "We lucked out."

32

ALEX

"Fucking hell," I groan. Here I am, trying to sink my boner while my girl jumps around in the sea in her itty bitty black bikini.

Life is so fucking cruel sometimes.

"You doing okay over there, Bro?"

"Fuck off, you smug prick."

"How is it possible you found someone who is as crazy as you?" he asks.

"I've no idea," I murmur, refusing to take my eyes off her. "Not fucking letting her go, though."

"Good."

The girls' joy and laughter float around us.

"Didn't really see myself as a sun and sand holiday kinda person, but this trip has been pretty epic," Daemon confesses.

"Yeah, it has," I agree. "Not sure I'm ready to return to reality."

"Oh, I don't know. I think I'm ready to make some motherfucker's life just that little bit worse."

"Sadist," I tease.

"What can I say? I love it. Ready to join them?" he asks, jerking his head toward the ocean.

"Too fucking right, I am."

"Last one there is a loser," he calls, jumping to his feet.

We take off running side by side, splashing into the warm water, making a beeline for our girls.

They shriek and try to swim away from us, but they stand little chance.

Wrapping my fingers around Evie's kicking ankles, I drag her into my body.

"You're a tease, Vixen."

"So are you," she purrs, spinning in my arms, wrapping her arms and legs around me like a koala.

"Jesus," I groan as she grinds herself against me.

"I see you didn't fix your little issue."

I scoff. "Little, puh-lease."

Threading her fingers in my hair, she drags my head back and attacks my neck with gentle kisses and sharp bites.

My hands flex on her arse until one dips lower, teasing her over the fabric of her bottoms.

"Gonna fuck you, Vixen. Right here. Right now. In front of all of our friends," I warn darkly in her ear, my cock only getting harder with every word I say. "Any of them could be watching as I take you."

Her movements get more frantic as I speak.

"My dirty girl wants that, doesn't she?"

"Alex," she moans against my throat.

She holds me tighter, allowing me to release my hands in favour of shoving my swim shorts down.

"So fucking hard for you, Evie."

All I get in response is a needy whimper.

The second I'm free, I tug the fabric covering her pussy aside and line myself up.

"You gonna be quiet, or are you going to let everyone know exactly what's going on here?" I ask. Personally, I don't give two shits either way. All I need right now is her.

"Guess we're about to find out."

I thrust forward, filling her easily.

"So wet for me," I murmur against her lips.

"Of course; have you seen you?" she teases.

"Nah, I was too busy looking at you."

I claim her lips as we move together, the gentle waves lapping at our shoulders.

The sounds of our friends enjoying themselves rings through the air, reminding me that they're only feet away. It makes my release surge forward faster than I'd like.

This isn't our first underwater rodeo; nor is it any of theirs. I'm pretty sure every single couple here has fucked in either the pool or the hot tub at the house at some point in the last two weeks. Thank fuck for chlorine, or Theo would be refusing to go in it about now.

"You feel so good," I groan as Evie's breathing becomes erratic, her walls clamping down so tight on my dick, I have to fight not to let go.

"Yes, yes," she chants quietly.

"Come all over my cock, baby. Let me feel you."

I thrust my hips faster as I claim her lips, swallowing down her cries of pleasure as she crashes over the edge.

I do the same only seconds later, only to be followed up with a round of applause.

Evie barks out a laugh while I tuck my face into her neck as I enjoy my lingering high. "I fucking hate my friends."

"Was it as you hoped for?" Evie asks, ignoring our audience.

"What, baby?"

"Fucking me in front of them."

I think for a moment. "I'm not sure. Might have to do it again to check."

She laughs, forcing me to slip from her body.

"I love you, Evie Moore."

"I love you too, Alexander Deimos. More than I could ever put into words.

<hr>

The rest of the day is full of joy and laughter as we forget about our impending return home and live in the moment.

As the sun begins to set, Zayn and Nico hand out the last of the drinks.

"What's up with Seb?" Evie whispers in my ear. "He looks weird."

Following her line of sight, I find him sitting up on the rock, watching Stella with her friends.

"Maybe he just needs a shit," I joke, earning me a slap to the shoulder.

"He looks... nervous."

"Nah, Seb doesn't get nervous. Definitely needs a shit."

We watch him for a few more minutes before he finally climbs down and walks to the bag he brought with him. He rummages around for a bit and then stands tall once again and begins walking toward Stella.

He whispers something in her ear before taking her hand and dragging her into the middle of our group.

She looks around nervously, wondering what's happening, while his eyes remain locked on her.

"Oh my God," Evie breathes, predicting what's about to happen while the rest of us watch in confusion.

Movement to our right catches my eye as Calli and Daemon move closer.

"Is he going to—" Calli starts, but her words are cut off when Seb starts talking.

"Right here on this very spot last year, I told you that you were mine. I opened my heart to you and prayed that you wouldn't smash it under your foot after all the bullshit I'd caused."

"Oh my God, he is," Calli whispers excitedly.

"And now we're back, standing here again, and I want to make those words permanent.

"You're mine, Stella. You have been since that first night you stood up to me in the graveyard when no one else would have been brave enough. And I want you to be mine for the rest of my life."

"Holy shit," Nico gasps, while girls shriek in delight as Seb drops to one knee and produces a ring.

"Will you be mine for the rest of our lives, Stella? Will you be my wife?"

Sniffles come from beside me, and when I glance over, both Evie and Calli have tears streaming down their cheeks.

"Yes," Stella cries, stealing my attention once more.

As I look back, she's dropping to her knees with Seb and throwing her arms around his shoulders.

"They're going to fuck right there in celebration, aren't they?" Toby deadpans.

But thankfully, that isn't what happens. After a long,

dirty kiss, Seb rips his lips from hers and finally slides the ring he brought onto her finger.

"I hope you know that this is all your fault," Toby barks at Nico. "You got married and now it's going to be like a set of dominos."

"Whoa, hang the fuck on. Theo was first. Shouldn't it be his fault?"

"Fuck no," Theo pipes up. "I got stuck with this one without my knowledge. Totally different."

"This one?" Emmie snaps, offended. "If anyone got stuck with anyone here, it's me."

"That's not what you were saying this morning when I woke you up with my head between your thighs, wife."

"Hey, I never said that being stuck doesn't come with its benefits."

We're still laughing when a pop of a cork shoots past us.

Seb takes a swig from the bottle before handing it to his fiancée.

She swallows a mouthful before screwing up her face in disgust. "It's warm."

"Sorry. There's more back at the house waiting for us."

"Then what the fuck are we all still doing here? Let's go and fucking party," Stella announces.

"Fuck yeah, let's go," Seb agrees, bending down and throwing his future wife over his shoulder and running for the rock we need to wade around to get back.

"We'll get the stuff then," Theo calls.

Seb flips him off over his shoulder but quickly returns to molesting Stella's arse.

"I guess we're leaving then," Daemon says as he and Calli begin tidying up their things.

An hour later and we're back in our room, showered and ready to spend the night celebrating Seb and Stella's engagement.

My girl looks insane with her bronzed skin and floral playsuit covering another bikini. She's got her hair twisted up into some kind of knot with a flower poked in the side of it.

"You look beautiful," I say, dipping down to kiss the skin beneath her ear as she applies a little make-up.

Placing the tube of mascara back on the side, she spins around and checks me out.

"You're not looking so bad yourself, Deimos."

It's lies, all of it. I'm wearing a pair of tan shorts and a white polo-neck t-shirt. There is nothing special about me right now. Although, that look in her eyes might suggest otherwise.

"Last night," she muses, stepping around me toward one of her cases.

"Yeah. It's gone too fast, huh?"

"Just a little," she murmurs, searching for something.

"You're not about to pull a ring out too, are you?" I tease, although I can't deny that the idea makes my heart race.

"No, I'm not. But I do have something special for you."

"Oh?" I ask, watching as she finally locates what she's looking for and spins toward me with a black box in her hand.

"What's that?"

"Something you've been missing."

I narrow my eyes at her.

"Here," she says, handing me the box. "Open it and find out."

Doing as I'm told, I slide the lid off and stare down in disbelief. "My watch. How did you— Where did you—"

"Your dad found it while they were clearing out the church. It was in bad shape, so we had it fixed up. Turn it over."

Again, doing as I'm told, I pull the timepiece from its cushion and turn it over.

Engraved in the back, there's a message that makes my heart rate increase.

Evie and Alex, until the end of time.

"Baby," I breathe, totally choked up with emotion.

"You like it?" she asks nervously.

"Like it? I fucking love it. Thank you."

"You're welcome. But really, it's your dad who did all the hard work. You should be thanking him."

Shaking my head in disbelief, I pull her into my arms and kiss her until we're both breathless.

33

EVIE

We're last to the party again. But this time, it wasn't because we were fucking like bunnies but because Alex FaceTimed his dad to thank him for the watch, and then Zay overheard his voice and refused to let either of us go until we told him every single thing we'd done here since we last spoke... two days ago.

We should probably have been grateful that Blake was out, or we'd have been stuck there even longer while the others enjoyed themselves out by the pool.

"Don't even start," Alex says, when we step out onto the deck to find Toby, Nico, and Theo smirking at us. "There were no orgasms involved."

"Yeah right, I'll believe that when I see it."

"Bro, you're more than welcome to watch it—" Brianna slaps him as she and Jodie join them.

"Stop being a pig."

"Hey, Demon. Everything okay?" Toby asks when he spots tears in Jodie's eyes.

My heart sinks that while we've all been enjoying ourselves here, she's been suffering in silence.

"Jessie called me," she blurts, her tears spilling over.

"You spoke to him?" Toby asks, looking as invested and concerned as Jodie.

"Yes. It was so good to hear his voice. To know that he's okay."

She sobs and Toby pulls her into his arms, pressing his lips to the top of her head.

"That's all she would have wanted," she whispers. "For him to be okay."

"I know, Demon. And he will be."

Toby smiles at us, his own relief palpable, and we leave them to it, walking deeper into the garden where another huddle of people are.

Multiple sets of eyes look up, but mine lock with one familiar set I haven't seen for a few weeks.

"Hey, Braveheart. How's it going?" Reid asks with mirth dancing in his eyes.

He's spent quite a bit of time with Brianna and Nico this week, but this is his first visit to the house.

"Yeah, it's good. Your hometown is pretty awesome."

He laughs. "If only. Our hometown is about forty minutes that way, and it's fucking terrible."

"Well, you know what I mean."

A flash of blonde hair appears before a woman wraps her arms around his waist and smiles at me.

"You must be Evie," she says softly. "I've heard a lot about you."

"All good, I hope," I tease.

"Hell, yeah. There aren't many people in the world that would have propositioned Reid like you did.

Alex stiffens against me.

"I didn't proposition him like that; calm down," I whisper, making both Reid and his girl laugh.

"I'm Alana, by the way."

"It's nice to meet you."

"Drinks?" she says before gesturing for me to follow her.

We find everyone else in the kitchen, Stella and Emmie once again whipping up some potent cocktails.

"I've already had two of their slippery nipples. Pretty sure they took a layer of skin off my throat," Alana jokes.

"Can't say I'm surprised."

I grab my cocktail and a beer for Alex and after a few minutes, everyone heads out, the music is turned up, and the party really gets started.

We dance, we drink, we strip down to our swimwear once more and mess about in the pool. It's the perfect night full of incredible people.

At some point, two other guys join us and Nico introduces them as Reid's boys.

I don't think much of it until a little while later when I look up and find Alana lip locked with the slightly more friendly one of the two of them.

Elbowing Alex, I nod in their direction.

"I thought she was Reid's girlfriend," I whisper, although with the number of cocktails I've had, it doesn't come out that quietly.

Nico hears and throws his head back on a laugh while Brianna simply states, "She is."

Reid saunters over and lowers himself to a spare lounger, looking totally unfazed by the whole thing. Maybe he just hasn't noticed, but that seems unlike him.

"Reid," I say, the alcohol loosening my lips. "Isn't that your girl over there kissing one of your boys?"

Twisting around, he watches them over his shoulder for a few seconds—long enough for the other, slightly older and scarier guy to join them. I gasp as he takes her head and leans in for a kiss of his own.

"Don't worry; it freaked me out at first too, but you'll soon get used to it."

My lips open and close like a freaking goldfish as he turns back to watch.

I look at Alex and roll my eyes at the smirk on his face. Of course he'd be all over this.

I'm about to ask for an explanation when my phone starts buzzing in my pocket.

"It's Blakely," I say when I pull it free. "Do you mind?"

"Want me to come? Alex offers as I get up to find a quiet spot to talk to her.

"No, enjoy yourself. Find out about this..." I wiggle my finger between Reid and the others. "I need details." He laughs as I walk away.

Swiping the screen, I stare down at my sister's face. "Hey, don't tell me, you already know about everything we've done?" I ask, aware that Zay will have pounced on her the second she got back.

"Yeah," she agrees, but there's not as much lightness in her tone as there is in mine.

I know it's earlier there and that she probably hasn't had multiple cocktails, but it's unlike Blake to be so sombre.

"What's wrong?" I ask, curling my legs beneath me as I sit in the middle of the huge corner sofa in the living room.

She stares at me through the screen for a few seconds, blinking away tears that are pooling in her eyes.

"Blake, what is it? Is everything okay?"

"I'm sorry," she sobs. "I'm so sorry."

My heart sinks into my feet.

"What is it?" I repeat, concern flooding my veins, sobering me instantly.

"I'm pregnant," she wails, her tears finally spilling free. "You're—"

"I fucked up, Evie. I'm sorry. I'm so sorry, I—"

Footsteps sound out a beat before Alex appears in the doorway with a fresh cocktail in his hand.

"What's going on?" he asks, taking in my shocked expression and Blakely's sobs.

"Uh... Blakely," I whisper, not taking my eyes from Alex's. "Whose is it?"

She breaks down at that question, telling me everything I need to know.

"I'm sorry; I need to go." She cuts the call before I get a chance to say anything.

"Whose is what?" Alex asks confused.

Pushing the iPad aside, I stand and walk to him, taking the drink from his and twisting my fingers with his.

"Something to worry about when we get back," I say with a cringe. "Let's go and enjoy our last night. Reality is already too close."

He studies me for a beat, but he must see the determination on my face, because he gives in.

"One more night in paradise, baby," he says, pulling me into his arms when we make it out to what we've turned into a makeshift dance floor.

"But forever together," I finish, my lips finding his as I try to force down the unease of what's to come.

So much for the end of the drama...

We fall quietly into our own little bubble, but inevitably, it's broken when Seb bellows, "Last one naked and in the pool is a loser."

"Do they never stop?" I laugh.

"It would be boring if they did. Come on."

Together, and along with all our friends, we leave what

little we're wearing behind and all bomb into the pool, knowing that no matter what hits us next, we're all going to be ready for it.

Because together, we can overcome anything.

Did you say you wanted more?
Well... SURPRISE!
Knight's Ridge Destiny, the series epilgue is coming on 8th June.
PRE-ORDER your copy now!

In the meantime, make sure you're in my Facebook group, Tracy's Angels, so you can discuss the series with other KRE lovers!

And as for what's next. Well... Reid Harris is coming for you this fall...
Add Book One of the Harrow Creek Hawks to your TBR now!

ABOUT THE AUTHOR

Tracy Lorraine is a *USA Today* and *Wall Street Journal* bestselling new adult and contemporary romance author. Tracy has recently turned thirty and lives in a cute Cotswold village in England with her husband, baby girl and lovable but slightly crazy dog. Having always been a bookaholic with her head stuck in her Kindle, Tracy decided to try her hand at a story idea she dreamt up and hasn't looked back since.

Be the first to find out about new releases and offers. Sign up to my newsletter here.

If you want to know what I'm up to and see teasers and snippets of what I'm working on, then you need to be in my Facebook group. Join Tracy's Angels here.

Keep up to date with Tracy's books at
www.tracylorraine.com

Falling Series

Falling for Ryan: Part One #1

Falling for Ryan: Part Two #2

Falling for Jax #3

Falling for Daniel (A Falling Series Novella)

Falling for Ruben #4

Falling for Fin #5

Falling for Lucas #6

Falling for Caleb #7

Falling for Declan #8

Falling For Liam #9

Forbidden Series

Falling for the Forbidden #1

Losing the Forbidden #2

Fighting for the Forbidden #3

Craving Redemption #4

Demanding Redemption #5

Avoiding Temptation #6

Chasing Temptation #7

Rebel Ink Series

Hate You #1

Trick You #2

Defy You #3

Play You #4

Inked (A Rebel Ink/Driven Crossover)

Rosewood High Series

Thorn #1

Paine #2

Savage #3

Fierce #4

Hunter #5

Faze (#6 Prequel)

Fury #6

Legend #7

Maddison Kings University Series

TMYM: Prequel

TRYS #1

TDYW #2

TBYS #3

TVYC #4

TDYD #5

TDYR #6

TRYD #7

Knight's Ridge Empire Series

Wicked Summer Knight: Prequel (Stella & Seb)

Wicked Knight #1 (Stella & Seb)

Wicked Princess #2 (Stella & Seb)

Wicked Empire #3 (Stella & Seb)

Deviant Knight #4 (Emmie & Theo)

Deviant Princess #5 (Emmie & Theo

Deviant Reign #6 (Emmie & Theo)

One Reckless Knight (Jodie & Toby)

Reckless Knight #7 (Jodie & Toby)

Reckless Princess #8 (Jodie & Toby)

Reckless Dynasty #9 (Jodie & Toby)

Dark Halloween Knight (Calli & Batman)

Dark Knight #10 (Calli & Batman)

Dark Princess #11 (Calli & Batman)

Dark Legacy #12 (Calli & Batman)

Corrupt Valentine Knight (Nico & Siren)

Corrupt Knight #13 (Nico & Siren)

Corrupt Princess #14 (Nico & Siren)

Corrupt Union #15 (Nico & Siren)

Sinful Wild Knight (Alex)

Sinful Stolen Knight (Alex & Vixen)

Sinful Knight (Alex & Vixen)

Ruined Series

Ruined Plans #1

<u>Ruined by Lies</u> #2

<u>Ruined Promises</u> #3

<u>Never Forget Series</u>

<u>Never Forget Him</u> #1

<u>Never Forget Us</u> #2

<u>Everywhere & Nowhere</u> #3

<u>Chasing Series</u>

<u>Chasing Logan</u>

<u>The Cocktail Girls</u>

<u>His Manhattan</u>

<u>Her Kensington</u>

Chapter One

Letty

I sit on my bed, staring down at the fabric in my hands.

This wasn't how it was supposed to happen.

This wasn't part of my plan.

I let out a sigh, squeezing my eyes tight, willing the tears away.

I've cried enough. I thought I'd have run out by now.

A commotion on the other side of the door has me looking up in a panic, but just like yesterday, no one comes knocking.

I think I proved that I don't want to hang with my new roommates the first time someone knocked and asked if I wanted to go for breakfast with them.

I don't.

I don't even want to be here.

I just want to hide.

And that thought makes it all a million times worse.

I'm not a hider. I'm a fighter. I'm a fucking Hunter.

But this is what I've been reduced to.

This pathetic, weak mess.

And all because of *him*.

He shouldn't have this power over me. But even now, he does.

The dorm falls silent once again, and I pray that they've all headed off for their first class of the semester so I can slip out unnoticed.

I know it's ridiculous. I know I should just go out there with my head held high and dig up the confidence I know I do possess.

But I can't.

I figure that I'll just get through today—my first day—and everything will be alright.

I can somewhat pick up where I left off, almost as if the last eighteen months never happened.

Wishful thinking.

I glance down at the hoodie in my hands once more.

Mom bought them for Zayn, my younger brother, and me.

The navy fabric is soft between my fingers, but the text staring back at me doesn't feel right.

Maddison Kings University.

A knot twists my stomach and I swear my whole body sags with my new reality.

I was at my dream school. I beat the odds and I got into Columbia. And everything was good. No, everything was fucking fantastic.

Until it wasn't.

Now here I am. Sitting in a dorm at what was always my backup plan school having to start over.

Throwing the hoodie onto my bed, I angrily push to my feet.

I'm fed up with myself.

I should be better than this, stronger than this.

But I'm just... I'm broken.

And as much as I want to see the positives in this situation. I'm struggling.

Shoving my feet into my Vans, I swing my purse over my shoulder and scoop up the couple of books on my desk for the two classes I have today.

My heart drops when I step out into the communal kitchen and find a slim blonde-haired girl hunched over a mug and a textbook.

The scent of coffee fills my nose and my mouth waters.

My shoes squeak against the floor and she immediately looks up.

"Sorry, I didn't mean to disrupt you."

"Are you kidding?" she says excitedly, her southern accent making a smile twitch at my lips.

Her smile lights up her pretty face and for some reason, something settles inside me.

I knew hiding was wrong. It's just been my coping method for... quite a while.

"We wondered when our new roommate was going to show her face. The guys have been having bets on you being an alien or something."

A laugh falls from my lips. "No, no alien. Just..." I sigh, not really knowing what to say.

"You transferred in, right? From Columbia?"

"Ugh... yeah. How'd you know—"

"Girl, I know everything." She winks at me, but it

doesn't make me feel any better. "West and Brax are on the team, they spent the summer with your brother."

A rush of air passes my lips in relief. Although I'm not overly thrilled that my brother has been gossiping about me.

"So, what classes do you have today?" she asks when I stand there gaping at her.

"Umm... American lit and psychology."

"I've got psych later too. Professor Collins?"

"Uh..." I drag my schedule from my purse and stare down at it. "Y-yes."

"Awesome. We can sit together."

"S-sure," I stutter, sounding unsure, but the smile I give her is totally genuine. "I'm Letty, by the way." Although I'm pretty sure she already knows that.

"Ella."

"Okay, I'll... uh... see you later."

"Sure. Have a great morning."

She smiles at me and I wonder why I was so scared to come out and meet my new roommates.

I'd wanted Mom to organize an apartment for me so that I could be alone, but—probably wisely—she refused. She knew that I'd use it to hide in and the point of me restarting college is to try to put everything behind me and start fresh.

After swiping an apple from the bowl in the middle of the table, I hug my books tighter to my chest and head out, ready to embark on my new life.

The morning sun burns my eyes and the scent of freshly cut grass fills my nose as I step out of our building. The summer heat hits my skin, and it makes everything feel that little bit better.

So what if I'm starting over. I managed to transfer the

credits I earned from Columbia, and MKU is a good school. I'll still get a good degree and be able to make something of my life.

Things could be worse.

It could be this time last year...

I shake the thought from my head and force my feet to keep moving.

I pass students meeting up with their friends for the start of the new semester as they excitedly tell them all about their summers and the incredible things they did, or they compare schedules.

My lungs grow tight as I drag in the air I need. I think of the friends I left behind in Columbia. We didn't have all that much time together, but we'd bonded before my life imploded on me.

Glancing around, I find myself searching for familiar faces. I know there are plenty of people here who know me. A couple of my closest friends came here after high school.

Mom tried to convince me to reach out over the summer, but my anxiety kept me from doing so. I don't want anyone to look at me like I'm a failure. That I got into one of the best schools in the country, fucked it up and ended up crawling back to Rosewood. I'm not sure what's worse, them assuming I couldn't cope or the truth.

Focusing on where I'm going, I put my head down and ignore the excited chatter around me as I head for the coffee shop, desperately in need of my daily fix before I even consider walking into a lecture.

I find the Westerfield Building where my first class of the day is and thank the girl who holds the heavy door open for me before following her toward the elevator.

"Holy fucking shit," a voice booms as I turn the corner, following the signs to the room on my schedule.

Before I know what's happening, my coffee is falling from my hand and my feet are leaving the floor.

"What the—" The second I get a look at the guy standing behind the one who has me in his arms, I know exactly who I've just walked into.

Forgetting about the coffee that's now a puddle on the floor, I release my books and wrap my arms around my old friend.

His familiar woodsy scent flows through me, and suddenly, I feel like me again. Like the past two years haven't existed.

"What the hell are you doing here?" Luca asks, a huge smile on his face when he pulls back and studies me.

His brows draw together when he runs his eyes down my body, and I know why. I've been working on it over the summer, but I know I'm still way skinnier than I ever have been in my life.

"I transferred," I admit, forcing the words out past the lump in my throat.

His smile widens more before he pulls me into his body again.

"It's so good to see you."

I relax into his hold, squeezing him tight, absorbing his strength. And that's one thing that Luca Dunn has in spades. He's a rock, always has been and I didn't realize how much I needed that right now.

Mom was right. I should have reached out.

"You too," I whisper honestly, trying to keep the tears at bay that are threatening just from seeing him—them.

"Hey, it's good to see you," Leon says, slightly more subdued than his twin brother as he hands me my discarded books.

"Thank you."

I look between the two of them, noticing all the things that have changed since I last saw them in person. I keep up with them on Instagram and TikTok, sure, but nothing is quite like standing before the two of them.

Both of them are bigger than I ever remember, showing just how hard their coach is working them now they're both first string for the Panthers. And if it's possible, they're both hotter than they were in high school, which is really saying something because they'd turn even the most confident of girls into quivering wrecks with one look back then. I can only imagine the kind of rep they have around here.

The sound of a door opening behind us and the shuffling of feet cuts off our little reunion.

"You in Professor Whitman's American lit class?" Luca asks, his eyes dropping from mine to the book in my hands.

"Yeah. Are you?"

"We are. Walk you to class?" A smirk appears on his lips that I remember all too well. A flutter of the butterflies he used to give me threaten to take flight as he watches me intently.

Luca was one of my best friends in high school, and I spent almost all our time together with the biggest crush on him. It seems that maybe the teenage girl inside me still thinks that he could be it for me.

"I'd love you to."

"Come on then, Princess," Leon says and my entire body jolts at hearing that pet name for me. He's never called me that before and I really hope he's not about to start now.

Clearly not noticing my reaction, he once again takes my books from me and threads his arm through mine as the pair of them lead me into the lecture hall.

I glance at both of them, a smile pulling at my lips and hope building inside me.

Maybe this was where I was meant to be this whole time.

Maybe Columbia and I were never meant to be.

More than a few heads turn our way as we climb the stairs to find some free seats. Mostly it's the females in the huge space and I can't help but inwardly laugh at their reaction.

I get it.

The Dunn twins are two of the Kings around here and I'm currently sandwiched between them. It's a place that nearly every female in this college, hell, this state, would kill to be in.

"Dude, shift the fuck over," Luca barks at another guy when he pulls to a stop a few rows from the back.

The guy who's got dark hair and even darker eyes immediately picks up his bag, books, and pen and moves over a space.

"This is Colt," Luca explains, nodding to the guy who's studying me with interest.

"Hey," I squeak, feeling a little intimidated.

"Hey." His low, deep voice licks over me. "Ow, what the fuck, man?" he barks, rubbing at the back of his head where Luca just slapped him.

"Letty's off-limits. Get your fucking eyes off her."

"Dude, I was just saying hi."

"Yeah, and we all know what that usually leads to," Leon growls behind me.

The three of us take our seats and just about manage to pull our books out before our professor begins explaining the syllabus for the semester.

"Sorry about the coffee," Luca whispers after a few minutes. "Here." He places a bottle of water on my desk. "I know it's not exactly a replacement, but it's the best I can do."

The reminder of the mess I left out in the hallway hits me.

"I should go and—"

"Chill," he says, placing his hand on my thigh. His touch instantly relaxes me as much as it sends a shock through my body. "I'll get you a replacement after class. Might even treat you to a cupcake."

I smile up at him, swooning at the fact he remembers my favorite treat.

Why did I ever think coming here was a bad idea?

Chapter Two
Letty

My hand aches by the time Professor Whitman finishes talking. It feels like a lifetime ago that I spent this long taking notes.

"You okay?" Luca asks me with a laugh as I stretch out my fingers.

"Yeah, it's been a while."

"I'm sure these boys can assist you with that, beautiful," bursts from Colt's lips, earning him another slap to the head.

"Ignore him. He's been hit in the head with a ball one too many times," Leon says from beside me but I'm too enthralled with the way Luca is looking at me right now to reply.

Our friendship wasn't a conventional one back in high school. He was the star quarterback, and I wasn't a cheerleader or ever really that sporty. But we were paired up as lab partners during my first week at Rosewood High and we kinda never separated.

I watched as he took the team to new heights, as he met with college scouts, I even went to a few places with him so he didn't have to go alone.

He was the one who allowed me to cry on his shoulder as I struggled to come to terms with the loss of another who left a huge hole in my heart and he never, not once, overstepped the mark while I clung to him and soaked up his support.

I was also there while he hooked up with every member of the cheer squad along with any other girl who looked at him just so. Each one stung a little more than the last as my poor teenage heart was getting battered left, right, and center.

With each day, week, month that passed, I craved him more but he never, not once, looked at me that way.

I was even his prom date, yet he ended up spending the night with someone else.

It hurt, of course it did. But it wasn't his fault and I refuse to hold it against him.

Maybe I should have told him. Been honest with him about my feelings and what I wanted. But I was so terrified I'd lose my best friend that I never confessed, and I took that secret all the way to Columbia with me.

As I stare at him now, those familiar butterflies still set flight in my belly, but they're not as strong as I remember. I'm not sure if that's because my feelings for him have lessened over time, or if I'm just so numb and broken right now that I don't feel anything but pain.

It really could go either way.

I smile at him, so grateful to have run into him this morning.

He always knew when I needed him and even without knowing of my presence here, there he was like some guardian fucking angel.

If guardian angels had sexy dark bed hair, mesmerizing green eyes and a body built for sin then yeah, that's what he is.

I laugh to myself, yeah, maybe that irritating crush has gone nowhere.

"What have you got next?" Leon asks, dragging my attention away from his twin.

Leon has always been the quieter, broodier one of the duo. He's as devastatingly handsome and as popular with the female population but he doesn't wear his heart on his sleeve like Luca. Leon takes a little time to warm to people, to let them in. It was hard work getting there, but I soon realized that once he dropped his walls a little for me, it was hella worth it.

He's more serious, more contemplative, he's deeper. I always suspected that there was a reason they were so different. I know twins don't have to be the same and like the same things, but there was always something niggling at me that there was a very good reason that Leon closed himself down. From listening to their mom talk over the years, they were so identical in their mannerisms, likes, and dislikes when they were growing up, that it seems hard to believe they became so different.

"Psychology but not for an hour. I'm—"

"I'm taking her for coffee," Luca butts in. A flicker of anger passes through Leon's eyes but it's gone so fast that I begin to wonder if I imagined it.

"I could use another coffee before econ," Leon chips in.

"Great. Let's go," Luca forces out through clenched teeth.

He wanted me alone. Interesting.

The reason I never told him about my mega crush is the fact he friend-zoned me in our first few weeks of friendship by telling me how refreshing it was to have a girl wanting to be his friend and not using it as a ploy to get more.

We were only sophomores at the time but even then, Luca was up to all sorts and the girls around us were all more than willing to bend to his needs.

From that moment on, I couldn't tell him how I really felt. It was bad enough I even felt it when he thought our friendship was just that.

I smile at both of them, hoping to shatter the sudden tension between the twins.

"Be careful with these two," Colt announces from behind us as we make our way out of the lecture hall with all the others. "The stories I've heard."

"Colt," Luca warns, turning to face him and walking backward for a few steps.

"Don't worry," I shoot over my shoulder. "I know how to handle the Dunn twins." I wink at him as he howls with laughter.

"You two are in so much trouble," he muses as he turns left out of the room and we go right.

Leon takes my books from me once more and Luca threads his fingers through mine. I still for a beat. While the move isn't unusual, Luca has always been very affectionate. It only takes a second for his warmth to race up my arm and to settle the last bit of unease that's still knotting my stomach.

"Two Americanos and a skinny vanilla latte with an extra shot. Three cupcakes with the sprinkles on top."

I swoon at the fact Luca remembers my order. "How'd you—"

He turns to me, his wide smile and the sparkle in his eyes making my words trail off. The familiarity of his face, the feeling of comfort and safety he brings me causes a lump to form in my throat.

"I didn't forget anything about my best girl." He throws his arm around my shoulder and pulls me close.

Burying my nose in his hard chest, I breathe him in. His woodsy scent mixes with his laundry detergent and it settles me in a way I didn't know I needed.

Leon's stare burns into my back as I snuggle with his brother and I force myself to pull away so he doesn't feel like the third wheel.

"Dunn," the server calls, and Leon rushes ahead to grab our order while Luca leads me to a booth at the back of the coffee shop.

As we walk past each table, I become more and more aware of the attention on the twins. I know their reps, they've had their football god status since before I moved to Rosewood and met them in high school, but I had forgotten just how hero-worshiped they were, and this right now is off the charts.

Girls openly stare, their eyes shamelessly dropping down the guys' bodies as they mentally strip them naked. Guys jealousy shines through their expressions, especially those who are here with their girlfriends who are now paying them zero attention. Then there are the girls whose attention is firmly on me. I can almost read their thoughts—hell, I heard enough of them back in high school.

What do they see in her?

She's not even that pretty.

They're too good for her.

The only difference here from high school is that no one knows I'm just trailer park trash seeing as I moved from the hellhole that is Harrow Creek before meeting the boys.

Tipping my chin up, I straighten my spine and plaster on as much confidence as I can find.

They can all think what they like about me, they can come up with whatever bitchy comments they want. It's no skin off my back.

"Good to see you've lost your appeal," I mutter, dropping into the bench opposite both of them and wrapping my hands around my warm mug when Leon passes it over.

"We walk around practically unnoticed," Luca deadpans.

"You thought high school was bad," Leon mutters, he was always the one who hated the attention whereas Luca used it to his advantage to get whatever he wanted. "It was nothing."

"So I see. So, how's things? Catch me up on everything," I say, needing to dive into their celebrity status lifestyles rather than thinking about my train wreck of a life.

"Really?" Luca asks, raising a brow and causing my stomach to drop into my feet. "I think the bigger question is how come you're here and why we had no idea about it?"

Releasing my mug, I wrap my arms around myself and drop my eyes to the table.

"T-things just didn't work out at Columbia," I mutter, really not wanting to talk about it.

"The last time we talked, you said it was everything you expected it to be and more. What happened?"

Kane fucking Legend happened.

I shake that thought from my head like I do every time he pops up.

He's had his time ruining my life. It's over.

"I just..." I sigh. "I lost my way a bit, ended up dropping out and finally had to fess up and come clean to Mom."

Leon laughs sadly. "I bet that went down well."

The Dunn twins are well aware of what it's like to live with a pushy parent. One of the things that bonded the three of us over the years.

"Like a lead balloon. Even worse because I dropped out months before I finally showed my face."

"Why hide?" Leon's brows draw together as Luca stares at me with concern darkening his eyes.

"I had some health issues. It's nothing."

"Shit, are you okay?"

Fucking hell, Letty. Stop making this worse for yourself.

"Yeah, yeah. Everything is good. Honestly. I'm here and I'm ready to start over and make the best of it."

They both smile at me, and I reach for my coffee once more, bringing the mug to my lips and taking a sip.

"Enough about me, tell me all about the lives of two of the hottest Kings of Maddison."

"Okay... how'd you do that?" Ella whispers after both Luca and Leon walk me to my psych class after our coffee break.

"Do what?" I ask, following her into the room and finding ourselves seats about halfway back.

"It's your first day and the Dunn twins just walked you to class. You got a diamond-encrusted vag or something?"

I snort a laugh as a few others pause on their way to their seats at her words.

"Shush," I chastise.

"Girl, if it's true, you know all these guys need to know about it."

I pull out my books and a couple of pens as Professor Collins sets up at the front before turning to her.

"No, I don't have diamonds anywhere but my necklace. I've been friends with them for years."

"Girl, I knew there was a reason we should be friends." She winks at me. "I've been trying to get West and Brax to hook me up but they're useless."

"You want to be friends so I can set you up with one of the Dunns?"

"Or both." She shrugs, her face deadly serious before she leans in. "I've heard that they tag team sometimes. Can you imagine? Both of their undivided attention." She fans herself as she obviously pictures herself in the middle of a Dunn sandwich. "Oh and, I think you're pretty cool too."

"Of course you do." I laugh.

It's weird, I might have only met her very briefly this morning but that was enough.

"We're all going out for dinner tonight to welcome you to the dorm. The others are dying to meet you." She smiles at me, proving that there's no bitterness behind her words.

"I'm sorry for ignoring you all."

"Girl, don't sweat it. We got ya back, don't worry."

"Thank you," I mouth as the professor demands everyone's attention to begin the class.

The time flies as I scribble my notes down as fast as I can, my hand aching all over again and before I know it, he's finished explaining our first assignment and bringing his class to a close.

"Jesus, this semester is going to be hard," Ella muses as we both pack up.

"At least we've got each other."

"I like the way you think. You done for the day?"

"Yep, I'm gonna head to the store, grab some supplies then get started on this assignment, I think."

"I've got a couple of hours. You want company?"

After dumping our stuff in our rooms, Ella takes me to her favorite store, and I stock up on everything I'm going to need before we head back so she can go to class.

I make myself some lunch before being brave and setting up my laptop at the kitchen table to get started on my assignments. My time for hiding is over, it's time to get back to life and once again become a fully immersed college student.

"Holy shit, she is alive. I thought Zayn was lying about his beautiful older sister," a deep rumbling voice says, dragging me from my research a few hours later.

I spin and look at the two guys who have joined me.

"Zayn would never have called me beautiful," I say as a greeting.

"That's true. I think his actual words were: messy, pain in the ass, and my personal favorite, I'm glad I don't have to live with her again," he says, mimicking my brother's voice.

"Now that is more like it. Hey, I'm Letty. Sorry about—"

"You're all good. We're just glad you emerged. I'm West, this ugly motherfucker is Braxton—"

"Brax, please," he begs. "Only my mother calls me by my full name and you are way too hot to be her."

My cheeks heat as he runs his eyes over my curves.

"T-thanks, I think."

"Ignore him. He hasn't gotten laid for weeeeks."

"Okay, do we really need to go there right now?"

"Always, bro. Our girl here needs to know you get pissy when you don't get the pussy."

I laugh at their easy banter, closing down my laptop and

resting forward on my elbows as they move toward the fridge.

"Ella says we're going out," Brax says, pulling out two bottles of water and throwing one to West.

"Apparently so."

"She'll be here in a bit. Violet and Micah too. They were all in the same class."

"So," West says, sliding into the chair next to me. "What do we need to know that your brother hasn't already told us about you?"

My heart races at all the things that not even my brother would share about my life before I drag my thoughts away from my past.

"Uhhh..."

"How about the Dunns love her," Ella announces as she appears in the doorway flanked by two others. Violet and Micah, I assume.

"Um... how didn't we know this?" Brax asks.

"Because you're not cool enough to spend any time with them, asshole," Violet barks, walking around Ella. "Ignore these assholes, they think they're something special because they're on the team but what they don't tell you is that they have no chance of making first string or talking to the likes of the Dunns."

"Vi, girl. That stings," West says, holding his hand over his heart.

"Yeah, get over it. Truth hurts." She smiles up at him as he pulls her into his chest and kisses the top of her head.

"Whatever, Titch."

"Right, well. Are we ready to go? I need tacos like... yesterday."

"Yes. Let's go."

"You've never had tacos like these, Letty. You are in for a world of pleasure," Brax says excitedly.

"More than she would be if she were in your bed, that's for sure," West deadpans.

"Lies and we all know it."

"Whatever." Violet pushes him toward the door.

"Hey, I'm Micah," the third guy says when I catch up to him.

"Hey, Letty."

"You need a sensible conversation, I'm your boy."

"Good to know."

Micah and I trail behind the others and with each step I take, my smile gets wider.

Things really are going to be okay.

DOWNLOAD NOW TO KEEP READING